JUSTICE HUNTER

Jennifer Morey

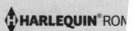 

HARLEQUIN® ROM

Recycling programs
for this product may
not exist in your area.

ISBN-13: 978-0-373-27972-2

Justice Hunter

Copyright © 2016 by Jennifer Morey

Printed in U.S.A.

"Please tell me what's going on, Rachel."

His grip tightened in her hair. Rachel stared breathlessly up into his intense face, seeing the strength of his concern for her and his angst that she wouldn't trust him.

He brought his head down for an energy-packed kiss.

The impact stunned her, and an instant later fire melted any thought of resisting. She let him take her mouth and fell into the velvety passion, desire so strong she couldn't comprehend where she ended and he began.

His kiss eased into a series of gentler, quicker ones.

"He almost killed you." He kissed her again, hard, seeking reassurance that she still lived. "I thought he was going to."

"Lucas."

His mouth covered hers yet again, his tongue going in for more drugging passion. Then he eased off. "I can't lose another woman, Rachel. I can't fail again."

As he continued kissing her, she answered with equal fervor.

"Tell me," he rasped.

Hearing his desperate need for her to trust him in at least that, Rachel nearly capitulated. But she could not trust him this way.

"I can't," she whispered harshly.

* * *

Be sure to check out the next books in this miniseries.

Cold Case Detectives: Powerful investigations, unexpected passion...

If you're on Twitter, tell us what you think of Harlequin Romantic Suspense! #harlequinromsuspense

Dear Reader,

If you like cold case action, my new miniseries is for you. In *A Wanted Man*, you met Kadin Tandy, a sexy former New York detective who lost his daughter to kidnapping and murder. Now he's focused all his intelligence—and bold brawn—on solving victims' cases that have gone cold. He's out to make criminals of violent crime pay, and he hires only the best to do the job.

Meet Lucas Curran, ex-marine, former LAPD SWAT cop who's got personal reasons to solve the next Dark Alley Investigations murder case. Mystery. Murder. Action. What more could you ask for? How about another story after this one? I'd love to entertain you.

Jennie

Two-time RITA® Award nominee and Golden Quill Award winner **Jennifer Morey** writes single-title contemporary romance and page-turning romantic suspense. She has a geology degree and has managed export programs in compliance with the International Traffic in Arms Regulations (ITAR) for the aerospace industry. She lives at the foot of the Rocky Mountains in Denver, Colorado, and loves to hear from readers through her website, jennifermorey.com, or Facebook.

Visit Jennifer's Author Profile page at Harlequin.com, or jennifermorey.com, for more titles.

For Mom. Thanks for visiting me in my dreams. Moments cherished.

Chapter 1

Lucas Curran bent his head against the biting Wyoming breeze, wondering for the hundredth time why a man like Kadin Tandy would choose a place like this to headquarter his renowned cold-case investigations agency. Similar to Lucas's hometown in Montana, Rock Springs offered Wild-West isolation. No concrete jungle here. Very few violent crimes and yet…that was exactly what Dark Alley Investigations fought.

Crossing the street, he took in the classy sign jutting out from an old, two-story brick building. Quaint. Understated. No one would guess what grisly crimes this agency took on. A row of shops lined Main Street, Christmas lights off on this cringe-worthy, overcast day. Some cars crept along the sleepy, snow-swept road. A few hearty geriatrics walked the sidewalks.

A couple hurried into a coffee shop. Other than that, only the snow looked busy and bustling.

He stepped up to the charming storefront, which had been renovated with tinted, bulletproof windows. His salvation. His ticket to revenge.

Excitement surged forth again, as it always did with the prospect of taking charge of his sister's murder investigation. He wouldn't rest until he avenged her, until he cornered and caged her killer—whoever thought he'd gotten away with the crime. Lucas couldn't wait to look into his eyes the very moment realization struck that Lucas had caught him.

Charming or not, Dark Alley was his weapon. Above the hanging sign, a second story promised warmth, clean white blinds and gossamer scarves, hinting at a feminine touch. Kadin Tandy lived there— with a woman. No wonder the place looked so deceiving.

Opening the door to the jingle of a bell he would more expect in a bookstore or gift shop, Lucas stepped inside. Kadin Tandy had opened this godsend to those who'd given up on more traditional methods, and he intended to take full advantage of all its resources.

"Can I help you?" a woman behind a desk across the entrance asked. A little on the heavy side, but a real beauty.

The door swung closed with another jingle, shutting out the biting wind and snow. Pictures of cities hung on the walls, and a freshly painted bookshelf to the right had more than books artfully arranged on its shelves. More feminine touches. A Christmas tree dead-center in front of the window had wrapped presents beneath its pine-smelling branches. So cozy.

So welcoming…for a hard-core violent crimes special ops unit. He wouldn't put a mere private investigations label on this agency. Not with a man like Kadin in charge, not with his past and experience, and not with his thirst for bringing ruthless justice down upon the destroyers of innocence.

He walked forward, his black leather combat boots thudding on the refurbished wood floor. "I have an appointment."

"Lucas?" she asked with a friendly smile. That congenial trait must have helped her land this job. Dealing with grieving, scared families had to be akin to dealing with death in a funeral home.

"Yes."

"Come on back," Kadin called from his office, the door left open.

The woman stood up, and when Lucas went inside the office to see Kadin getting up from his chair, she closed the door. All very sensitive to the nature of the business.

Lucas shook Kadin's hand.

"Welcome aboard," Kadin said.

He'd contracted him earlier this week and asked him to come in for what he called *orientation*. All of his operatives were contracted, not hired directly. *To allow more freedom,* Kadin had explained. Freedom to take risks. Freedom to use force. All without any liability to the company.

"Thanks. I'm happy to be part of the team."

"Have a seat."

Lucas sat on a black, real leather chair separated by a table. Kadin took an identical one on the opposite side. Reaching for one of two envelopes on the table, Kadin then handed it to him.

Lucas took it and parted the opening to slide out the pages within. Kadin opened his file on the table and leaned over to read the first page.

"These first few pages summarize what's in your contract."

"I read my contract."

"This is just to make sure you didn't miss the most important parts."

"I didn't miss anything."

Kadin's eyes lifted to look at him. "I'm not going to tell you how to carry out an investigation. You should already know that. If you screw up, that's your responsibility."

Ah, the price of freedom. Lucas didn't mind. He'd rather have freedom than let others do the doing for him. And he wouldn't screw up.

"That wasn't in the contract."

"I have three rules that can never be broken," Kadin said, gaze unflinching. "If you break any of them, I reserve the right to terminate your contract and possibly turn you over to the feds."

"Rule number one," Lucas said before Kadin could. "Make sure the evidence can stand up in court." No cheating when it came to evidence. No lawbreaking. "Rule number two—no vigilante kills."

"And the third?"

"Always put the victim first."

That seemed and sounded like a no-brainer to Lucas, but in Kadin's terms and conditions, he referred—in coded language—to lawbreaking as opposite from evidence gathering. The law could be broken to save victims. Freely broken. Protect the innocent, no matter the cost. If saving a victim meant losing key evidence, then justice took on a different set of rules, an unwritten set of rules. Meaning, there were none. Unfortunately, people came to Dark Alley long after the victims had died. Kadin referred to the danger of chasing killers as the collateral damage.

"Do you think you'll have any trouble with any of those?" Kadin asked.

"No." Not when Lucas didn't see it as a vigilante kill.

"Not even rule number two?" Kadin probed, as though predicting his thoughts.

He'd worried over Lucas's motive when he'd first met him.

"Especially rule number two." He had an un-quenchable thirst for the freedom Kadin offered, and he couldn't promise he wouldn't kill his sister's mur-derer, but he could promise he'd do it justly. Kadin may not agree with his brand of justice, however.

Kadin stared long and hard at him. He didn't quite believe Lucas had come to Dark Alley out of a deep sense of nobility. But instead of calling him on it, he said, "Good. Now let's talk about your sister's case."

On some level, Kadin must understand how Lucas felt. Four years had passed since his sister's murder. Police had little to go on and no witnesses. An inno-cent life had been taken, and a guilty one still lived on.

"The last person to see her alive was her husband, Jared Palmer," Kadin said. "He looks like a suspect."

Lucas gripped the arm of the chair, squeezing his fingers to stave off the wave of anger just the mere mention of Jared's name stirred. "She was alive when he left for work the morning of her murder."

Kadin's eyes rolled up from the page in the open file for another hard stare.

Lucas continued. "When he came home that evening, she left dinner ready for him before she went out for her monthly outing with friends at the country club. That's all been verified. Her club friends said she left at ten. Jared claims she arrived home at ten twenty and came to bed."

Kadin sat back, elbow on the arm of his chair, rubbing his chin before dropping his hand. "And he claims he saw, heard or noticed nothing else the rest of the night."

"Correct." That had always infuriated Lucas. He'd always felt Jared had lied, although his story had never changed, not one detail. That made him either a really good liar or innocent.

"I can see why you'd think he did it," Kadin said.

"I still think he could have done it."

"Were it not for the affair," Kadin said.

That was the newest piece of information that had developed in the case. Jared had recently called a woman named Rachel Delany. Police hadn't known about her, but the conversation clearly indicated the two had known each other before Luella's murder. Intimately.

"The woman has an interesting résumé," Kadin said. "Have you read her background?"

Lucas nodded. "In and out of juvie. All grown-up now but can't hold a job. Doesn't have many friends." He showed Kadin a photo he'd pulled out from the envelope. "Beautiful."

Kadin's brow lifted and he nodded. "Very beautiful. But even pretty women are capable of murder."

"How did they meet?" Nothing in the file indicated that, and Lucas found it odd that a man as well-off as Jared would end up in an affair with a woman like Rachel.

Lucas turned the photo so he could see her again. Rachel's shiny hair tapered into a sophisticated chocolate bob, drawing striking lines on each side of golden-brown eyes rimmed by liner and long thick black lashes. Those eyes looked right at the camera, sultry, daring and full of dangerous mystery. This woman had seen the rough side of the tracks, but must have found a way into the pinkies-up crowd.

"Has she done this before?" Lucas asked, not liking how the woman's hotness stirred baser instincts. He flipped the pages, skimming through them and finding a paragraph on her previous relationships.

"Yes," Kadin said as he read. "She's had other affairs, not with married men, but with wealthy men. The relationships never last."

Lucas closed the file. "No surprise there. She's not very together, and the type of men she chooses must figure that out sooner or later."

"Let's not jump to conclusions. She might be innocent." Kadin leaned forward again. "What's your plan?"

"I'm sorry, folks. We're going to have to get another bus and transfer you. Engine problems."

Rachel Delany stared at the bus driver, unable to believe the bus had broken down now, today of all days. She'd just finished her last college final before the Christmas break and had a thirty-minute window to get to work. She had five minutes left. Grabbing her backpack, she stood and walked down the aisle toward the front, where the midfifties black driver saw her in the rearview mirror.

"It'll be a few minutes before the other bus gets here, Rachel," he said.

"I don't have time, Larry. I'll walk the rest of the way."

"It's a couple of miles to the next stop," he said. "That mean ol' boss of yours can wait. Let me take you the rest of the way."

She smiled big. Larry knew all about her troubles. "A little snow won't hurt."

His dark, bushy eyebrows lifted over trouble-free eyes and he smiled back. "What'd you say your degree was? Weather girl?"

Rachel laughed on a soft breath, envying his humble existence. Whenever she felt the struggle of her own life too much, all she had to do was think of him. He made a happy living on a low wage.

"Don't stop to talk to anyone on the way, now," Larry called.

Still smiling, she waved and stepped off the bus. She talked to people on the bus all the time. Strangers had such interesting stories, like sitting with Forrest Gump on a park bench.

She tipped her head back and let the cold flakes peck her cheeks. A little cold and a long walk never bothered her. Bozeman, Montana, wasn't known for its balmy weather, and she hadn't chosen this area for the fluff. She had a little Larry in her—along with a dream to make something of her life.

Checking the time, she broke into a jog. Her female boss had already warned her about being late. One minute didn't seem too late to Rachel. She wished she could tell her boss where to go every time she nit-picked over silly things, but she needed this job until she graduated and found one with more requirements than clock-watching.

Reaching the mall, she entered with a few stomps to shed the snow and then decided rushing wouldn't make any difference. She'd get her last check and leave. One more job to dribble into her past.

Dodging someone coming the other way down the mall corridor, Rachel's backpack bumped against the metal door as she cut the corner too close at the store entrance. Her boss stood behind the counter, alone. Leaning against the back wall, she watched her with disapproval marring her pudgy, wrinkled face. She made a show of looking up at the clock on the wall above her head.

Two thirty-four. More than thirty minutes late. Even Rachel would call that late.

"I had a final and the bus broke down," she said, only for the slight chance that the woman would listen to human logic.

Her boss sighed in that huffy way that so annoyed Rachel and then walked around the counter. "Rachel, I've given you more than enough chances to prove yourself here."

"It was my last final. I'm on break now until January."

"At which point you'll only be late again," the woman said. "I need someone more devoted."

Rachel humphed. "It's a retail job."

The woman immediately took offense. "Any job has its responsibility. You've shown me none with yours. You're late more than you're on time."

True, but Rachel considered this a means to achieve something more rewarding. "I rely on public transportation. I depend on bus schedules. They don't always match my work schedule. I've asked you to consider that when you write my schedule." She began to wonder why she even tried to defend herself and come up with excuses.

"I'm sorry, Rachel," she said. "I can't arrange everyone else's schedule to suit yours."

"This is the first time I've been more than a few minutes late."

The woman eyed her upper body as though her jacket didn't cover enough of her shape. "Late is late."

She'd often eyed her like that. Rachel let the spitfire that lower-class living had set free in her take over.

"You've never liked me," she said, a revelation. Why hadn't she seen it before?

The woman's eyes flitted all over Rachel now, down her trim body and back up to her blemish-free face. "Liking you has nothing to do with why I'm firing you today."

"You've looked for ways to fire me. One or two minutes late isn't late. You censure the way I talk to customers."

The woman stiffened, telltale offense. "Flirting isn't professional."

"I never flirt here." The woman invented things!

"I did you a favor by hiring you. It isn't my fault you turned out to be a disappointment." She reached over to the counter and picked up an envelope. "This is your last paycheck."

Rachel took the money. The envelope, its feel in her hand and the knowledge of what it contained, nearly did her in. No more checks would follow. Her will spared her from crumbling. Slowly, she looked up.

"Thank you," Rachel said. "This is best for both of us."

The woman's lower jaw fell slack, and misunderstanding twitched above her nose. She expected another reaction. Would seeing Rachel hurt satisfy her, a woman driven by jealousy?

"I can do better than this." With that, Rachel pivoted and walked toward the exit.

"If you're thinking about filing a complaint, you should know I've documented everything," the woman called after her.

File a complaint. As if she'd wasted her time on that negativity. Rachel didn't turn or respond, just left the store. A man in a nice suit stood at a sunglasses kiosk. He didn't look her way as she passed.

Rachel checked her phone. Her boyfriend still hadn't texted her. She'd tried to get ahold of him all day, but he hadn't responded. Someone to talk to right now would be nice.

She saw a woman dressed to the nines, carrying four bags and looking into the window of a jewelry store as she passed. Did she have a husband taking care of her, or had she made her own way in this vicious world? Rachel slowed her pace and watched her come to a clothing store and go inside, her face peaceful and tastefully made up, giant rock on her ring finger sparkling under the store lights. Rich husband. Pampered woman. But happy.

Rachel loved seeing people this way, comfortable in their environment, the world they created with decisions. The beautiful, sophisticated woman didn't give off any airs. She had money, her man's money. Rachel imagined her man treated her as though his money belonged to her just as much as it belonged to him. Equals.

Why did life have to be such a struggle for some people and so seemingly easy for others? Rachel wanted that. Just once, she'd like to know what it felt like to be that woman, the willowy one with shopping bags, admiring a sparkly dress as though contemplating an upcoming party, no worries in the world.

All her life, nothing had ever come easy for Rachel. Granted, she'd gotten herself into trouble as a teenager, but that girl had grown up. Finally. Now that she wanted a good, honest life, life seemed to oppose her every effort. What was she doing wrong? She tried so hard and never got ahead. The constant battle had become routine. She'd gotten fired today, and it had barely fazed her. Routine.

Leaving the mall, she didn't feel like going home. Somehow, getting fired deserved some kind of memento. Rachel adjusted her backpack as she crossed the street, glancing back to see the man in the suit had left after her. Was he crossing the street, too?

As she walked down the sidewalk, she began to get an uneasy feeling. Nothing like this had happened in years, not since the disastrous affair she'd had with that executive. He'd contacted her last week, trying to reconcile. After all this time, why? His call frightened her. She'd gently refused his invitation to dinner. Had that started up trouble again?

O'Shuck's was a few blocks from here. She covertly looked back. The man in the suit still trailed behind her. He seemed to catch her notice of him but didn't stop following her. She didn't recognize him, but he was far enough away not to be sure. Would Jared stalk her?

Alarm kicked up the knock of her pulse. She walked another block and looked back. Still there. He was following her.

Rachel walked faster. O'Shuck's was just up the street now. She could see the lights. Almost at a jog by the time she reached the door, she checked the sidewalk. The man walked toward her, looking right at her.

Rachel entered the pub and breathed her relief. What was she going to do now? What if the threats started again? She wasn't sure if it had been Jared who'd threatened her the last time, and she didn't recognize the man following her now.

Trying to appear calm, Rachel walked toward the bar. O'Shuck's drew a nice working-class crowd and boasted Haggis and Irish coffee. She came for the short walk to her apartment, the company and the atmosphere, which was much better than her apartment. Anything was better than that.

Dropping her backpack and putting her cell phone on the bar, she took a seat and waited for Hans to see her. Glancing back toward the door, she didn't see the man in the suit.

"Hey, Rachel." Hans had a deep-creased grin for her and a sparkle in his Viking blue eyes. He stepped over to her. "The usual?"

"Make it a vanilla latte."

"Coming right up. Special occasion?"

"I was fired."

Hans winced and then said, "Ooh. That is rough. That old bitty come up with a reason?"

"The bus broke down and I was thirty minutes late." She looked back again and saw the man in the suit standing just inside the door, looking right at her. What the...

He was tall and well built and now that she saw him close-up, blond with a buzz cut and a handsome face. Definitely not Jared Palmer. But had he been the man who'd threatened her before?

Hans put the drink before her. "Sorry, Rachel. You're good peeps. You don't deserve that."

The stranger began to approach.

"That man followed me from the mall," she said.

Hans looked to the man. "You sure?"

"Positive."

"Sir," Hans said to the man as he stopped next to her chair. "The lady says you followed her. Do I need to call the police?"

Hans to the rescue. She felt safe...for now. But what about when she went home?

"You're very observant," the stranger said.

Of all the things a dangerous man could say, Rachel didn't expect that. She sensed nothing sinister about him, not as sinister as she'd felt the last time.

The ding of her cell phone indicated someone had texted her. She looked down and saw her boyfriend had finally answered her. What the text said made her pick up the phone.

Sorry. No easy way to say this. I met someone else. You've been great. Take care.

That effectively shifted her focus. Rachel read the text again to make sure it said what she thought.

"You've been great?" She scoffed as the insult began to mushroom. "Take care."

Had she really dated someone this insensitive and clueless? Lowering the phone, she looked up at the stranger, who reached into his jacket for something while clips of the last six months passed in her mind. Her boyfriend had been fun to be with but now that she had a bird's-eye view, his superficiality became obvious. She hadn't known anything deep about him.

"I believe this is yours."

Startled, she looked down at what the man had taken from his jacket. Her wallet. He put it down on the bar.

"How did you—"

"I'll have what she's having," the stranger said to Hans as he sat on the stool next to her. "And put hers on my tab."

"How did you get my wallet?" she demanded. Then she recalled what he'd said.

She backtracked what she'd done with her wallet. She'd had lunch and put it back in the zipper pouch. Hadn't she zipped it shut?

"I saw you go into a shop at the mall. Your backpack bumped the door frame and your wallet fell out. I started to go over but I heard you talking to your boss."

She had bumped the door frame. But had it been hard enough for her wallet to slip out?

"I'm Luke Bradbury." He swiveled to face her better.

She looked down at his offered hand and then back up at his drool-worthy blue-gray eyes, crinkling with an all-out charm-packed grin. Now that she wasn't afraid of him, she could appreciate his looks. He was a great package. Dressed as though he had money, too.

Ordinarily, a man like him would capture her interest. He did capture her interest. But something about this one had her holding back. No, not him. Her boyfriend had just broken up with her in a text message. He was a successful businessman like Luke must be. She'd dated a lot of men like that. Successful men attracted her. Their stability. They had what she wanted. But maybe her criteria needed some tweaking.

Beyond his attractiveness, Rachel began to wonder why he'd come to this pub.

"Why did you follow me here?" Why hadn't he approached her after she left the shop?

"I confess." More charm oozed from him. "You looked so upset. I didn't want to intrude."

Intrude? "You had my wallet." Hardly an intrusion to return it…

While he didn't frighten her the way the other man had after her affair, she had to be careful. She didn't know who'd threatened her back then. And Jared contacting her may have stirred danger. She snatched up her wallet and put it into her backpack, this time making sure she zipped it shut.

"Yes." His smiling eyes made a pointed journey down her body and back up. "A perfect excuse to meet you."

She gaped at him. Was he for real? She kept going back and forth between seeing him as an attractive man and someone untrustworthy. "Not interested."

His confident grin slipped as she turned back to her coffee and sipped.

"In what?" he asked, as if he didn't know.

Seeing his genuine perplexity, she said, "Thanks for returning my wallet, but I'd like you to leave me alone now."

"Uh…sure…okay." He continued to look at her.

Rachel decided to hurry and finish her coffee and go.

"I'm sorry."

She turned to him. Why was he sorry?

"I shouldn't have come on to you like that."

"That's not the only reason I want to be left alone." She didn't know why she kept talking to him. She really did want to be left alone now. "My boyfriend broke up with me in a text message."

"Is that the, 'You've been great. Take care' guy?"

Rachel reeled again from the callousness of those heartlessly chosen words. "Yes." She leaned a little closer to the stranger. "Do you all do that?"

"No. I always break up in person. If I'm the one doing the breaking up."

Rachel didn't think that happened to him very often. And she didn't want to hang around to be the next woman he broke up with in person. She stood from the stool, lifting her backpack and tucking her phone in the same compartment as her wallet, zipping it shut.

"You're leaving?" Luke asked.

"Yes. I came here for company but now I need to be alone."

As she put the backpack on, Luke watched her, reluctant to let her go.

"When will I see you again?" he asked.

"You won't." She waved to the bartender. "Thanks, Hans."

Luke noticed her friendly exchange, and Rachel realized she'd just revealed she knew the bartender, which also revealed she came here regularly.

Luke stood. "All right. I'll see you here again sometime, then."

She stopped from turning to go and his towering height flustered her, as did his impossibly blue-gray eyes. "Will I have to avoid my favorite hangout?"

"You'd avoid it?" His flirty grin returned.

Rachel feared her unwanted interest had begun to show. "No. Just you."

He chuckled. "Have dinner with me, then. Somewhere nice. Quiet."

"I told you I wasn't interested."

"I could have kept your wallet. Thank me for returning it by having dinner with me," he said.

"You'd have kept my wallet?"

"No."

She started for the door with a "Goodbye" tossed over her shoulder.

He didn't say anything. When she glanced back, he didn't seem so confident anymore. She'd shot him down, and he couldn't believe why.

Rachel smiled before going outside. Luke Bradbury wasn't a man accustomed to being rejected. His tenacity flattered her, but the cautionary instinct that had reared up when he'd said he'd followed her remained.

Walking up the street in falling snow, she caught sight of a car parked across the street and a man sitting inside. He looked right at her. Another admirer? The way he just sat there made her think not.

She walked faster toward her apartment.

Chapter 2

Lucas's stepfather slapped his hand down onto the wooden desk, more indignant animation than anger. "I can't lie!"

Joseph Tieber owned Bozeman, Montana's, busiest private air transportation and tourism company. A pilot for more than thirty years, he now sat behind a desk and employed several young airplane and helicopter pilots and numerous other staff. Lucas wasn't the executive he'd personified for Rachel, but his stepdad did make a lot of money on his passion for flight. He and Luella had been young when their dad died and their mother married Joseph less than a year later. While the transition had been rough, growing up with Joseph had always been an adventure.

"Even for Luella?" Lucas hated lowballing, but his motive had a lot of bite.

His stepdad sighed, full of defeat. He lowered his head as sorrow weighed him down, running a hand through his hair.

After a moment he rested his hands on the desk and lifted his head. "If you want me to hire this woman, why not create a job for her?"

"I mean to win her trust. Offering her a job like this will go a long way toward achieving that." He hoped anyway. He may have difficulty convincing her to take the job. He hadn't believed how quickly she'd shot him down. He'd dangled a subtle money carrot and she'd gotten up and left, refused an expensive dinner.

"I may be able to get her to talk, too," his stepdad said.

Lucas was relieved he was coming around to his way of thinking. "Yes."

"What if she recognizes me?" his dad asked.

"There wasn't much news about Luella's murder. There was something about the search for her for a while but nothing that will lead back to me. And you never adopted us. Luella and I are Curran, not Tieber."

"She may have looked Luella up after she found out about the affair."

"Luella didn't like social media. There isn't much about her on the internet. I checked. The news didn't mention her maiden name. Right now Rachel only knows Luella as Luella Palmer, not Curran. She might put it together, but not before I get what I need from her."

After mulling that over a little, his stepdad said, "I'll swear my assistant to secrecy and temporarily reassign her elsewhere in the company. But I'm only doing this for Luella. For the record, I don't approve of your deception."

"Thanks, Dad." Lucas stood.

Joseph stood with him. "Before you go, I want to talk to you some more about this vigilante agency you've gone and joined."

"On my own I don't have access to databases or certain types of equipment. Dark Alley has everything I need and more. Kadin even arranged for my fake identity. I have a driver's license and everything." He'd be a believable Luke Bradbury for Rachel. "I can work anywhere, too. Right here."

"Your mother and I are thrilled you came home, Lucas, but we're concerned with how far you're taking this. We're wondering if you should leave the investigation up to the local police."

"Her case is cold."

"They're going to be pursuing the affair just like you are. I don't see why you have to get involved. You should be concentrating on your own life. When are you going to settle down? We didn't raise you to be an ineligible bachelor the rest of your life. Your mother would like grandchildren. Are you going to take that away from her?"

This had become an issue after his sister's murder. It had been a small issue before, but now his mother had grown anxious over her reduced family. She was lonely, Lucas supposed, and mourning, still, the loss of her only daughter. His mother had crumbled after Luella's death. Lucas would never forget the call early one morning. Some hikers had found a body, and police believed it was Luella. She would never be the same woman. A lot of his dad's light had dimmed, too. Once a vivacious man who yearned to explore, he now went through his days with less fizz.

His father had never been one to push this before. His mother must be having a rough time. That only gave him more of a reason to be involved. The sooner he solved his sister's murder, the sooner they all could move on with their lives.

"I'm doing this for all of us, Dad. I'll give Mom grandchildren." Just not right now. His first marriage had ended badly. He wasn't in a rush to try that again.

A few days later Lucas waited for Rachel to leave her apartment. He'd planted a listening device in her wallet, a small, thin USB-like wireless voice-activated transmitter with a range of more than fifty feet and long-lasting batteries. He'd tucked it into one of the pockets behind the credit card sleeves. So far she hadn't noticed it. He'd followed her the few times she'd left her apartment and heard her working on a computer, most likely looking for a new job. She'd walked to the grocery store once. Now he spotted Jared Palmer's BMW, and sat up straighter in the driver's seat.

Jared parked along the street and walked toward the apartment building entrance, glancing around as though making sure no one saw. Lucas had purchased a car with tinted windows. He also had an SUV. When Jared's gaze passed over his vehicle, he paused a second and then looked elsewhere before facing the doors. He disappeared inside and moments later, Lucas heard Rachel let him up to her apartment.

"What are you doing here?" she asked when she let him in.

"You haven't returned my calls."

Lucas heard them move into the apartment, which was small enough for him to hear everything.

"I thought we decided not to see each other anymore," Rachel said.

"It's been a long time since Luella died. I haven't forgotten you, Rachel."

The rustle of clothes indicated Jared touched Rachel.

She moved away, going into the kitchen and turning on water. Did she need something to do? Did she still have feelings for Jared?

"I love you," Jared said, having followed her.

Still? After all this time? Lucas found that peculiar. Why hadn't they kept seeing each other? His wife had been murdered, but if he truly loved Rachel, wouldn't he find a way to keep seeing her? Maybe he had. Maybe no one knew.

Rachel turned off the water and didn't respond. Did she love him back? Maybe she'd loved his money.

"I've apologized for not telling you I was married."

"Yes, but it doesn't change the fact that you deceived me."

So his lie about being married had run her off. But her heart may still be invested in him, even if her mind wasn't.

This, Lucas hadn't anticipated. That Jared had lied to Rachel, that she might not have gotten involved with him if she'd known he was married.

"Enough time has passed," Jared said. "We can be together again. For real."

For real. Their relationship had been a secret, until now, if Rachel agreed with whatever he proposed.

Again, Rachel said nothing.

"I can make your life easier, Rachel. I'm not a poor man."

Lucas heard something metallic falling into the sink. Rachel must have dropped a utensil.

"I don't care about money."

Didn't she? Jared must have doubts, too, because he chuckled and said, "Yes, you do."

"I used to. Now I can see it just brought me unhappiness. I need to figure out what I really want in a man."

She continued to surprise Lucas. Was she telling the truth?

"No one knows about us," Jared said. "We can say we just met." Had they split up to avoid suspicion? Lucas found this conversation highly questionable, at least on Jared's side. He wasn't sure about Rachel.

"I need you to stop calling me and coming over here. You don't know what finding out you were married did to me. You hurt me."

"I know that. I didn't mean to. I met you and…it just happened. I'm sorry. I told you that. I've never been unfaithful to anyone until I met you."

"I did have feelings for you, but that doesn't matter anymore. You should go. And don't come back."

"We can be together," Jared insisted. When she again didn't respond, he said, "Think about it. I'll call you in a few days."

"No. Don't."

Jared sighed hard, her rejection frustrating him. "Just think about what I've said. Think about how good it was with us."

Before she'd discovered he'd cheated, the ultimate betrayal.

"Go. Please."

After a long pause, Lucas heard him going to the door.

The door closed and Rachel sighed. A thumping suggested she'd let her head fall against the door.

How did she feel about Jared? Something in the tentative way she'd sounded made him think she feared him.

Rachel brought her laptop to O'Shuck's and sat at a table with her diet soda, logged on to the free Wi-Fi, searching for work on an online job board. It had been more than a week and still no prospects. She'd hoped to be back to work by now so she wouldn't have to dip into her savings.

"May I?"

Startled, Rachel looked up to see Luke standing at her table, indicating the chair beside her. Before she could say no, he pulled out a chair and draped his leather jacket over the back.

"I thought I made myself clear the last time." Although she'd known he'd try to catch her here, she'd hoped he'd show up at the wrong times. Had he followed her again? Apprehension made her tense. Jared's visit couldn't be a coincidence. Could it? Was it all starting again?

"Yeah, but I know you're at least a little curious about me." He sat down.

Curious. In a scary way. A weird way. Wary of his true purpose, but not wary of the genuine attraction they had. He'd picked up on that hint. Maybe he thought he could use it to his advantage. She'd play along for now.

She noticed he wore jeans tonight. No suit. Leaning back against her chair, she said, "Dressing down tonight?"

He gave himself away when he glanced down at his chest—a very impressive chest in the snug black Henley. "Not working."

"You work?" She deliberately goaded him. What was his story anyway? The way he'd waited to return her wallet, claiming to be attracted, felt true but something rang off about him.

He smiled in a staged way. "You don't think I work?"

"I think you wore that suit for a reason, but I don't think it was work."

"Really? Why not?" He seemed impressed by her keen observation, and a little wary.

"Who goes to the mall in a suit at dinnertime?"

Leaning back, he propped his ankle on his knee. "Probably lots of people."

"Not you." She drank some of her soda, eyeing him with acute awareness.

After a few moments studying her, his smile smoothed into genuine sincerity.

"All right. You've got me. I've seen you before I found your wallet. I dressed in the suit to impress you. You losing your wallet presented me with what I thought was a perfect opportunity to meet you," he said.

"So you're admitting to spying on me."

"No. I didn't spy on you. I saw you at the mall when you were working. After I couldn't get you off my mind, I went back."

"So, you're a stalker?"

He grunted a laugh. "No. I saw you in passing. I didn't hang around to watch you."

"Go to the mall often?"

"Men need clothes, too." He put his foot down and sat relaxed in the face of her interrogation.

She eyed him, not completely buying his story. Maybe he had dressed in the suit to impress her, and when that had failed, he'd dressed as he normally did. Why the suit, though?

He may be sincere, but she still felt unsure of his true motive. Had he ever taken no from a woman? With his hot looks, she didn't think so. Unfortunately for him, she'd had too many bad experiences with men to be interested in giving another a chance anytime soon.

"I told you before, I wasn't—"

"I'd like to help you with a job," he cut her off.

Offer her a...

"What?"

"I have a friend who runs a transport company. His assistant quit, and he needs someone to replace her."

She scrutinized his face, looking for signs of falseness. She found none. He'd come here to help her find a job.

"I heard you talking to your boss. I heard her fire you. You're beautiful. I wanted to meet you, but the timing seemed bad. I followed you and here we are."

She bought that he'd been attracted. She also maybe bought her getting fired had ruined his plans to meet her. But she didn't feel he'd given her the whole truth. Did she want to start something with him?

He might have a job for her.

"You must have other intentions," she said.

He grinned. "Of course. I buy time to woo you out to dinner with me."

By arranging work for her—with his friend—he'd have opportunities to come and see her, to try and get to know her, to try and...

She ran a look down his broad, muscular chest and back up to the tough planes of his blond, stubbled face. Maybe she should say no. Then she thought of her graduation, how close she was to achieving her dream. If she took this job, she didn't have to date Luke. He couldn't make her do anything she didn't want to do.

"How do you know your friend would hire me?" she asked.

"I've already spoken with him. Do you know how to use Microsoft software?"

"Yes. I've actually...done that kind of work before." She didn't say where or for whom.

"Then it's settled. All you have to do is call him." He took out a card and handed it to her.

After staring at him through her uncertainty, questions racing over whether she should follow her impulse and trust him, she reached out and took the card. She read the name. Joseph Tieber, Chief Executive Officer and founder of Tieber Air Transport.

She moved her gaze to him, dumbfounded. He offered her a lifeline, this stranger who found her attractive. A thousand red flags waved in her mind, but if he was going to hurt her or threaten her, wouldn't he have done so by now? The man who'd threatened her before wouldn't have offered her a job. He had to be someone different. Luke wasn't that man.

"Why are you doing this?" she finally asked.

He grinned, and she thought he looked a little triumphant. "Because I can. And I've told you, I have a selfish reason. I'd like to take you to dinner."

Rachel placed the card on the table and rested her hand over it. She needed a job. Desperately. Her plans would be ruined without income. She patted her hand up and down on the card.

He reached over and put his on top of hers, stopping the nervous action. "Give it some thought."

It was the second time in a short period a man had told her to think about something personal. She looked from his ringless hand to his muscular chest and strong biceps, up to his amazing eyes. Warmth zinged her unexpectedly, a purely physical reaction to a drop-dead gorgeous man.

Unsettled over her quick and passionate reaction that could get her into trouble, she said nothing as he stood.

"Wait." She wasn't sure why she stopped him. Something nudged her to get to know him better. He'd just offered her a job, a perfect stranger. She had to know why, and it had to be more than finding her attractive. What was his story? Why had he singled her out?

He turned back to the table, studying her and coming to some conclusion he didn't share. Had she caught him off guard? Did he know she had questions about him and did he not like that?

Rachel prided herself on being street-smart. She could tell when someone wasn't being completely open and honest, and this man fit the bill.

"Why don't you have a soda with me?" She gestured to the chair he'd vacated.

He looked down at her glass as though surprised. "Soda?"

She smiled, content her tactic had worked. Distraction for extraction. Extraction of information, that is. "I always have soda when I come here. I only drank coffee the last time because I was fired that day and I was feeling reckless."

He grinned, sitting down while she waved to Hans.

"One more for him. No diet, though." She checked him to confirm and he nodded once.

She watched him settle back against the chair, eyes shrewd and onto her.

"All right," he said, "now you've got me. What do you want to know?"

She held back the smile that pushed to spread. His sharp intelligence tickled her senses despite her reservations. But did he think she'd invited him to stay out of sexual interest or interest in his motives?

"I'd like to know more about the man who's supposedly getting me a job just because he thinks I'm sexy."

"Supposedly?"

"Nothing's sure until it's sure."

He hesitated, seeming reluctant to continue, catching on that her interest was not sexual. "I recently bought some property outside of town. I've been working on it for a few months."

That was something personal, all right. "A ranch?"

"Yes, but not a working ranch. It's purely for my selfish enjoyment."

He had money. A lot, from the sound of it. Normally, that would appeal to her, but now she wanted to be more careful. Her financial hardship should not stain her decisions when it came to men, as it had in the past. When she graduated, she'd get a great job and take care of herself. She'd have fine things, things she wanted—whatever she wanted. She didn't need a man to obtain that.

"I'm the son of a dot-commer," he said in her silence.

So his rich parents would give him everything. Weird how that disappointed her. Affluent men had always intrigued her. Their ambition. Their way of life. Their intelligence. She may have had a tough start to life, but she would finish grandly. Her intelligence matched any man with money. If she was totally honest, though, she'd say money made life easier. She wanted an easier life. That was why she'd gone to college.

"Did you ever want to do anything professionally with your degree?" she asked. "Or have you?"

He hesitated again. "No, not professionally. I trained to be a SEAL after college."

That took her aback. "Really?" He was a big man. Tall. Muscular. But not overly so. He had the rugged appearance to be good at something like that.

His gaze dropped, and he turned the glass of soda on the table.

"You're a SEAL?"

"No." He hesitated yet again. "I quit before the end of training."

She could tell he had difficulty talking about this. His quitting bothered him. Uncertain as to whether she should question him further, Rachel held off. She didn't know him and wasn't sure she wanted to know him any more than she did. She liked successful men. She didn't consider his being born into money his own success. And he'd quit SEAL training. The fact that it bothered him didn't make him a quitter.

She resisted real attraction brewing, deeper than

any suit could ignite. This man had a heroic streak in him. No corporate executive could compare to that.

He turned away, giving her time to calm her stirring excitement.

"Why did you quit?" she couldn't resist asking.

Slowly, he faced her again, in control of his emotions. "I didn't want to."

Rachel didn't press him to say more. He'd quit; he hadn't been disqualified. He hadn't failed the training. He'd quit. He'd aspired to be a SEAL, and something had happened to make him quit. She caught herself looking all over his face and upper torso. Sexy. Strong. A definite fit for SEAL material...but...heir to a dot-commer...

It didn't fit.

How many pampered men like him tried out for SEAL training? Did he think he was special, or was he the real deal?

"What about you?" he asked, turning on the charm again. "All I know about you is that you're beautiful."

She couldn't help smiling. What girl didn't like compliments like that? "I graduate in May next year. Business. I'm getting my MBA."

He whistled. "MBA? How long have you been going to school?"

"Years. I take classes when I can." When she could afford to.

He looked at her differently now, as though he'd just learned something unexpected about her.

"What," she teased, "haven't you ever met a poor college student before?"

"No."

She supposed he wouldn't, growing up with all that money.

"How old are you?" he asked.

"Thirty-one. I started college after…" She drifted off, not meaning to take the conversation there.

"After…"

She turned to him. "That's all you need to know… for now."

He sat there, relaxed on the chair, comfortable, confident and wholly absorbed in her—in her sharp wit… and her looks, of course. She felt the draw to that.

"I'm thirty-seven." He stood up. "I should get going. Call my friend. He'll give you a job. It's a good job."

A good job. Would it be?

"See you soon, Rachel." With that, he walked out of the pub without a glance back.

When he vanished from sight, Rachel picked up the card. She almost picked up her cell and called right then. Instead, she refrained. His job came with strings, invisible ones.

Chapter 3

Rachel decided her future took precedence over her wariness of Luke. She needed a job. Her landlord came by last night, asking for rent again. This morning she called Joseph, and he told her to come meet him at two o'clock. Dressed in gray slacks and a collared white blouse, she sat in the reception area, open to four floors above, closed doors off the square and light streaming in through the atrium overhead.

A woman appeared through one of the double glass doors, walking like a runway model in her sleek black skirt suit and blouse peeking through the opening of her fitted jacket. She checked Rachel out as though sizing up the competition.

"Rachel Delany?"

"Yes." She plastered a smile on her face and stood, reaching for the woman's hand.

The woman looked down at her hand and then turned without taking it.

"Something I said?" Rachel muttered.

The woman didn't glance at her so maybe she hadn't heard.

"Do you have a name?" Rachel asked.

"Marcy Sanders," she said without looking her way.

"Nice to meet you, Marcy."

The woman stopped at an office and pushed the door open wider, backing out of the way to allow Rachel to pass, bestowing her with unfriendly regard as she passed.

"Thank you," Rachel said.

Marcy shut the door.

"Rachel Delany." The tall, trim man with salt-and-pepper hair and glasses stood from his mahogany desk and leaned across the shiny wood to extend his hand.

She took it for a brief shake. "I can't thank you enough for this."

"No need. My... Luke's told me all about you. I'm happy to help out when I can."

"This is a big way to help out. My landlord will be relieved."

He smiled and sat down as she took a seat.

"Will I be stepping on toes taking this position?" she asked.

"Never mind Marcy. She'll recover just fine when I tell her what she's being compensated for shifting positions."

"Oh, so I'm taking her job." Rachel nodded. "Mr. Tieber, I really don't want to—"

He held his hand up to stop her. "First, call me Joseph, and second, you aren't taking anyone's job.

Marcy wanted to transfer anyway. She'll be working for General Counsel."

"Does she know that?"

"She knows she's transferring. I haven't told her where yet because I had to make arrangements with General Counsel first. She'll be happy, don't worry."

Rachel felt better. "Then I'm excited to be a part of your team."

"After I tell Marcy the good news, she'll show you around and train you for your new role. Welcome to Tieber Air Transport."

Rachel couldn't subdue a beaming smile, one that Joseph noticed.

"How exactly did you meet Luke?" he asked.

Embarrassment threatened to flush her face. "He returned my wallet to me after I lost it."

"He said as much. He also said you were fired the day you met."

"Yes. The bus broke down and I was late getting to work."

"Will you have trouble getting to work here?"

"No. I'll take the bus."

"Well, if you're going to be late because of the bus, just call me and let me know."

"I will. Thank you." What a nice man. He made her feel so welcome.

He picked up the phone. "Marcy, would you please come in?"

Rachel started to stand.

"No, you stay here."

Marcy came into the office with her stormy scowl. She stood beside the chairs. "Yes, Mr. Tieber?"

"I spoke with Mr. Jordan this morning. His assistant put in her notice last week, and he has an opening. You'll start there in the morning."

Marcy's mouth opened, and her eyes brightened. "Really?"

"Yes, so I'll expect you to be nicer to Rachel, here. I need you to train her to do your job."

"Of course. I'd be happy to." She smiled at Rachel. "Come on, let's get started."

Rachel left the office and followed Marcy to her new cubicle. Marcy sat down, and Rachel pulled a chair beside her.

"Did you really get fired because the bus broke down?" Marcy opened her email. When Rachel turned in silent question, Marcy added, "I listened to you talking to Joseph. Sorry."

"That's my luck."

"You're that unlucky?" Marcy breathed a laugh. "It can't be that bad."

"Oh, yes, it can. It started when I was thirteen."

"A handful for your parents, huh?"

"My parents are dead. But yes, I was a handful." The regret in her tone rang true. Rachel couldn't hide the emotion and wished she'd never brought it up.

After giving Rachel a few days to get settled in, Lucas arrived at his stepdad's company. Rachel wasn't at her desk when he went into Joseph's office.

"It's about time you showed up here," his dad said.

Lucas shut the door and went to the chair before the big desk.

"When are you going to tell Rachel the truth?" his stepdad asked.

"When I'm sure she had nothing to do with Luella's murder."

"She isn't the type of woman to do that. Marcy just told me all about her. Apparently, they've been getting close through her training. Did you know her parents died when she was thirteen?"

"Rachel's?" She hadn't mentioned it, but then, they didn't know each other yet. And she kept her distance from him.

"Ran away from two foster homes. Arrested for theft."

She sounded like a perfect suspect. "And you want me to tell her who I am?"

"She stole food and money. She lost her parents. She was going through a rough time. She's a sweet girl, Lucas."

He couldn't believe it. His stepdad had fallen for Rachel.

"She just might be good for you."

"I barely know her. And you don't, either." It hadn't even been a week, and Joseph had him seeing Rachel romantically.

"She got her GED at twenty, and now she's going to graduate with a business degree. She's turned her life around. You should tell her before it's too late. You should have never lied in the first place."

"I want her to talk about her relationship with Jared."

"Well, hurry up and do it. I don't like being part of this deception."

All right. Lucas would step up the pace, turn on the heat a little more—seductive heat. With Rachel, that would be easy.

* * *

Rachel looked up as she heard Joseph's office door open, startled to see Luke appear. She hadn't seen him come in. She shouldn't be surprised to see him. He and Joseph were friends.

"Rachel," he said with a disarming smile.

She prepared herself to be wooed. "Hello."

"Have dinner with me tonight."

For a moment he tempted her. But something about him still kept her wary. "I have to study."

"I've given you a few days. Now it's time for you to thank me for getting you this job."

"Thank you for getting me this job."

"I'm not taking no for an answer."

Behind him, Joseph stood in the doorway. "Go on, Rachel, he doesn't bite."

She caught the wily way Luke glanced at him and wondered what the exchange meant. Well, she had an opportunity to ask him, get him to open up.

"All right. Dinner." She reached for her purse.

"I'll have a car brought around," Joseph said.

While Rachel wondered why he went out of his way to accommodate, Luke extended his hand to her.

She stood without taking it. "Slow down, fancy man."

Joseph had a limo waiting for them by the time they made it down to the lobby. Her suspicion grew.

"What did the two of you talk about?" she asked.

The driver opened the door and she got in, Luke behind her.

"You," he surprised her by saying.

"Me?"

"He told me about your parents."

Not expecting that, Rachel faced forward.

"I'm sorry. That must have been rough on you."

Rough. She didn't think she'd ever get used to not having them around, or the sudden way they had been ripped out of her life. All through junior high and high school, she'd felt so different from everyone else. No one understood her loss. Other kids had parents who picked them up and took them to activities and showed up for events at school. Not her. She had to take care of herself. As an only child, she'd been close to both her parents.

"They were a lot of fun to be with," she said.

"Any kid would have rebelled. I hope you don't regret what you did."

She didn't respond for a while. "Maybe I shouldn't have said anything to Marcy." She'd been so easy to talk to, though, once she realized she had nothing to fear from her.

"You straightened your life out."

She breathed out a scoff.

"You're not in jail."

No. Not in jail. She'd been close to crossing a bad line.

"What changed it for you?" Luke asked.

She found the question awfully insightful for a man who knew so little about her. He and Joseph must have really had a talk about her. He got her thinking about that. The only thing she hadn't told Marcy was about Jared. The juvenile record must have come up in her background check through the hiring process.

"After my third arrest, the judge made me go to counseling and said if I didn't go he'd keep me in jail. The counselor helped me. He talked to me about my parents and reached me. He asked what my parents would think of the way I was behaving." That still had the power to choke her up. Such a simple thing to ask, and yet such a profound impact on her. "They would have been upset. Disappointed. Unhappy. I didn't want to do anything that would make my parents unhappy. It took me a few years to figure out what to do. I worked a job or two but stayed at my third foster home until I got my GED and saved enough money to get a place of my own."

"So it was the counselor who changed it for you?"

She hadn't thought about the path in her life like this before, that there had been some exterior trigger that had steered her in the right direction. But it hadn't been the counselor. He'd helped her emotionally.

"No," she said. "It was the job I got at an insurance company, my first real job. I made good money for someone who had a juvie record. I felt really lucky." And then she'd discovered something about the company that had ruined it all. As her thoughts ran into everything that had followed, she didn't feel like talking anymore.

"What company?"

The limo had stopped in front of the restaurant.

"We're here," she said, and got out before the driver could open her door.

Stepping up to the entrance, she endured Luke's curious glances. He'd noticed her unwillingness to talk further about her one and only good job. She stole a closer look at him. He met her gaze and in the brief moment, they connected, enough for her to see suspicion…or maybe disappointment.

* * *

Lucas rode in the back of the limo with Rachel, neither of them saying anything since leaving the restaurant. He'd tried to get her to talk about her job at the insurance company over dinner, but she'd fielded his questions—or more like blatantly changed the subject. She handled herself professionally, graciously countering his attempts with questions of her own.

How did your friend get his business going?
How long have you known Joseph?
Have you ever worked for him?

After the third question she refused to answer, he'd given up. He could tell she hadn't missed his probing. She must realize he wanted to know more, even, perhaps, that he found her reluctance suspect.

While his wariness of her remained intact, her golden-brown eyes kept flashing up to his—strong, unflinching and magnetizing. Her beauty threw him off when he least needed.

The limo came to a stop in front of her apartment building. Cracked concrete, missing bricks, boarded-up windows and next to no exterior lighting brought the gentleman out in him. Frustrated or not, he couldn't allow her to walk to her apartment alone at this time of night.

"I'll walk you."

"No need. Thanks for dinner." She opened the car door.

Lucas got out with her, stopping the driver from doing so, as well. His long strides easily caught up to her as she headed for the front doors.

"I can handle myself just fine," she said.

She must have lived like this for a long time to say

something like that. Ignoring her, he opened one of the doors for her, not seeing a doorman anywhere, or even anyone at the enclosed desk.

She went to the elevators, facing him after pressing the up button. "You can go now."

He couldn't leave on a note like this, with her bothered by his probing and him bothered by her secrecy. "The door isn't locked. Anyone can come in here."

"Of course they can. This isn't Manhattan."

The elevator doors opened. Rachel got in and reached for the close button, but he stepped in before she could shut him out.

She moved to the back and leaned with her arms folded, her avoidance in talking about her past hanging between them. If he was going to win her trust he had to ease up on her, and maybe lighten the mood. Even dressed conservatively in a knee-length, slightly flaring gray skirt and white, ruffle-collared blouse, she looked sexy. Silky brunette hair draped over her shoulders to the tops of her round breasts. Her outfit didn't conceal her curves. Lucas doubted anything would do that. She'd have to be wearing a bag for that to happen.

He noticed how she became aware of his inspection, a warming one, and she responded. He loved how she did that, such an unconscious reaction. Her instincts kicked in and their attraction heated the elevator. He took a step toward her just as the doors opened.

Grinning, he offered her to precede him. With the tiniest of smiles, she did. One small step toward winning her back over to his side.

He glanced at her on the way to her apartment. She noticed, and the physical awareness worked in his favor. Even if she sidestepped him with her secrets, a baser part of her had other ideas. At her door, she faced him.

"Well, here I am," she said. "Safe and sound."

He stepped forward, testing her space. Her eyes grew less playful, but heated curiosity remained. Never before had he deliberately kissed a woman. He'd always waited for the right moment. Not this time.

She put her hand on his chest, and for a moment he thought she'd refuse him. "Are you always this pushy with women?"

"Is this pushy?" He leaned in slowly, watching her eyes, feeling her hands press firmer on his chest, but not enough to pass as refusal. He hovered over her mouth just in case. Those golden-brown orbs blinked. Softly, he caressed at first, moving over her lips awhile before reaching with his tongue to ask for entry.

She parted her lips, and he kissed her as expertly as he could. He put all his experience into this kiss. A lot rode on its success. But as she responded with a warm sigh and an answering tongue, he lost control. No longer deliberate, desire made him slide his arm down to her rear and angle his head for a deeper connection. The sweet confection of her mouth, the soft curves of her breasts now crushed against him, the feel of her firm butt in his palm, all swarmed into his consciousness, obliterating reason.

Nearly a full minute later, he withdrew, so inflamed he didn't think he could step back and leave. No, he wanted to go inside with her.

He stood breathing with her, his forehead against hers.

She tipped her face up, and he found himself kissing her again. Blood rushed to his groin. Already hard from the first kiss, he could burst now.

"Let me in," he said, kissing down her neck to the top of her blouse.

"Oh," she breathed. "I don't even know you."

"We can talk first." He came back up to her mouth. "Maybe."

She laughed with him, deep, sultry sounds. Then she turned in his arms and unlocked her door while he kissed her neck. She managed to get the door open and he followed her inside.

Those few seconds opened enough clarity for him to slow down. As she backed up with fiery eyes cooling, he could see she'd begun to simmer down, as well.

"Uh… Coffee?"

"Sure." He followed her into her kitchen, just a couple steps from the entrance. A two-chair table took up most of the small dining area. Her apartment was little more than a hotel room, with a daybed on one side of the studio and living area on the other.

Rachel went about preparing a pot of coffee. "You never did tell me why you quit the SEAL training."

For a moment he wondered if she'd asked on purpose, digging for the most personal information on him. To douse the passion? How could she know the weight of her question? He considered doing as she'd done, blatantly changing the subject. But then he'd lose ground in winning her trust.

Clamping down angst, he said as neutrally as he could, "I got married."

Rachel paused in her task to look back at him. "Didn't she support your wishes?"

"She told me she was pregnant. I didn't want to

quit, but I didn't want to have a baby and be gone all the time. My plan was to work as a SEAL for a few years and then settle down. I thought being careless with her was just as much my fault as hers." He wished he didn't have to continue.

The coffee had begun to brew, the rich aroma filling the apartment. Rachel got out two cups and put them down.

"What happened?" she asked when he didn't go on.

Bitterness welled up as always when he thought of this. Was telling her worth using it to gain her trust? Luella's smiling face and laughter came to him, a memory of the time when they were kids and she threw water balloons at him. He'd just come home from his job as a burger-flipper, his first one. He'd had a really bad day and yearned for college so he could get away from fast food. As soon as he'd gotten out of the old Camaro, she'd sprung out from the garage with an armful of balloons. She'd dropped some, but a couple had gotten him good.

He'd found her stash and broke a few of them on her. They'd both been dripping wet by the time they ran out of balloons. That was Luella, spontaneous, worry-free, always looking for her next source of laughter. That day the source had been him.

Later, he'd found out his mother had told her he'd had a rotten day. He'd talked to his mother after he left work because she'd left a message asking him to stop for a pound of hamburger meat for dinner.

He and Luella had been so close growing up. And now she was dead. All her bubbly life had been taken from her.

Yeah. She was worth telling Rachel about his ex-wife.

"After we were married, she told me she wasn't pregnant. She tried to tell me she had a miscarriage, but when I asked her to show me her medical records, she wouldn't produce them. That led to a long fight. Finally, she confessed and said the only way I'd marry her is if she told me she was pregnant."

Rachel's mouth dropped open, an automatic response.

"I got a divorce," he said. "But that didn't get me back in SEAL training."

Now Rachel shook her head. "Why do people lie about things like that?"

"She fought for me to stay married to her, too." He scoffed at the audacity.

"I might be able to forgive but, yeah, never able to trust or love that person again. If anyone can carry out a lie that size, what else are they willing to do to get their way?"

She meant Jared. Like her, Lucas had learned the hard way that people could say things that sounded believable when inside their thoughts ran another agenda. His ex had been that way. He'd believed her teary profession that she was pregnant, that she was so sorry, that she hadn't planned on it happening. The one thing he believed most was her claim that she hadn't been thinking when they slept together. He hadn't, either. But she *had* been thinking afterward.

He recalled how she'd pursued him, a hot navy SEAL trainee. Young. Virile. She'd been upset when he'd told her he quit. She wanted a SEAL for a husband. No doubt she'd have enjoyed his deployments, freeing her up for affairs.

"You're really upset about that," Rachel said.

He looked down to see the steaming cup she offered. "I made a mistake quitting. I'm not a quitter, but the SEALs see it differently."

"You think you should have married her and not quit."

"Yes. I'd have learned she lied either way."

"You put fatherhood first. There's nothing shameful about that. She lied to you. You did nothing wrong."

"Justify it any way you like. The fact remains that I quit."

"There are worse things in life."

"Dying. That's it."

She sipped her coffee. "Well, you didn't die, so be thankful instead of bitter. There's nothing you can do to change the past."

Everything happens for a reason? "Is that how you view your juvenile record?"

Holding the cup with both hands, she averted her gaze and then returned it to him. "I'm not perfect. I wish I could change my past, but yes, I know I can't."

"You're bitter about it?"

"No, not bitter. Just…regretful. I used to be angry at the world and the universe and God for killing my parents. Now… I realize it's just…life."

They shared a long look. She seemed so good. Nice. Honest. Nothing like what he'd expected. Maybe he should give her a chance. Maybe he should tell her the truth.

He'd just gotten finished telling her how his ex-wife had lied to him. She could see how much that had hurt him. How could he do the same to someone else? Granted, his lie wasn't as life-altering as his ex's, but it was still a lie.

She stepped toward him, reaching for his face, caressing him, and then pressed her body to him.

"Rachel…" How could he begin?

"Shh." Her forefinger ran across his lips and stopped in the middle. Then she slid her hand around to the back of his neck as she rose up onto her toes to kiss him.

"There's something…" *I need to tell you* stayed in his mind as she opened her mouth and kissed him in earnest.

He drew her closer, intense passion firing. Just a little more of this and then he'd tell her. He felt her fingers in his hair, felt her move as though yearning to be closer. Kissing her became strained. He wanted her naked. Sexual desire gnawed at him.

"This is crazy," she whispered against his mouth.

He kissed her. Crazy. Yes. She had no idea.

"Why do you turn me on so much?" She dug her fingers into his hair again, pressing him to her mouth for another firecracker kiss.

"I want you so much," she said. "I've never felt this kind of passion before." And then, with that, she stepped back, her hands still on his chest as though stopping touching him was the most difficult thing she'd ever had to do. "Why you?"

Logic sank through the drugging desire. What a question. He didn't have an answer. He could ask the same about her. *Why her?*

Chapter 4

Rachel couldn't stop thinking about Luke. Over dinner he'd been so obsessed with her job at the insurance company she wondered if he had something wrong with him. Would he turn into a stalker or something equally weird or more dangerous? But then that inexplicable attraction she had, and he for her—she felt it between them, a living thing that kept expanding. That was what made her invite him in.

Talking the way they had changed her perception of him. He'd revealed himself, more than he had so far. Where before she felt he'd played a role, last night she'd gotten to know the real Luke Bradbury. And she liked him.

Leaving the break room toward the end of her workday, she started down the hall toward her desk. Hearing a laugh that sounded like Marcy's, she stopped and headed in its direction. Might as well say good-night.

"I know. She thinks this is real," Marcy said. "Like we're all really her friends."

Rachel stopped short on the other side to the cubicle wall.

"What's Joseph going to do when she finds out?" another woman asked.

Was she talking about Rachel? She had to be.

Rachel felt coldness spread through her face, and prickles of apprehension sank down her arms, making her hands tremble.

"Hire somebody else, I guess. I'm not going back to work for him. He knows I want the job in Legal."

They *were* talking about her. *No.*

Betrayal snaked into her. In seconds she added up what this meant.

"Why did Lucas lie to her? Why not tell the truth?" Marcy's friend asked.

Yeah, Rachel wanted to know the same thing. Lucas? Was that his real name? He'd lied to her about his name? His identity?

"His ex-wife's been calling, did you know that?" Marcy didn't answer her friend's question.

"No. Are they getting back together?"

Rachel swam in confusion. Who was this man? Did his ex-wife really lie to him? Had he made it all up?

"I bet she'd like that. Who wouldn't? He's hot."

"And rich."

The two laughed in borderline giggles.

"I almost feel sorry for Rachel," Marcy's friend said.

"She's going to find out what he's up to eventually," Marcy said. "It won't be too hard for her to figure out."

"Did Joseph tell you why Lucas wanted him to hire

her or why they lied about who they were?" Marcy's friend asked her question again.

"No, but I heard Lucas joined some hotshot private detective agency. Have you heard about that guy whose daughter was kidnapped and killed a few years ago? Kadin Tandy?"

"No. Who is he?"

"He's famous for his involvement in cold cases. Dark Alley Investigations is the name of his agency. He only takes cold cases. People go to him for help in finding their lost kids or family members, or to help them solve their murders."

"Really? Lucas was sexy before, but that makes him even more so. Maybe we should tell Rachel about him. Have you seen the way he looked at her yesterday?" Rachel pictured Marcy's friend fanning her face in her pause. "Could have lit the place on fire."

"Are you sure?"

"Oh, yeah. I don't even think he's aware of what he's doing."

Marcy's cell phone chimed. "Gotta go. My new boss is texting me."

"Don't stir up any trouble," her friend said.

Marcy laughed softly and left the cube. She saw Rachel and froze.

Rachel pivoted and headed for Joseph's office. He was still in his meeting. She didn't care. She went to the boardroom and flung the door open so hard it banged against the wall.

Joseph sat at the head of the conference room table, four other men in suits lining both sides. He looked up at her and didn't have to be told what she'd just found out.

"Why did Lucas lie to me?" Of course, she already knew. This must have something to do with her job at the insurance company. And Jared...

"Rachel." Joseph stood up while the other four men watched in riveted interest. "I didn't want to go along with this."

"Why?" She felt tears threaten and refused to give in to them now.

"Lucas should explain it to you. I warned him not to lie to you. I told him he should be honest."

He wasn't going to tell her. Rachel turned and walked fast to her cubicle—no, not *her* cubicle, *Marcy's* cubicle. Except Marcy wouldn't take her job back, one she'd had to vacate to allow for this farce to play out.

"Rachel, we found out about you and Jared, and Lucas wanted to try and get you to talk about it."

Talk about what? What about her and Jared. Not needing to hear another word, afraid of what might come to light, she grabbed her purse and hurried for the exit.

Joseph followed her. "Rachel. Just let us both explain."

She reached the front entrance, security guards and a few visitors stopping what they were doing to watch.

Joseph took hold of her arm and stopped her.

Rachel looked away but didn't try to pull away. He'd seemed so nice to her, like a father figure. That stung most of all.

"I told him what a lovely young woman you are. You aren't what he initially thought. I knew this would end badly. And now it has, and I regret my part in it. I offer you my sincerest apology. Please believe I have tremendous respect for you and sympathize with all you've been through. You are a kind, giving and brave woman. I can only ask that someday you'll forgive at least me."

That softened her marginally, but not enough to make up for the hurt.

"I thought this was for real," she said, tears threatening again. The last time she'd cried was the last night she'd spent in jail.

"It can be. The job is still yours if you want it. Take all the time you need." With that he let go of her arm.

Rachel saw genuine regret and apology in him and had to believe he'd meant what he said.

"Unfortunately, I think it's too late." She turned and left the building, wiping a tear away, angry it had slipped free.

She walked to a faraway bus stop and finally boarded, staring out the window all the way to the stop near her apartment. Had everything Luke—Lucas— told her been a lie? Last night had seemed so genuine. But he'd left out a few facts, more than just his real name. He worked for a place called Dark Alley Investigations, a place that investigated cold cases. It could mean only one thing.

Lucas had joined the agency to look into Luella Palmer's murder. Was Joseph her father? Was Lucas his friend, as he'd said?

She took out her older model smartphone and began to slowly navigate the internet, searching for anything relating to Joseph Tieber. She searched for Luella as well, and found a news story on her murder. An obituary said Joseph Tieber was her father and Lucas her brother. Lucas Curran, not Bradbury. Reading that stung. Who was he? She didn't know him at all, a man she'd slept with.

Was Joseph his stepfather? They had different last names. Had Luella been Tieber or Curran before she married Jared? She had an urgent need to know and berated herself for allowing her feelings to run her out of the office before making Joseph tell her. Humiliation didn't make her eager to face him again. Or Lucas.

Not wanting to go home with all the chaos mixing in her mind, Rachel stayed on the bus, and then two hours later found herself walking toward Joseph's house. She remembered his address from some documents that had required she list it. All she needed was information. The truth. Not knowing who Lucas truly was would prevent her from getting closure. She'd rather face Joseph than Lucas. Joseph should be home from work by now. She'd talk to him and then she'd put this behind her and move on with her life.

Another hour later she walked up Joseph's spectacular street, huge and luxurious houses spaced far apart on giant lots. She went up to the front door and knocked.

A woman answered. Dyed blond hair, average height and weight, she looked well preserved and warily curious.

Rachel heard a television somewhere inside; the sound echoed in the cathedral-like entry. She had never seen anything so grand in her life. On TV, but not in person.

"Yes?" the woman asked.

"Is Joseph here?"

"He isn't home from work yet. Who…" The woman searched Rachel's face as though trying to place her.

"I work for your husband. A-at least, I used to work for him."

More understanding smoothed the woman's face, but her confusion remained. "What are you doing here?"

"I…" Rachel lowered her head, at a loss for how to explain and not sure she should. This woman was a stranger, and Rachel didn't feel like explaining what had occurred.

"Wait a minute." The woman pointed her finger as something dawned on her. "You're that girl. The one who had the affair with our daughter's husband."

"I'm sorry." Rachel started to turn, expecting animosity. "I intruded. I'll go now."

The woman stopped her with a gentle hand on her arm. "Wait."

Startled, Rachel looked into blue-gray eyes much like Lucas's, and instead of wrath, she saw kindness. Warmth.

"I assume you found out?" Lucas's mother said.

"Really, I should go. I shouldn't have come here."

"Joseph said you would."

Rachel didn't understand what she meant.

"Find out," the woman clarified, hooking her arm with Rachel's. "Come in. Let's talk."

The woman guided her inside, taking her to a wide-open living room that magnetized Rachel.

"Have a seat and we'll talk this through. My son and husband don't give the technique much credence when they really should."

Rachel didn't resist the woman's wishes. Joseph must have told her some things, things he'd asked Rachel to believe.

She sat on a gigantic sectional. Something shifted in her, a deep, long-forgotten sense of caring, of being cared for. This woman could have turned her away. Instead, she welcomed her. Since her affair and the loss of her one good job, Rachel had alienated herself from her friends. She had no family, other than a few distant cousins too far removed to count.

"I'm Gloria Tieber. Why don't you start by telling me how you did find out?"

Rachel would have retreated, were it not for Gloria's simple approach. "I overheard Marcy talking." She turned away with the renewed sting that memory packed.

"Don't mind her. Whatever she said, she said it because she's jealous. Joseph was going to transfer her no matter what. He isn't a game-player. He won't tolerate anyone who is. He prefers people who shoot straight. Like you."

Rachel brought her thoughts back around.

"It's not like him to lie," Gloria said. "But he'd do anything for Lucas. They've been close ever since Joseph and I met. Took to each other right away."

"Lucas isn't his son?" She already knew, only needed confirmation, or maybe just to have it embedded into her head so she didn't imagine there'd ever be any hope for her with Lucas.

"Next best thing. Stepson. My first husband died at a young age, when Lucas was just four. Luella was just a baby back then."

Rachel watched as the woman's thoughts wandered. The awfulness of losing a husband and the good memories of Luella had to feel like sorrow sprinkled with sugar.

"That must have been very difficult," Rachel said.

Gloria smiled, the sorrow remaining. "It was such a long time ago. And Joseph is a wonderful man."

Rather than continue down that line, Rachel asked, "Lucas and Luella weren't adopted?"

"We decided not to arrange for Joseph to adopt them, in memory of their father."

She could see Joseph being the kind of man to go along with that. An insecure man may not be so understanding. Lucas was a lot like that, too. As that thought popped into her head, the hurt churned on a new wave. "Why did he lie?" Rachel asked. "Does he think I had something to do with Luella's murder?"

"I think he needs to investigate every possibility."

The neutral way she answered told Rachel that he hadn't ruled out any possibility.

"I didn't know about Luella until after her murder," Rachel said, feeling obligated to, as though she had to defend herself. "I saw it on the news."

"Joseph told me."

One morning she'd awakened like any other, with the sunrise, the news and a cup of coffee while she prepared for work. Her new schedule. She'd finally arrived. She was one of the commuters in the traffic report. Might seem insignificant to most, but she'd never had a job with hours that coincided with rush hour.

Then a breaking story had come on with video of Luella Palmer's crime scene. When the screen changed to her place of residence, she'd recognized the house instantly. Jared had taken her there on a few occasions, not often, but often enough to keep her from becoming suspicious. Luella must have been traveling or out with friends. She'd stood there, stunned with a mounting storm of emotion. Betrayal, disbelief, a surreal unreality. He couldn't have...

But he had.

How could he?

Next, the news showed Jared Palmer walking into the police station for questioning. The husband was always one of the first suspects, but what motive would he have?

"He tried calling me afterward," Rachel said. "I didn't answer. I never wanted to talk to him again. I didn't even want to hear his explanation, because to me, there was no explanation worthy enough to hear. He lied about being married. He made me the other woman without my awareness."

"Why didn't you go to the police?"

Had Lucas already judged her for not doing so? She had to be careful how much she said. "I wanted nothing to do with him. I had nothing to do with Luella's murder. I didn't even know she existed. I wasn't with him the night she was killed. For all I could see, he could have killed her. What if he lied to police?" Part of her had hoped he'd be sent to prison. If she could have helped that process along, she would have.

Gloria leaned back, crossing one leg over the other. "Lucas has always believed Jared killed her."

"Why? What has he discovered?" Surely, Lucas must have unearthed something. And then another thought came. "If he's so convinced Jared killed Luella, then why go after me?"

"Your affair, of course." Gloria bestowed her with a shrewder look. "And the fact that you didn't go to the police."

Rachel didn't back down. But neither did she offer

any further explanation. No one would look out for her except herself, and revealing too much could draw danger to her door.

"And I wouldn't say he's *gone after* you. He just… needed a way to get information."

Rachel wasn't sure she liked this woman. She put on a friendly front, but boy, look out for what lay beneath.

"I should get going." As she stood, she saw Lucas step out from the entry.

She froze with shock. How long had he been there? Had he listened to her conversation with Gloria?

"Hello, Rachel."

The way he said *Rachel* had her on edge. She replayed all she'd said. Nothing too terrible.

Hearing Gloria stir, she watched her stand and smile at her son. "Lucas." Going there, she hugged him. It all looked genuine. "I can't imagine what's brought you here."

In other words, she had a crystal clear idea. He held his mother, but hard eyes targeted Rachel.

Why did he look at her like that? The kissing. His touches. The passion. None of that mattered now. Flustered, unable to grapple with the conflict between him last night and him now, she stepped toward the entry, intending to pass Lucas and his mother. She would have walked right past them, but Lucas moved in her way.

"You're not going anywhere."

What would he do to stop her? Rachel stepped back and out of his reach. Passion had stolen her mind last night. Today she saw his true agenda. She should have never let down her guard. She'd sensed something off in him. She should have listened to the silent warning.

Well, she'd listen now.

"You told my mother you haven't spoken with Jared," he said.

Why had he zeroed in on that? What interest did he have in Jared, other than his possible involvement in his sister's murder?

"I didn't," she said. "Not after I found out he was married."

"But you *have* talked to him."

She began to have a bad feeling. How would he know if she'd spoken with Jared or not?

"He tried to restart things with you," he said.

His mother turned sharply to her, and Rachel drew her head back, an involuntary flinch.

"How do you know that?" Then her jaw went slack as the reason came to her. "You spied on me?" Not only had he lied to her, he'd spied on her! He knew about Jared. Furthermore, his ex-wife was trying to restart things with him. All the distrust she felt with Jared rushed forth with Lucas. She refused to be victimized again.

Giving him a shove, she went to the door.

He caught up to her, taking hold of her arm and pulling her back toward him. "What are you hiding, Rachel?"

"Let me go." She'd feared consequences like this, both the danger to herself and those close to her. While she even now didn't second-guess her decision, she often wondered if she should have been braver.

"Tell me about your job at the insurance company. It was Jared's, wasn't it? You worked for him."

Oh, God, no. This could not come out now. She yanked her arm free and left the house.

Lucas followed her. She walked down the street.

"If there's something you know, you have to do the right thing and tell me."

She ignored him and kept walking.

"Rachel."

"Leave me alone. I wish you well and that you find your sister's killer. I don't know anything that will help you or the investigation." She glanced pointedly at him. "If I did, I'd have gone to the police." If she had something concrete.

"The smallest detail could change the direction of the investigation," he said.

The smallest detail...

Telling him about the first and last time she saw his sister wouldn't hand him the killer, and she didn't qualify what little she did know as a small detail. Or the things that had occurred afterward. But dare she reveal anything?

Without responding, she kept walking. He sighed with resignation.

"Where are you going?" he finally asked.

"Bus stop."

"Wait."

He seemed awkward over a shift in his mood, going from angry and frustrated to needing something from her. Information.

"I'll drive you home," he said, his persuasive side coming out in a forced way. He must have sensed she held back and didn't like that, but he'd try to get her to talk. To what extent would he go? He'd already lied to her. She had to expect he could lie again.

"No, thanks. You did that last night." And he had

his ex-wife to deal with. She wanted no part of him with even the slightest chance he'd go back to her.

"This has nothing to do with last night."

How could he say that? "Last night was based on a lie."

"I have to find my sister's killer, and you aren't exactly a fountain of information."

She wasn't helping him at all. She couldn't. "I didn't kill her."

"Do you know who did?"

Rachel thought of the faceless man who'd stalked her, frightened her and still did. "No." She reached the bus stop, where she'd have to wait twenty minutes.

"Let me drive you home."

She eyed him, seeing his distrust and lack of appreciation. He'd like to let his irritation loose, she'd bet.

"You lied to me, and all you care about is what you think I might know, which is nothing," she said.

His attitude changed in an instant. He softened and regarded her contritely.

"It's cold out here," he said. "Come on. I'll drive you home."

"There's nothing I can say that will help you," she said. "So maybe you'd rather not waste your time on a girl like me."

He blinked acknowledgment of her insight. "I won't be wasting my time. And I'm sorry for lying. But as you can see, this case is very important to me. Come on, Rachel." He held out his hand. "Come with me."

She wasn't ready to let him off that easy. "What about your ex-wife? Won't she mind if you take me home?"

He took a second or two to piece together what she'd said. "I don't care if she does."

Jared would have said something like that to her. Experienced liar.

She looked away.

"Hmph," Lucas scoffed. "You think I'd actually take her back after what she did?"

She rolled her eyes his way. His lying bothered her more than the threat of his ex-wife.

"I'm not Jared," he said. "And I resent you comparing me to that."

Again, she turned away.

Lucas took her hand and pulled her toward him. "I get why you don't trust easily, especially since I lied to you. But you aren't in any danger if all I do is drive you home."

Pulling her hand free of his, she started toward his black SUV.

"Where's your car?" she asked.

"In my garage. I have more than one vehicle."

Of course he did. He had money.

It was the cold, not him, that made up her mind. She'd be a fool to trust this master manipulator.

Chapter 5

Lucas pulled to a stop in front of Rachel's apartment building.

"Don't walk me to my door." She started to open the SUV door.

"Rachel." He had to agree; walking her to her door obviously presented danger to both of them, but words still had to be said before he let her go. "Don't hold my dad responsible for what I did. You should keep your job with him."

Glancing over, he caught her slow blink before turning toward the window.

"He's a good man. And I know you need the income."

"Unlike you?" she asked.

"That I don't need the income?"

"No, the other."

That he wasn't a good man. Lucas suppressed a grin, hearing the hint of teasing sass. "I'm a little rough around the edges."

She turned from the window as he pulled into the parking lot. He met her look, watching sass go sober. "Were you really in training to be a SEAL?"

She liked that part about him. "Yes." He would have liked to have kept being a SEAL. And she would be the kind of woman who'd support a man like that.

Why he'd thought that, he didn't know. Reaching for his door handle, he stopped when she asked another question.

"What about the dot-commer?"

"Lie. I'm sorry."

Her mouth pressed tight but she recovered to ask, "And the ranch?"

"All mine."

"Did your dad buy it?"

"I have a trust fund, but I also earned money as a SWAT cop."

"You're a cop?" Her voice rose high with the last word.

Pleasant surprise and interest sparked, the way it had when he'd told her he went to SEAL training. "Yes. LAPD. Until I joined Dark Alley Investigations. Local police weren't getting very far." His time with the Los Angeles Police Department had provided an adequate diversion. Every day brought new disorder to bring to order. Murder. Robbery. Domestic violence. Rape and crimes against children had been the worst.

He noticed Rachel had turned away again. She hadn't gotten out of his SUV, though. Maybe he had hope, after all.

"What about your ex-wife?" she asked.

"I'm not getting back with her. That's not a lie."

Her distrust had built a robust wall of defensiveness to protect her against lying, cheating men. He understood why she kept going back to that.

She mulled that over awhile, debating whether to believe him on any topic.

"Dark Alley seems very elite," she said without looking at him.

He kept a grin from sprouting. She was curious about his job with DAI. "*Elite* isn't a word I'd use."

Now she turned to him. "What word would you use?"

He searched for something adequate. "Facilitative."

Those golden orbs slid over from the angle of her head, losing some of her distrust and becoming seductive. Attracted…

"Facilitative?"

He had to actually curb an outright chuckle. A moment more to overcome the impact of her lovely face, and he had the wherewithal to respond.

"I have a lot more room to investigate with them than I would in LA as a cop."

"Meaning, they look the other way when you do something illegal but in favor of the investigation."

"Something like that. I wouldn't call myself a mercenary, but I could be a mercenary with a heart."

He watched her struggle to hold back a grin. Opening the door, she said, "You're a liar," and got out.

Seeing her glance back on her way to the dimly lit, cheap front apartment door, Lucas fought a tickle of adoration. Her hair sailed with the turn of her head, and her hips swayed like a confident woman misplaced in her current setting. She opened the front door and went inside.

Lucas leaned his head back, basking in a mysterious glow. Still parked where he'd let her go, he took a few moments to settle back down to Earth.

Then dread marched a slow invasion. He hadn't felt that tight pull in the pit of his stomach since the last time he'd met a woman who touched his heart. He'd met her a year after his divorce, after he'd started as an LAPD cop, after he'd acclimated to the ugliness of crime and set his sights on becoming a detective.

Nicole had been an administrative assistant in his department. She always had a cheery hello for him and had a young, sexy body. Her fun personality had masked what grew between them. Then she'd invited him up to her apartment after dinner and a movie. They'd made love, and Lucas felt as though he could be with her, really *be* with her.

That tight pull inside had preceded a sick feeling and reminders of how he'd been fooled before. Fear of being fooled again hadn't been what made him withdraw from that sweet, funny girl. She hadn't understood and he hadn't explained anything to her, just stopped calling and going by her desk. She'd tried to intercept him, and the last time he saw her, she cornered him and demanded an explanation.

I'm not interested in anything lasting, he'd said.

He hadn't been prepared to talk about his feelings. He hadn't understood them himself. But after that girl had quit her job and left LA and he'd read the email she'd sent him, he'd thought of nothing else for months. He'd broken her heart. His dishonesty had crushed her. He'd never explained about his ex.

After he'd sorted out his thoughts, he realized he wasn't ready to be with another woman. He'd told the truth that he wasn't interested in anything lasting, but he'd left out that he didn't think long relationships were worth the investment of trust. Becoming a damn good detective had taken priority. He had to be good at something. He'd quit SEAL training. He would rather die than give up his career as a detective. He had something to be proud of, and that went a long way in making up the loss of a dream.

Now, though, he wondered how so many years had gone by without thinking of that sweet, funny girl. Would he spend the rest of his life single? That thought didn't bother him. The thought of spending the rest of his life with a woman did. That tug in his stomach tightened, as though Rachel could draw him away from all he'd built. She could send him down a different path, just like his ex.

Just as he put the gear in Drive, he spotted someone climbing up a fire escape. Lucas had parked opposite the alley beside the run-down apartment building. Silhouetted against light coming from a streetlight near the next building, the man reached the fifth floor. Rachel's floor.

Without hesitation, Lucas put the gear back in Park, turned the engine off and pushed open his door. He jogged toward the man and the fire escape, staying in the shadows.

The man worked on the window, testing the lock and then using something to pry the window open. Was that Rachel's apartment? He pictured her getting ready for bed, unsuspecting.

Lucas began to climb the fire escape, seeing the

man disappear into the building, leaving the window open. He ran up the metal stairs to the window. No sound came from inside. Did the man think Rachel wasn't home, or had he waited for her to return?

Lucas didn't think so. He would have seen Rachel get out of Lucas's SUV. It was late. Maybe he hoped to sneak inside while she slept. Except she wasn't asleep. Not yet.

Climbing through the window and into Rachel's small dining area, Lucas heard the shower running and then saw the man turn from the bathroom door. He was just under six feet tall with dark eyes and dark hair, and he wore black jeans and a black fleece jacket. Lucas didn't recognize him.

The man suddenly noticed him and charged. Lucas blocked a trained kick and the chopping swings of the man's arms. He sparred with his feet and hands, connecting two blows to the man's head. Realizing he had a formidable opponent in Lucas, the man ducked and rolled to escape, standing in the middle of the living room. Lucas kicked his torso, and the man slammed against the wall opposite the window. Before Lucas could continue his assault, the man jumped into a somersault and landed by the front door.

Rachel appeared in the bathroom doorway with a towel wrapped around her. Distracted just long enough, Lucas couldn't stop the man from running through the door.

He ran after him, shouting to Rachel, "Stay here!"

The man took the stairs.

Lucas ran after him, leaping over the railing to the lower level stairs to gain distance. The other man was fast. He raced down to the lobby level.

An old man in worn clothes stumbled out of the way as the intruder pushed by. He banged through the front doors and sprinted down the street. Lucas chased after him, dodging a homeless person's grocery cart heaped full of all his meager belongings.

The man shouted something unintelligible.

Lucas ran around the corner where the intruder had gone. The man glanced back quickly and then veered into a car wash. A lone man sprayed his new Lexus sedan, the only car there at this time of night.

The intruder reached the car and shoved the washer down to the ground. Lucas made it to the car door just as it closed. The man looked at him as he locked the door and started the engine. Lucas pulled out his gun and as the man drove off, he shot the rear tire out.

The man drove haphazardly without stopping. Lucas ran after the car, but it raced away.

"It has run-flat tires."

Catching his breath, Lucas turned to the man who'd just lost his car. He spoke with both pride and dismay.

"Report it stolen."

"Why were you chasing him? Are you a cop?"

Without answering, Lucas jogged back toward Rachel's apartment. He'd follow up with the police in the morning. In the meantime, he'd snatch Rachel and take her to his place.

She was dressed by the time he returned. She'd hastened to put on jeans and a long-sleeved flannel shirt. He could tell she wore no bra. As she moved toward him, her breasts jiggled more than they would if confined.

"Pack your things," he told her, annoyed that he found her so irresistible.

She stopped short. "What?"

"I'm taking you to my place."

"Your ranch?"

"No, my place in the city."

She went into the kitchen and opened her refrigerator. "That isn't necessary."

Summarily dismissed, Lucas ignored her reaction and moved toward her, stopping at the threshold of the eight-foot-wide kitchen. "It is." She was just going to have to put her distrust aside.

"I would have handled that man just fine by myself."

Her overconfidence almost inspired him. "With a towel wrapped around you?"

"I'd have dropped the towel." She let the refrigerator door close and twisted off the top of a bottle of water.

He looked up from the vicinity of her breasts. "Exactly what that intruder would have liked, I'm sure."

"I know how to fight." She held up the water. "Want one?"

He turned and headed for the rickety armoire she'd set up next to her daybed. The doors didn't latch so he swung them open, looking around for luggage.

"What the hell are you doing?"

He knelt to look under the bed and found a duffel bag. After sliding that out, he unzipped it and began putting clothes inside.

"Hey." She took hold of his arm.

He stopped and faced her, dropping the pants he held into the open duffel. "I'm taking you with me if I have to tie and carry you."

"Why would you want to do that? I thought you had

me pegged a murderer." She lowered her arm, releasing him from her soft hold.

"I don't think you murdered anyone, but I wonder if you know something important. That makes you a person of interest." He caught himself grazing her body with a hot gaze.

She caught him, too. Folding her arms, lips pursed, she spoke without words.

He stepped aside. "Pack."

At first she didn't move. But then she glanced around her apartment and toward the window she'd closed in the dining area. He couldn't call it a room. It was too small. He couldn't tell if she felt she didn't have much to leave behind or if worry drove her decision-making.

What did she have to worry about? Him? Or the secret she harbored, because he had no doubts now she had at least one—a big one.

"I'll protect you," he said.

She slowly moved her eyes back toward him. She had nowhere else to go. She could stay here and risk the stranger coming back, but she needed a job to afford that, and she may not want to go back to work at Tieber Transport.

"And I won't treat you like a suspect." Not until he had proof. Or he discovered what she was keeping hidden.

She continued to contemplate. Then she stepped to her duffel bag. "All right, but only until I find a new job."

"Or keep the one you already have." He moved farther out of her way, liking the sexy glare she bestowed on him.

Strange, how he could go from dread to excited sexual anticipation all in one night.

Lucas's city house was a mansion compared to Rachel's apartment. He pulled into the three-car garage that also had a car with dark windows parked in it, and she went inside the house behind him. The smell of potpourri greeted her as she walked through the laundry room and entered the entry with a grand staircase on the opposite side. Well, the staircase looked grand to her. It curved to an upper-level loft and a double doorway leading to the master suite. The entry branched off into a formal living room and a larger family room that extended to the back of the house, the kitchen and dining room adjacent.

Rachel had been in lots of nice houses with the men she dated, so seeing Lucas's didn't surprise her. It was the personal touches that stood out more than all those others. He had pictures of his family on a built-in bookcase, including some old ones that must have been of his biological father. In one, the man wore a police uniform. His father had been a cop.

"Where is your dad?" she asked. "What happened to him?"

"He died in the line of duty."

She saw the regret in his eyes, the flash of *if only*.

"He answered a domestic call and was shot on his way to the door. The boyfriend of the woman who called for help shot him. He'd already killed his girl-friend. A few days later, the law found him, and he was killed in the resulting shoot-out."

"That's terrible."

Lucas moved to the photo and picked it up. "I was so young, and my sister was only a few months old."

"Your poor mother." Rachel knew that kind of loss all too well. She hadn't been that young when her parents died. Sometimes she wished she could have been.

"She had a rough time for a while, but then she met Joseph. He changed her life. And ours. I think of him as my father."

Joseph did strike her as a good man. Even with his role in Lucas's deception, he had an ethical moral compass. She moved on to a hand-painted sculpture of a ship on one of the end tables. Paintings on the wall looked original.

"You like art?"

"An informant I knew was an artist. I bought some of his work." He looked up at the oil painting of a fisherman on a pier at sunset. "He had trouble with a drug addiction, and I tried to help him."

"Where is he now?"

"He overdosed on cocaine." He turned. "Come on. I'll show you to your room."

Upstairs, he led her through the loft to one of the other bedrooms. Inside, he opened the walk-in closet. There were clothes inside. Women's clothes.

Rachel stepped into the closet and began going through the items hanging up. "Did your ex leave these?"

"No. I bought them from a rape victim who owned a secondhand store."

He helped people a lot. She began to see him in a different light and had to restrain the inclination to forget that he'd lied to her.

"If any of them fit you, go ahead and keep them."

"Thanks." She stood there, as he looked at her face, aware that the temperature had warmed between them.

Wearing vintage jeans and a white knit sweater she'd found from the closet, Rachel bobbed her leg as she waited with Lucas for the detective he'd contacted regarding the stolen car last night. She'd watched and listened to him maneuver around conventional channels to find the right man. He'd called his boss, Kadin Tandy, who'd taken just an hour to locate someone they could talk to.

The police station bustled with activity, mostly clerical. Rachel loved people-watching, and this morning, she couldn't stop staring at the hooker who'd just been released. She wore a tired scowl and didn't look like a hooker. She dressed nicely. Although tight, the black dress came to her knees, and the jewelry being returned to her that she put back around her neck and wrists looked real. The only reason Rachel knew she was a hooker was because she heard her talking to the clerk.

The tall tattooed man with her must be her pimp, and he dressed in a suit and tie. Rachel marveled over them, fascinated. People fascinated her. All different walks of life, each had their own journey. While she appreciated those who shared her struggles, those who had fortune or an average but sustainable existence drew her equally.

"Stop staring," Lucas said.

Seeing the hooker direct a glare her way now, Rachel turned to Lucas. "Do you ever wonder how people like that end up?"

"Not usually."

"She can't do what she does the rest of her life. Does she have family? Will she find a new profession?" She'd like to think everyone found their way, but life wasn't that kind. And it wasn't kind because of the people in it. Only the strong survived. Darwinism at its cruelest. Who really cared when people lost their homes and livelihoods? Who cared what happened to them? She did. And if she was rich, she'd help them, not turn her back.

"Mr. Curran?"

Rachel still hadn't gotten used to his real name. The reminder of his deception pricked her ire as she stood with him and he shook the five-foot-nine-inch balding detective's hand.

"Bob Newman. I've heard a lot about Kadin Tandy. I never thought he'd call me."

He looked like a Bob Newman. "I appreciate you seeing us."

"Come this way." The detective led them past a maze of desks to a conference room.

Rachel sat next to Lucas, and the detective sat across from them. There were papers on the table in front of him.

"You work for an extraordinary man," Detective Newman said. "It's a shame tragedy drives a man to do what he's done. His daughter's kidnapping and murder is a case we use to train our new officers. There are lessons to be learned, not just from that case but many others like it. Cold cases."

"Yes. They do require a certain expertise."

"Kadin tells me you come from a strong investigative background."

"I was a detective before I joined SWAT."

His clipped tone told Rachel his emotion had stirred with the topic. Being a SWAT member must have satisfied whatever urge had inspired him to become a SEAL, but it must have fallen short.

"A man like that wouldn't hire just anyone. He's got quite a reputation in this country."

Detective Newman didn't skimp on praise. Or envy.

"About the stolen car..." Lucas said. Clearly, he didn't want to talk about the great martyr Kadin Tandy, a man driven by grief and justice.

"Ah, yes." Newman pushed the file over to him.

"We found the car abandoned outside of town."

Rachel leaned over to see the location, reading the cross streets. There was an old dive bar near there, just far enough out of town to be dangerous.

Newman slid out a three-by-five photo, a color-printed copy from a digital source. She recognized the man who'd broken into her apartment.

"Have you ever seen this man before?" Newman asked Rachel. Evidently, he'd been briefed on what had happened. Lucas must have told him.

"No."

Lucas watched her as she answered, and she felt his distrust. He didn't discount she might be lying.

Well, then, he'd just have to keep not trusting, because some things she couldn't divulge.

Lucas pulled up to the ramshackle bar Rachel had told him about after they left the police station. She'd surprised him by revealing that, and then he'd realized she must have told the truth about her intruder. She hadn't known him.

That was something. But she still had her secrets.

At almost noon, a fair amount of cars had already gathered in the gravel parking area. The Lexus had been abandoned about two miles up the road. There was a chance the thief and intruder had stopped in for a drink.

Inside, the stench of stale beer assaulted his nose. Beer spilled and left to dry had caused stains in the torn industrial brown carpet. The cushions of black vinyl booths pushed through tears and cracks, and the laminate peeled back from tabletops or had broken away long ago.

Lucas started with the bartender, who shook his head when asked if he'd seen the man in the picture. He showed the photo to all in the room, and no one recognized the man.

Just as he would have left, he spotted the bartender talking to a newcomer, pointing to them. The newcomer looked over.

Lucas stopped and Rachel followed his gaze, seeing with him the man walking toward them.

"You looking for Marcus Henderson?"

Lucas showed him the photo. "Is this him?"

"Yeah, that's him. Bastard owes me money. I loaned him a few thousand to help him get into a new place, and he blew me off."

So now he'd like to get even. Lucas didn't mind how he obtained information, as long as he got it.

"Do you know where we can find him?" Lucas tucked the photo back into his jacket.

"What's he done this time?"

"Broke into a house. Stole a car."

"You a cop?" The man checked him out up and down. "You don't look like one."

"I'm a private investigator."

The man checked out Rachel with much more leisure.

"This is my deputy," Lucas said, drawing his attention back to him. "Where can we find him?"

"You gonna make him pay me back?"

"You'll have to go through the proper legal channel. But I can remind him for you." Lucas put his hands on his hips, something he did when he meant for someone to see his gun.

The man did and, with a grin, told them the address. "Anything else you need to know about him?"

"Anything you can tell us. Where he works. Anything about his family. Friends. His hangouts."

"He doesn't work. He sells drugs. Rumor has it he does odd jobs for his dealers, you know, dirty work like roughing up people who owe money. Ironic, isn't it?"

"Who hires him?"

"Nobody knows who. Marcus kept that quiet, as anyone would expect. He might be a thief but he isn't stupid when it comes to that sort of thing."

"Do you deal drugs?"

Lucas glanced over at Rachel with her innocent question that no smart criminal would answer honestly.

"Oh, hell no. I sell cars at the Ford dealer downtown. I make a good living." He said the last part to Rachel, who stiffened into a straighter stance.

"What about other friends? Family?"

"His family lives on the East Coast. He doesn't keep in touch with them. I don't know about any friends. He runs with a different crowd now."

That would be all they'd get from him, all that might help to find out who had sent him to Rachel, or if he'd done that on his own.

"Thank you for your time." Lucas turned with Rachel. "You've been a big help."

"You go on and tell that slime I'll be expecting payment."

Lucas lifted his hand in friendly farewell. "I'll do that."

A short drive later, Rachel headed for a nice middle-class house about twenty minutes from downtown Bozeman. She stood next to Lucas at Marcus's front door. He'd already rung the bell and knocked.

She looked over at the BMW in the garage, the door open. Someone should be home.

Lucas met her eyes. He agreed.

Testing the doorknob and finding it locked, he gave the neighborhood a scan. Then he produced a small tension wrench and pin that he used to work the lock. Lengthy seconds passed. Rachel glanced around. No one walked by. No cars appeared. Everyone was at work or inside. She couldn't see into any windows very clearly. If anyone saw them, they'd not know until the police arrived.

The lock snapped open.

He pushed the door so it swung slowly.

Rachel stayed behind him as he entered and pulled out his gun. She peered past his big shoulders and saw the mess.

Lucas stopped.

"Don't even think about telling me to stay outside," she said.

He glanced briefly back, mildly annoyed but not arguing.

A standing lamp had fallen. Beer bottles had tipped over onto the floor, a puddle of beer still on the coffee table. A throw blanket lay askew on the floor along with the couch pillows. Kitchen chairs had tipped over. There had been a struggle here.

She touched Lucas's back as he moved cautiously into the house. As they moved closer to the kitchen, she caught sight of a pair of feet sticking out from the island counter.

Lucas stopped again.

"What is that?" She'd seen crimes before. She'd seen robberies. She'd seen gang members try to shoot each other. She'd lived next door to a drive-by shooting. She'd seen a lot. But this. This pushed the boundary.

Was that Marcus, and was he dead?

She thought she saw the rim of a pool of blood.

Lucas started forward. "Don't touch anything."

Crime scene…

Stepping forward, she stopped when she confirmed it was blood she saw. Turning her back, she covered her mouth. She'd never seen a dead body before. She'd never seen a murdered body.

The man who'd broken into her house was dead. Murdered.

Why?

Chapter 6

"Are you sure you don't know him?"

Rachel shook off the image of the dead man. "Yes, I'm sure." She noticed they weren't headed for his city house. "Where are we going?"

"To see Jared."

Alarm electrified her. To see Jared? For real? Why? Aware of her elevated pulse and breathing, Rachel pretended calm.

"You'd rather not?" He saw right through her. He knew she kept facts from him.

She steeled herself against her failing strength. He could not break her. "No. All right. Let's go see him." She looked out her window as he parked in front of a familiar building, the location of her dream job, when she'd believed that dream had come true.

Lucas held the door for her, and she resented his

gloating. He looked forward to her squirming through this. He had no idea why she'd squirm, though.

He asked the receptionist to let Jared know they were here. Rachel didn't doubt Jared would drop whatever he was doing. She concealed a stressed exhale.

There he was. Jared walked with a low brow toward them, suit lapels flowing, tie swaying. He hurried too much. Talk about making it obvious.

"Rachel," he said as he came to a stop. Then to Lucas, he extended a professional hand. "Lucas. It's been so long."

"Jared."

The tone Lucas used piqued Rachel. She couldn't see any animosity in his face, but the clipped name clued to some underlying tension.

Jared glanced to her as though wishing she'd clue him in to the purpose of this impromptu visit. She offered no help. If not for him, she wouldn't be in her current situation, one that hadn't gone away since she'd discovered Jared's lie. She'd been a fool to think it would.

With a wary look at Lucas, Jared said, "Why don't we talk in my office?"

Rachel followed him first, Lucas's hand going to the small of her back. The contact gave her a shock. Had he done that unconsciously? He didn't pay her much attention, so maybe he had.

In Jared's office, she preferred to stand—a good distance from where Jared faced them in front of his desk, arms folded defensively. Lucas stood beside her, his hand dropping from her back, leaving her bereft for the few seconds before she braced herself for the conversation to come.

"What can I do for you?" Jared asked.

"We're not one of your clients, Jared," Lucas said, low and dark.

Jared barely looked his way before going straight to her. "How do you know him?"

"How do you think I know him?" Rachel couldn't keep a little of her own animosity out of her voice.

She didn't expect the hardening of his eyes. And then the aloofness. "He's always thought I killed his sister."

"Did you?"

Jared scoffed. "You know I didn't."

"How would she know?" Lucas asked, pouncing, and probably trying to get Jared to reveal something, whether willingly or not. And include her. Implicate her.

Rachel sent Jared her best warning, direct eye contact he glanced over and dismissed. He better not try to implicate her, too. She put her hand on the edge of one of the guest chairs, hoping Lucas didn't notice her dig her fingers into the supple black leather.

Stepping forward, Lucas stood beside her and in front of Jared, who'd moved back with Lucas's advance. He now stood beside the desk.

"I'll ask again. What can I do for you? I presume you came here for a reason?"

"Someone broke into my apartment," Rachel said, not adding it couldn't be a coincidence after he'd come to see her.

Jared turned to her, genuinely shocked. "A burglar?"

She grunted at the funny joke. "No, Jared. As you recall, I don't own anything of value."

"Whoever broke into her apartment must think she's a threat." Lucas moved closer to her side.

Rachel tensed. Why had he moved closer? She watched him regard her softly, glancing at Jared to see him notice the act. And it had to be an act. Why was Lucas doing this? Why make a point to show her affection now?

"You went to see her," Lucas said to Jared, whose eyes shifted to him in defense.

"My relationship with Rachel is our private affair."

"Affair," Lucas scoffed. "Yes, it was that, wasn't it? You cheated on my sister. You haven't changed."

"Oh, don't start that again, Lucas. So I dated a lot of women. I don't know why that bothered you so much. It's not as though you had a shortage of admirers."

"Luella was my sister. Do you think I wanted her to end up with you?"

"She loved me. I loved her."

"Until you met Rachel?" Lucas glanced at her, a silent reassurance that he meant her no insult, and then a hardening that stopped the sentiment. She had, in fact, had an affair with his sister's husband. Maybe he believed it hadn't been intentional. It hadn't. Rachel had a strict moral code when it came to that sort of thing.

"Luella and I started to have problems the year before I met Rachel," Jared said. "We were going to get a divorce. If you were close to her, she'd have told you that."

When Lucas took a menacing step forward, Rachel put her hand on his biceps.

He stopped, heeding her gentle request to remain calm.

Jared again noticed this exchange and pinned her with his gaze. "How long have you known him?"

Rachel chose not to answer and after a few seconds, caught Lucas's subtle, repressed grin.

"We just met," he said to Jared, playing him again.

"Well, if we're through…?" Jared moved behind his desk.

"When was the last time you saw my sister alive?" Lucas demanded in the most intimidating tone that Rachel had ever heard from him.

Jared stopped in the process of sitting down. He slowly straightened. "I've told it before. The last time I saw her, I left for work. When I came home, dinner was in the refrigerator. It was her night to go out with her friends. I went to bed at nine thirty."

"You didn't hear her when she came home?" Lucas asked with less force, more of a manipulating detective now. A hunter.

"No."

Luella's keys had been found in her purse. Her car was in the garage. There had been no sign of forced entry. No blood. Rachel had read the news.

"You told police she came to bed," Lucas said.

"She did." Jared glanced at Rachel as though seeking her support.

She eased her grip on the leather chair.

"You told them the time. Ten twenty," Lucas said.

Jared turned from her to him, paying closer attention. "I was asleep when she came home."

He should not get lackadaisical with a man like Lucas in the room. Lucas could ferret out a lie expertly. And he had a physical presence that commanded obedience.

"Then how did you hear her? How did you know the time?"

"Look, I'm not lying. I estimated the time. And I did hear her. I fell right back to sleep. She must have gotten up in the middle of the night."

Rachel still found it difficult to believe Jared didn't wake up or notice his wife missing from bed. Had Luella never come home that night? Had something happened before ten twenty? Her car had been in the garage. No sign of forced entry. Someone she'd known must have lured her away.

"Are you sure you don't know anything about why someone would break into my apartment?" Rachel asked as amenably as she could. She did not trust him. A man who could deceive his wife and the mistress he obtained did not deserve trust. In that, she agreed with Lucas that he could be the prime suspect in Luella's murder.

Jared absorbed that awhile. "Why do you think I had anything to do with that?"

Rachel decided it was best if she didn't respond. She saw Lucas study her in frustrated disappointment. He needed to hear why.

"What's going on with the two of you?" Jared asked.

Why did he ask? Rachel glanced at Lucas, who still regarded her with heated, hidden emotion. Feeling that heat begin to seep into her, she realized perhaps Jared had picked up on some undercurrents. Her secretiveness put him at odds with her because of the attraction neither of them could control. The animal, physical desire couldn't be turned off.

Jared swept his arm from Lucas to her, but his growing angst arrowed on Lucas. "You had your hand on her back on the way in here, and I can see the way you look at her."

The personal reference took Rachel aback.

"Jared?" She had to check to see if she'd read him right.

"Why are you with him?"

"What?" She put her hand to her upper chest, not understanding.

"Did you kill my sister to be with Rachel?"

Rachel sucked in an appalled breath and turned on Lucas. "Stop!"

"No," Jared said, "I did not. I wouldn't have had to kill anyone to have Rachel." He slid unrecognizable, mean eyes to her. "Until she found out about Luella, but by then Luella was already dead."

"Jared—"

"Why are you with this man?" he cut her off.

"I am not *with* him." Then she said to Lucas, "My relationship with Jared had nothing to do with her murder."

"That remains to be determined."

Stung by his indifference and cold regard, Rachel went for the door. "Stay out of my life, both of you!"

"Rachel, wait," Lucas said, concern in his tone.

But as she cleared the door, she heard Jared say, "Now you've done it. If you want to be on her good side, you're doing a lousy job." He let out a wicked chuckle. "You must not know her very well."

No one knew her very well. Her mother had known her. No one since. As she wondered about that. A sinking feeling settled over the idea that maybe she'd done that to herself.

She jogged to the elevator, catching the closing doors and squeezing into a full car. As the doors closed, she saw Lucas rush to a resigning stop before he was blessedly blocked from her view.

Staring at the numbers going down, Rachel wished she didn't feel like running every time something or someone cornered her. As an adolescent, that had been juvenile court. As an adult, anything that threatened her chances for a normal life, a life like she saw in other people like the woman at the mall. She feared being sucked down into a cesspool her adolescent choices had created, forever circling the consequences.

Meeting a man like Lucas didn't help. He could be something good for her, if he could open himself to that. His sister's murder, her association with Jared and his lack of trust made that an impossible dream.

That was what made her run. Lucas. His perception of her. And her inability to change anything. She had to stay her course. Graduate. Work hard to secure her future. For herself. That was why she'd left everything and everyone behind. She needed to prove her worthiness not only to herself, but also to all who'd witnessed her downfall after her parents died.

Getting involved with Lucas would only spin her back into a cesspool. She cared too much about her reputation and her future to allow that to happen.

"What is going on between the two of you?"

Lucas turned from the elevator doors to see Jared had followed him. "That's a question I'd like to ask you."

"You may not like to hear this, but I fell in love with Rachel."

"You fell in love with the last woman you slept with while you were with Luella." Satisfied he'd sur-

prised his ex-friend, Lucas said, "Yes, I knew about
your affair before you married my sister. I didn't say
anything to her because I hoped you'd be faithful once
you were married." That Lucas hadn't told Luella had
plagued him ever since. After her murder, the burden
had grown. How he regretted not telling her. Maybe
she'd have left Jared and still be alive today.

Jared stepped back as two women in business skirts
and jackets approached the elevators. "Is that why you
started hating me so much?"

One of the women glanced back at Jared and then
at Lucas.

Lucas moved across the hall to the wall where Jared
stood and kept his voice low. "No, I recognized what
a snake you were shortly after I introduced you to Luella." That had been after Jared had gotten this job and
he'd partnered with Eldon Sordi, a man with a high
taste for the good life. He'd gone through four wives
so far, and went on glamorous poker tours. Jared had
never told him and didn't have to, but Eldon also had a
drug problem, one he'd picked up after meeting Jared.

Lucas had warned Luella but she'd been taken in
by the promise of a rich life. He'd had words with
Jared, who'd dismissed his recreational drug use as
merely that.

Then, after he married Luella, she had called Lucas
crying one night after Jared had come home from
work late, drunk and wired on cocaine. Lucas had
urged her to divorce him, but she'd said she loved him.

Lucas had flown home and gone to see Jared two
days later. He'd given him more than an earful. He'd
sported a black eye after going nose to nose with him.
That had been the beginning of their falling-out. The

last and final hammer slamming down had been when Eldon's fourth wife hired a private investigator, who'd snapped several photographs of Eldon and Jared on a yacht with two strange women. Eldon's wife had sent them to Luella.

The call Lucas got from his sister had infuriated him.

That was six months before her murder.

More people got off the elevator and walked down the hall.

"You were always too righteous," Jared said when they were alone again. "Your dad died in the line of duty, and you made it your life's goal to martyr him. You would never have become a cop."

Lucas didn't know how Jared had drawn that conclusion. His dad had died when he was a young boy. True, having only photos of him and his mother's narrations, his dad had seemed like a superhero.

"Is your life's goal infidelity and greed?" he asked his old friend.

Jared scoffed. "I do love money. The rest just happened."

And he'd let it happen. "That's what people without integrity say. It's much easier to let things happen than to take care not to hurt those closest to you. Hurting others never concerned you. I didn't realize that until Luella started seeing you."

"Like I said, righteous. You'd be a lot less stressed out if you let go a little, Lucas. Relax and just live."

His partner Eldon appeared in the hall, walking as though his tight schedule pressed him. "Ah, there you are." He passed an uninterested look at Lucas. "We've got that HealthFirst policy meeting in fifteen. I need to talk to you."

"I was just heading there." Jared turned to Lucas. "You remember Lucas Curran?"

"Your wife's brother. Of course." Eldon reached out an impersonal hand.

Lucas shook it briefly.

"I'm sorry to cut this short, but…" Eldon stepped back and then waited for Jared to go with him.

"Next time you stop by, let me know first. Maybe we could meet somewhere more casual." Jared started off with Eldon.

"One more thing, Jared." Lucas waited for him to turn, Eldon doing the same with a hint of annoyance. "I'd have become a cop whether my dad died or not. It's in my blood. And I'm good at it."

Eldon turned away first, Jared lingering as the unspoken message dawned on him.

If he killed Luella, Lucas would bring justice to his door.

When they disappeared back into the office area, Lucas faced the elevator. A few seconds later the doors opened, and he stepped in. Someone hurried inside after him. As he faced forward, he saw Marcy.

"Oh, hello, Mr. Curran."

"Marcy. What are you doing here?"

"Oh." She glanced back toward the offices. "I'm seeing one of the executives here."

How had she met an executive here? Joseph's company had nothing in common with this one.

"I'm glad I ran into you," Marcy said, full of bright energy. "I wanted to apologize for your girlfriend overhearing me talking. I didn't mean for—"

Nothing about her indicated she felt caught. Lucas wasn't sure why he thought she should. He just found it peculiar to find her here.

"Don't worry about it."

She moved closer, putting her hand on his upper arm. "But I do. With your sister's murder still unsolved, you might have learned something if she hadn't found out you got her that job as a ploy. Your dad told me she might know something about your sister's murder."

His dad had a big mouth.

"If there's anything I can do to help, all you have to do is tell me."

What did she think she could do, besides stick her nose where it didn't belong and then spread rumors? And have affairs with one of Lucas's estranged friend's executive peers.

She lowered her hand, coquettish now. "I was real glad to hear you moved back to Bozeman."

She'd flirted with him before. Marcy had the reputation of flirting with every available executive. She'd gone her rounds in Joseph's office, and for some reason had moved on to Jared's. Lucas couldn't compare her to Rachel. Though when he'd first met Rachel and thought she practiced the same dirty tactics as Marcy, the two were completely different. Rachel sought successful men because she had aspirations for a better life. Marcy pounced on them out of greed. Rachel looked for love. Marcy looked for money.

Rachel looked for love?

Since Rachel lost her parents, he couldn't see how she wouldn't, whether she realized that or not.

The elevator doors opened, and Lucas stepped out.

Marcy trailed behind, trotting to catch up to his longer strides.

"I heard your ex-wife moved here. Tory Curran?"

Did she say her last name on purpose? She'd kept his last name, a sore point with him.

"I've got to get going, Marcy."

"Don't want to talk about it? I'm sorry. Too personal." She made a Valley Girl face, impish smile and flashing eyes. "Are you making any progress on the investigation?"

The abrupt question alerted him to motive. Why did she ask? "I can't discuss the details."

"Do you think Rachel killed her? She could have, you know, in a jealous rage and all. I heard she claims to have found out he was married after Luella was killed. What if she's lying?"

Lucas kept walking to the exit in the lobby.

"Why would Jared kill her?" Marcy asked.

That's what he intended to find out.

"Rachel would have more of a reason than him," Marcy pressed.

Lucas began to think her interest in his sister's murder went beyond hunger for gossip. He stopped and she nearly bumped into him.

"Why do you say that?" he asked with a demanding tone.

"Uh…" She stammered and struggled for a reply. "Because Jared has no motive. He makes a lot of money. Luella came from a well-off family, your family. Maybe he would have to free himself for Rachel, but why do that? Why risk it? Rachel must have been upset when she heard he was married."

"She ended the relationship." Even as he said that

he wondered why he felt inclined to defend her. She'd had so many bad breaks in her life, maybe he felt sorry for her. Or…maybe he felt something entirely different for her.

"Still…"

Marcy seemed eager to put the blame on Rachel. Why? Did she want her out of the way so she could pursue Jared? Or Lucas? She'd said she was glad to see him back in town.

"Well, if Rachel killed Luella, I'll find out and then you can celebrate." With that, he turned and walked toward the exit, leaving her standing there with an open mouth, watching him go.

Something bothered him about the way Marcy had approached him. She must have waited until he'd finished talking with Jared, and then rushed after him. What about Luella interested her so much?

He decided to wait until she left work. Maybe he'd follow her, see what she did in her personal time. A gold digger like her might have more motive than a destitute woman like Rachel.

He didn't have to wait long. An hour later Marcy appeared through the doors of the company, and Jared held the door for her. The two of them went to a waiting sedan and got inside.

Why had Jared left the meeting that had seemed so important to Eldon? Maybe it hadn't been a long meeting. Maybe the more important question was: Why were Jared and Marcy leaving work early?

The sedan moved through the parking lot and out to the street.

Lucas carefully followed.

A short time later he stopped near an upscale club

with a chalkboard out front that advertised happy hour. At just after three, Jared and Marcy were right on time. Had Lucas been looking at the wrong people over the years since his sister's murder?

Lucas left the restaurant. Before he went to patch things up with Rachel, he'd stop at Marcy's house and plant a listening device. Marcy may have made a mistake showing her cards by talking to him. She might just be his first big clue in this case.

Chapter 7

Rachel's cell phone rang after she finished a long bath. It was after five, and Lucas hadn't come by yet. She'd come here to get away from him. Maybe he'd leave her alone. Even for one night, she needed some space between them. Her cell rarely rang so she wondered if it was him.

With a towel wrapped around her and another twisted on her head, she went to the kitchen counter where she'd left her phone. Seeing the unknown number, she debated over whether to answer or not. What if it was a creditor?

Reprimanding herself for cowering, she answered. "Hello?"

She heard the sound of a television in the background of the caller. That and steady breathing.

Alarm chased through her with an all-too-familiar dread. "Hello?" she repeated.

"We had an agreement."

The muffled voice, deep and deathly calm, hurled her back in time. The same voice had haunted her before.

Rachel said nothing, too terrorized to think of anything other than the danger that had returned—just as she feared it would.

"Who are you? Why are you calling me?"

"You know why, Rachel." The man's muffled voice lilted with cynical wickedness, a complete lack of empathy. The sound sent chills through her. He must have put something over the phone to disguise his voice.

"I think the only reason I didn't kill you before is because I found you very attractive," he said. "But now you're with Lucas Curran. That changes things."

How did he know that? Rachel faced her window. Was he spying on her? That elevated this to a new level.

"At first I thought he was just another one of your boyfriends." The man further filled her with anxiety. He'd been watching her all this time. "But then I found out he's a detective from Dark Alley Investigations. Luella's brother joined a high-profile agency, didn't he?"

Rachel refrained from begging him to leave her alone.

"Maybe I should have taken care of you four years ago," he said.

"I haven't told anyone." She hated the quiver in her voice. Moments ago she'd scolded herself for being a coward. This stranger had made her the grandest of cowards. Although he didn't know, he preyed on insecurities developed after her parents died, through her struggles in foster care and juvenile court.

"If you don't st-stop calling me, I will go to the police," she said, heart slamming in heightened apprehension.

"St-st-st," the man mocked. "Not the response I hoped to hear, Rachel. Mr. Curran is working his spell on you. I looked him up, you know. Quite a crusader, that one. I read an article about him when he was an LAPD cop. Saved a young boy from his stepfather kidnapper. Another time, he ran down a would-be rapist when he was off-duty. The man never stops."

"Maybe I won't have to go to the police," she said, feeling her strength returning. She'd thought of that several times since discovering Lucas's true identity, like a fantasy. He'd solve his sister's murder and rescue her in the process. All along she'd hoped the law would catch the killer.

"No. All you need to do is stay away from him."

What if Lucas wouldn't stay away from her? What if she didn't want to stay away from Lucas? What if he was her only way out of this?

"If you don't," the man continued, "I'll kill you."

"I don't know anything," she said, having told him that before. And she truly didn't. Nothing she could say about Luella would implicate anyone in her murder, or hint to any promising leads. This man thought she knew something when she didn't. "You're wasting your time calling me. If I did know something, do you really think I wouldn't have gone to the police?"

"You know enough, sweet Rachel."

He sensed her fear. Ever since her dealings with the law, she feared police. She feared being accused of something she didn't do. She feared this man would succeed in doing that. He'd threatened it before.

Stay quiet, sweet Rachel, or you may find yourself the guilty one...

He'd referred to her affair with Jared. She could appear the jilted lover. With Jared's wife out of the way, he'd be all hers. Never mind if that wasn't true, if she'd been the one to leave him and never want anything more to do with him. Four years ago he'd alluded to things that had made her believe he could draw her into trouble.

"Who are you?" she asked again.

"This is the only warning you'll get, Rachel. Stop seeing Lucas Curran. Go back to being the quiet girl you were before he came to town."

Quiet girl...

She had been a quiet girl—too quiet. She'd convinced herself that her isolation had been a result of her determination to better her life, but shame had done that.

Hearing the line go dead, Rachel put her phone down with trembling fingers. She shouldn't have allowed him to control her fear the way he had four years ago. She should have gone to the police. She knew that. She'd known it a few months after he'd stopped terrorizing her.

Like the last time he'd threatened her, Rachel suspected she was talking to a killer, Luella's killer, or the one who'd hired her killer. She'd tried to find out more about him but ended up with nothing but more threats. When she'd stopped searching, he'd stopped terrorizing and it had been too easy to slip into a shell.

She had to do something. But what? The time for

doing had long passed. Now she'd only look guiltier. Rachel wasn't sure what was worse, cowering and not going to police, or being accused of Luella's murder.

Hearing her apartment door begin to open, she jumped and felt the lurch of her pulse. Pivoting, she saw Lucas enter and close the door. He stood there without saying anything.

"How…" How had he unlocked the door?

He held up a key. "I made a copy."

"You…sneak!" She moved forward and tried to take the key from him.

He raised his hand, out of her reach. She gave up and stepped back, folding her arms.

"Did you ever meet Marcy before you started working for my stepdad?" he asked.

She drew her head back, bewildered. "No. Why?"

"I ran into her at HealthFirst. She said she was seeing someone there. And then I saw her leave with Jared."

Rachel couldn't even be shocked by that news. "Well, Jared does like to fool around. And Luella was your sister. Jared could have gone to Tieber Transport."

He blinked slowly with the logic that made. "Yes. And I was in LA while they were married."

He wouldn't have known when Jared had gone to Tieber Transport, but he must have, and that's how he'd met Marcy.

"Now do you believe me when I say I'd never get involved with him again?" Rachel asked.

He didn't say anything, just looked at her while his thoughts went on. He probably debated whether to try and get her talking some more.

"Enough of that for tonight," he said. "We could both use a break."

"How do you propose we do that?" Rachel loved spontaneity.

"When's the last time you went to the museum?"

She had to think on that a moment. "Gosh. With my parents. Years." That suddenly seemed so sad. Yet another motivator to improve her life. If she had money, she could go do things like that. She could have a family and take her kids.

"We'll go tomorrow. Take a day off from all of this."

While that offered welcome reprieve, she had to question his motive. Sexy and big and full of masculine power, he had what it took to capture her heart. Was that where her thoughts of family had stemmed? She'd always assumed she'd someday have a husband and family, but she'd never put a time frame on it. When she could afford one. Or, when she met the right man.

Now that she really thought about it, she'd like to have a family sooner rather than later. Would she ever get the chance? After she graduated, she'd have to work hard to build her new life. That would take time. Her biological clock would keep ticking on. Which did she consider more important? Career and a new, great life? Or a family? What if she could have both? Lots of people worked and had families. But Rachel preferred either one or the other. She'd rather raise a family and not have to work a demanding job. Her mother hadn't worked. She'd spent time with Rachel growing up. That was how she'd gotten so close to her mother.

That was also why losing her had been so devastating. Dad, too. Dad had worked, but he'd come home every night with love in his eyes and a kiss for her mother. She'd seen what true love is. She wanted that.

Inside the Bozeman Museum of Natural History late the next morning, Rachel and Lucas started with the dinosaur exhibit. Rachel stayed alert for any strangers who could be the man who'd called. She didn't notice anything peculiar, but then, she was no detective.

Feeling safer inside the building, she relaxed and let herself appreciate the artifacts. Preserved skeletons posed behind glass and on pedestals. Rachel stopped at one where several smaller dinosaurs had gotten stuck in mud and died, fossilized in their mortal doom.

"Sometimes I feel stuck like that," she said.

"Don't we all?" He chuckled.

"You feel stuck?" She turned to him, eyeing him from his torso to his handsome, blond, stubbly face. "I wouldn't think a man like you ever gets stuck."

"A man like me?" He faced her a little more, his interest sparked.

She hadn't intended to do that. Sparks lit at the most unusual times with them. He lit her that way, too.

"SEAL, SWAT cop, private investigator. Take your pick. Men like you don't get stuck. You fight your way through."

He looked at the exhibit again, lost in thought.

She looked at the exhibit with him, waiting for him to move on.

"I got stuck with a dishonest wife, and I'm stuck now with Luella's murder case," he said.

Rachel hadn't expected him to talk about this. "You got away from your wife." For a price, but he'd gotten away. And now his wife had returned. Would she win her way back into his heart? She didn't let herself fall into that negativity. "How do you feel stuck with Luella's murder case? I mean, it hasn't been solved yet. Is that what makes you feel stuck?"

"No. I'll solve her murder. I'll just never be able to forgive myself for letting her die."

How in the world did he rationalize that being his fault? Before she could ask, he left the exhibit.

Rachel followed and caught up to him, scanning the crowd for anyone suspicious.

"She met Jared through me," Lucas said. "He and I were friends in college."

"What happened?" She spotted a man looking at her. Average in height, dark, receding hair, he appeared normal except the way he'd zeroed in on her.

"We were still friends after that, up until he showed me what kind of man he'd become. He studied finance." Lucas followed her gaze.

The man saw him and turned away.

"Maybe I should have seen that coming."

Rachel glanced toward the man who'd looked at her.

"I mean about Jared," Lucas said.

Rachel let out a breathy laugh, more self-conscious than anything. "Not everyone is an inside trader."

Finished with another exhibit, Lucas led her toward an exit. He held the exterior door open for her. This led to a large courtyard. In the distance she saw an old homestead in the wintery landscape.

"In summer the flowers are spectacular," he said as he walked the shoveled and icy path.

Her foot slipped, and she had to correct her balance.

Lucas offered his elbow, and she hooked her arm there, feeling instant warmth and not from his body heat—from her own.

"I tried to talk her out of marrying him, but she wouldn't listen."

She tipped her head up to see him. "Then how is that your fault? She made her own choice."

"I should have done more to stop her. She'd still be alive if not for me."

"Because she met Jared through you?" Anyone who lost a loved one went through stages of grief and the could-have and should-haves, but Lucas seemed to carry that to the extreme. "Are you that sure he killed her?"

"Can you tell me anything that will convince me otherwise?"

Rachel removed her arm from his as she stepped up to the homestead door. Would he try to get her to talk again?

"I thought we were doing this to take a break from that," she said.

He opened the door for her. "We are."

With him manipulating her? She went inside, and the charming farmhouse took her into a world long past. Museum employees dressed in costumes played out what life would have been like, cooking over a wood-burning stove, spinning yarn, weaving a rug.

After going through the house, they left through the back and took in more actors forging iron in a blacksmith's shop and tending to horses in the barn. Every once in a while she caught Lucas watching her.

For a moment she contemplated telling him. What

a relief that would be to get it off her chest, to lean on someone for a change. Except, could she lean on Lucas? How would he react to what she had to say?

In his pursuit of justice, he wouldn't react kindly. He'd be furious that she'd kept information, no matter how minuscule, from him or the law.

As they headed for the parking lot, he put his hand on her lower back. He'd been subtly attentive all afternoon. Manipulating.

"How about dinner?"

"Sure." She had to eat. Pausing for a slow glance around, she didn't see anyone watching her, nor did the man from inside appear.

Rachel glanced back once again and didn't see anyone follow. When she faced forward, she saw Lucas had reached his SUV. She liked his understated sophistication. Even though he had more than one vehicle, his choices were functional.

She walked there.

"Are you all right?" he asked.

"Yes." She got into the vehicle and feigned nonchalance as he moved around to the driver's side.

He sat behind the wheel and started the engine. "Why do you keep looking around?" he asked.

"Am I?"

He sent her a frustrated frown that said, *you know you are.*

"The whole meeting with Jared spooked me." While that didn't cover the entire truth, it wasn't a lie, either.

"Why?" He began driving.

She chose her answer carefully. "He wants to get

back together. He says he still loves me." She sent a pointed look his way. "You heard him."

He'd listened in on her without her knowledge.

"And you're afraid of his brand of love?"

"He's seeing Marcy." How could he love her and see other women? "It's like he's obsessed with me. Like it's a power thing."

"That's Jared. He feeds off power and money. He likes to be in control. He probably felt that way when you were seeing him."

In control of his wife. In control of his lover. In control of his business. The man. The boss.

"Yes," she said. How had she been so easily controlled? She supposed it was easy to control someone if they didn't know the truth.

He pulled into a casual venue with cheery neon signs and cottage-style architecture. An old house converted into a restaurant. Pine trees surrounded the parking lot. A pile of plowed snow would take well into spring to melt. Rachel zipped up her jacket to the chill. The sun had begun to set.

A car drove into the parking lot behind them. Hearing it approach, she felt Lucas put his arm around her waist and tug her off to the side.

The car came up to them.

Rachel saw it heading right for them. She moved to the side of the lane as Lucas gave her a shove. He pulled out a gun as the car sped up.

Lucas fired, and the driver veered away. But then it spun into a circle to face them again.

Rachel ran for the edge of the lot, toward the pile of snow. The car went for her. Lucas fired his pistol again. Rachel screamed and leaped onto the mound of snow, clawing and climbing up. Glancing back, she saw the car skid, and it slid into the side of the snowbank.

Snow loosened and fell. She lost her precarious perch midway up and began to fall.

She screamed again as she landed at the bumper of the car.

Gunfire compelled the driver to race off. Spinning tires spat snow and ice at her. She covered her head with her arms and rolled the rest of the way off the bank.

"Rachel!" Lucas ran to her, crouching and checking back to make sure the car had gone.

"I'm all right." She sat up and did a mental survey of herself, almost not believing she was okay.

"He went after you," Lucas said.

"But the man who broke into my apartment is dead." She met his hard eyes, his entire face strained with alert readiness.

"He got caught. Whoever paid him must have taken over."

"Damn." She shook her head, wishing she could make this all go away and she could get back to the task of improving her life. School. A good job. Why couldn't those two things be her only worry? That and money. Surviving.

This gave a whole new meaning to survival. That man had tried to kill her. Or had he?

She averted her face, remembering the caller. Was he trying to scare her?

Yes, but would he not try the next time? Maybe next time he'd try to kill her for real.

Lucas sank his fingers into her hair, gripping the

back of her head and moving her so that she had to look at him.

"Please tell me what's going on, Rachel." His grip tightened in her hair.

Rachel stared breathlessly up into his intense face, the strength of his concern for her and his angst that she wouldn't trust him.

He brought his head down for an energy-packed kiss.

The impact stunned her and an instant later, fire melted any thought of resisting. She let him take her mouth and fell into the velvety passion, desire so strong she couldn't comprehend where she ended and he began.

His kiss eased into a series of gentler, quicker ones.

"He almost killed you." He kissed her again, hard, seeking reassurance that she still lived. "I thought he was going to."

"Lucas."

His mouth covered hers yet again, his tongue going in for more drugging passion. Then he eased off. "I can't lose another woman, Rachel. I can't fail again."

As he continued kissing her, she answered with equal fervor.

He ended the kiss, and she drowned in the blue-gray force of his eyes.

"Tell me," he rasped.

Hearing his desperate need for her to trust him in at least that, Rachel nearly capitulated. She could not trust him this way. Where was his ex-wife? How did he really feel about her? Slighted, lied to, but if he'd loved her, love would prevail and mend whatever had transpired between them. His ex could have done what she'd done out of love. She loved Lucas. She'd made a mistake lying to him, trying to claim him for her own.

"I can't," she whispered harshly.

"Why not?" he demanded, his passion fading with anger.

"I'm afraid." That, at least, was the unaltered truth. She was afraid.

"I'll protect you."

Rachel let her head fall forward onto his shoulder. "You won't."

With his fingers still in her hair, he pulled her head back.

"Why do you say that?"

"I'll look guilty even though I'm not."

"Why will you look guilty? I believe you didn't kill my sister. Please. Tell me what you know."

Tears burned her eyes. The temptation to confide in him was so great, and yet, she'd spent so many years watching out for herself, she couldn't rely on anyone else.

"If I could help you find her killer, I would," she said. "Nothing I tell you will do that, Lucas. Please believe me when I say that."

"Then you have nothing to fear, least of all from me. I can help you, Rachel. I can protect you, from whatever it is you're running from. Just trust me."

Rachel rarely cried, but a wrenching sob broke free. "I want to." She put her hand on his cheek. "I do."

"Then do it. Tell me what you know. No matter how small of a detail it is, tell me. You may not realize that it would help. But what if it can help, Rachel?"

The wrenching sob eased into soft crying, a release of built-up tension she'd kept bottled up so long. "Lucas."

He used his thumbs to wipe her dropping tears. "Even if you don't trust me, trust that I'll do whatever it takes to solve my sister's murder. I know it wasn't you, Rachel. Trust me that I'll find her killer. Just trust in that."

Rachel closed her eyes to that sweet temptation, temptation that won her over. She didn't kill Luella. And she believed Lucas was capable of finding the person who had.

She opened her eyes. "I'm scared."

"Don't be. Not with me here."

She closed her eyes again, this time more briefly. When she opened them, she was ready. "I saw her in Jared's office late at night."

"Luella?"

"Yes. The night before she was murdered."

"Why were you there? Were you working?"

Oh, this would be uncomfortable. "I went to see Jared. It was late. After ten. I was just leaving. We had just… We were in a conference room. He had this fantasy—"

"Okay, okay, I get the picture. What was Luella doing in his office?"

"I don't know. I asked her what she was doing and she told me she'd gone to the wrong office and left. I didn't know who she was until the morning after her murder, when the news showed her picture and said she was Jared Palmer's wife and he was the prime suspect. I assumed she went to his computer to find out what he was doing. I don't think she realized I was the one he was with."

"She might have been looking for something else," Lucas said.

Rachel hadn't considered that. Luella had been Jared's wife. She hadn't thought it odd that she'd be there. Plus, she'd been absorbed in the realization that Jared had lied, and seeing his wife for the first time—and the night she'd been killed—had been a shock and a horror.

"What would she have been looking for?"

"Something that got her killed." Lucas stood up, taking her hand and helping her.

Reeling with the implications of that, Rachel slipped on the icy pavement and put her hands on his chest.

He held her with one arm around her waist. "Did anyone besides Luella know you were there?"

She shook her head.

"Jared?"

"He took a call and then said he had work to do. I left him in the conference room."

"What call? Who called him?"

"I don't know. Someone he works with."

"At what time of night?"

By then it had been about eleven. "I don't know exactly. Do you think that's significant?"

"It could be." He kept her hand and walked back toward the vehicle. "How about we pick up dinner and go to my place."

She didn't argue. Dinner in public had lost its appeal.

"The man who's trying to scare you isn't Jared."

"I know."

"But Jared could be paying someone."

She nodded wearily. "Maybe."

He opened the passenger door for her and then when she sank onto the soft leather seat, he leaned in. "How long has he been trying to scare you?"

She stared at him, astonished. How could he be so sure he was only trying to scare her?

"What?" she asked, dumbfounded.

"Come on, Rachel. You're scared. You always look over your shoulder when we go places. You've been scared a long time, haven't you?"

She looked straight ahead. Yes, she'd been scared. But never more so than now. The man who'd threatened her was out there, somewhere. He'd kill her. Could she depend on Lucas to protect her as he claimed? He may intend to, but what if he failed?

"It's all right," Lucas said. "You don't have to tell me anything more."

He went around to the other side and got in. Starting the engine, he didn't drive right away. "One thing confuses me."

His intelligence amazed her. He'd pieced together far more than she had or ever could have in just a few minutes. That made her uneasy. What if he figured out too much?

"What is it?"

"Why would Jared claim to love you if he wants you dead?"

Rachel leaned her head back against the seat, relieved he hadn't pieced everything together. "Maybe he doesn't want me dead."

Revealing any more to Lucas would put her life in danger. Because he'd start digging where he shouldn't, and that would set off more than her stalker. That would roll a boulder off something best left where it lay.

Chapter 8

Lucas had to work extra hard talking Rachel into letting him drop her off at Tieber Transport. He needed her safe while he went to investigate a lead he'd discovered last night, one he hadn't told her about.

"Why does it have to be your stepdad's company?"

"You'll be safe there."

Her head lolled in annoyance without looking his way. "That's what you keep saying."

"And I think you should keep your job." Another thing he'd kept repeating this morning.

"It was never *my* job."

She'd said that this morning, too. "Yes, it was. Are we going to argue about that again?"

She sighed.

"Joseph knows you're coming. He's happy. You don't have to work. You can sit in the cafeteria if you want. But he did ask that you meet with him."

Rachel propped her elbow on the window frame and bit her thumbnail.

He drove to a stop in front of Tieber Transport. "I'll be back in two hours."

"Where are you going?"

"I can't tell you." They'd already been over this.

"Why not?"

"Rachel..."

Dropping her hand, she turned to him. Unlike before, she conveyed an injured look. Brief. But he felt it deep down. She didn't trust him.

He didn't trust her, either. Whatever he had planned, he wasn't sharing. That was all she needed to know.

She got out and slammed the door.

He watched her walk to the entrance, her angered strides twitching her butt to a sexy tempo.

When she was inside, the doorman's head nodded down once. Lucas had prearranged his watch. He gave the man a salute.

Nan McNally lived in the country on a farm not far from where Rachel had lived when her parents died. Nan, he'd learned from a treasured box filled with old records in Rachel's apartment, had known her since they were kids. The last photo Lucas found placed the two at about age twelve, just before Rachel's parents died. Nan wasn't Rachel's only friend back then. She'd had several, but Nan was in more photos than any other. He found no other photos like that. Rachel had some on her computer, and even a few of Nan, but nothing as social as those as a kid. Losing her parents had alienated her, made her something of a loner.

He opened the hair salon door to the jingle of a

bell. The Clip and Color was Nan's salon. Kadin had zipped him over a quick background. At nine in the morning on a weekday, Nan was the only hairdresser in the wood-floored room. Three other stations and the small front counter were empty.

"Be right with you," she said as she picked up a hair dryer.

A five-foot-six slender woman with good-size breasts and shoulder-length hair with blond streaks, she was attractive and put together. She wore slightly heavy makeup around bright blue eyes and wore tasteful earrings with her silky green, blue and black shirt that hung over black leggings.

The shop was next to a grocery store and decorated richly in predominantly gold and black. The seating area looked more like a living room with a sofa and two chairs. A water fountain trickled along with soft pop music.

Lucas waited for her to finish with her customer; the elderly woman with freshly cut gray hair paid and left.

"Right this way."

"I didn't come for a haircut," Lucas said, seeing her go still with unexpected bewilderment and then slight annoyance.

"Did you see the no-soliciting sign in the front window?" she asked.

"I'm here to talk to you about Rachel Delany."

She stopped and turned. "Oh." She smiled, although not with welcome. "And here I thought you were going to try and sell me something. Do you know how hard it is to make a living as a hairdresser in a town like this? People think that just because you own a business, you have money to scatter to the masses." She braced her hands on the counter. "Who are you?"

Lucas had caught her off guard. She hadn't expected anyone to come to her about Rachel. In fact, it seemed she hadn't heard about or from Rachel in a long time.

"Lucas Curran. My sister was Luella Palmer."

Nan straightened from the counter, becoming wary. "So you found out about Rachel's affair and now you're hoping I can say something to implicate her."

Lucas moved closer to the counter. "No. I came here to understand why she hid her relationship with him."

Nan assessed him with new eyes. "You want to know about her relationship with another man? She captured you, didn't she?"

He'd rather not acknowledge that, especially since it stung with so much truth. "When was the last time you saw her?"

"Almost four years ago. She's had some rough times, but that girl has never lost faith. She believes someday she'll have the life she was meant to have before her parents died. How'd you find out about her?"

Rachel's affair had been a big secret up until Joseph found out through rumors that Jared had an affair around the time of Luella's murder. Now Lucas realized Marcy must have gotten Jared to talk.

"Word got around," he said. "Why has it been so long since you've seen her?"

"Probably the same reason she kept her affair secret."

Did Nan know that secret? He had to be careful not to clam her up. She'd protect Rachel. He'd make her feel comfortable and convince her that he meant her friend no harm. He would if she did have something to do with his sister's murder, but getting information was more important to him than anything. A few tiny lies wouldn't hurt.

"Why did she alienate herself from you?" he asked.

"From everyone. Not that she had any family. She had lots of friends. And she was beginning to flourish at that job. Jared ruined all that. And Luella's murder. She felt humiliated over his deception, and she was afraid Jared was the one who killed Luella."

"Why did she think that?"

"She wouldn't say. I've tried to call her and get her to open up, but Rachel isn't one to rely on others. She's been that way ever since her parents died. She feels she has no one to turn to. That sometimes upsets me. I've known her most my life. Why doesn't she rely on me?" Nan drifted off in silent thought, clearly mourning the loss of a good friend.

"She came to you after she discovered Jared's lies." But even if Rachel had been forced to toughen up and closed herself off, why run and hide from an affair and a murder? There had to be more. If she had nothing to do with it, she wouldn't hide. That made her appear guilty.

"How did she find out Jared was married?" Lucas asked.

"She saw the news about Luella." Nan blew air out as she remembered. "It's been so long."

Yes, a long time, and his sister's murderer still walked free. "Where was she the night of the murder?"

Nan eyed him suspiciously. "I thought you didn't come here to try and tie her to that."

"I didn't. Just being thorough." He smiled gently. Best not to frighten her off, not to make her feel she'd expose Rachel, even if unknowingly.

"Why not leave the investigating up to police?"

"I'm an ex-cop. And police are moving too slowly on the case. I'm trying to do what I can to help things along." At least he spoke the truth. And Nan had to realize he'd go to any extreme to catch his sister's killer.

She took a few moments to contemplate him, going over her options. She seemed an open book, an honest, good person, someone he could see Rachel chumming up with. Which made Rachel seem more innocent than he was ready to accept. He needed an open mind. If Rachel had been involved in Luella's murder... He couldn't be attached to her killer.

"Rachel was home the night of the murder," Nan finally said. "I spoke with her at about eight. She said she was going to take a bath and go to bed."

Rachel had no alibi the night of Luella's murder. Luella had been murdered between eleven and one that night. Jared had been home. Rachel had plenty of time to drive to Jared's house. Maybe the two of them had worked together.

"Did she ever say anything to you about Luella?"

"Only that she was Jared's wife and she'd been killed. It was all a big shock to her. She didn't know Jared was married."

That would be a shock—if she was innocent.

"Anything else stand out?"

Nan thought a few seconds. "You know, she did mention something. A woman came to see Jared one day and left in tears. Rachel said she heard the woman accuse him of fraud."

A cold chill channeled its way down Lucas's body. Rachel hadn't mentioned anything like that. Her words echoed, raising his ire.

I don't know anything that will help you or your investigation. If I did, I'd have gone to the police…

Didn't this qualify as knowing something? She suspected Jared of fraud. Insurance fraud?

"I think Rachel suspected Jared was up to something," Nan said, making it worse.

Fraud. Still poleaxed by the word, he asked, "What kind of fraud?"

"Can't say. Rachel didn't know, either. All she heard was that one small snippet of conversation. It may not mean anything."

Or it meant everything. Lucas fought to keep his temper under control, "When did she hear the woman accuse him of fraud?"

"Just after Luella's murder. She'd gone to pick up her personal things from her desk. That same week, in fact." Nan eyed him again. "I probably shouldn't be telling you anything. Rachel hasn't told you any of this?"

"No."

Nan's whole demeanor changed. She'd expected Rachel to be forthcoming, but Rachel had not been forthcoming. She'd hidden a big chunk of information that should have been revealed four years ago, immediately after she'd discovered it.

Lucas struggled to hang on to calm. Bullying Nan right now would not help his cause.

Another customer came into the salon. Nan greeted the woman and then took up a broom and began sweeping her station. "You should go and talk to her directly.

I'm beginning to feel like you're trying to get me to say something I'll regret."

He was. "My sister's murder is still unsolved. You may be able to shed light on something no one has seen before."

"I have a customer. You should get going now." She kept sweeping.

"How did Rachel feel about Jared's lie?"

"Humph. How do you think she felt? She was hurt. Up until then, she talked about how wonderful he was, how well he treated her, how intelligent he was, how handsome. He was her prince, her knight in shining armor. Too good to be true." Her sweeping slowed as she looked up at Lucas. "She said that to me once. *He's almost too good to be true.* That was about two weeks before she found out he was a snake in the grass."

Jared had played the role well. His estranged friend had perfected the art of deception. Lucas had experienced the treachery himself. "Did Rachel isolate herself because she was involved in fraud with Jared?"

Nan stopped sweeping. "Heavens, no. Rachel would never do anything like that. After going through her troubled teen years, she's been determined to turn her life around. When Jared happened, she had a setback. She was always leery of the law. Jared scared her."

"What do you mean she's leery of the law?"

"You should ask her that." Putting the broom away, Nan went to the front.

Passing Lucas, she greeted her customer and then said, "Come on back."

Lucas followed them to the station, watching her put an apron over the elderly woman, who looked up at him in silent question. What was he doing hanging around?

Getting answers.

"Why did Jared scare her?" he asked.

Nan asked the customer what she'd like today, and the customer said the same as last time. Nan sprayed the woman's hair with water, looking at Lucas through the mirror.

"You have to understand how important it is to Rachel that she improve her life," she said. "She has deep regrets over the things she did in her teen years. She wishes she wouldn't have disappointed her parents and will do anything not to disappoint them again. That makes her hypersensitive to the law."

Innocent people wouldn't feel that way. "Is she afraid of being arrested again?"

Nan began cutting her customer's gray hair, and the woman stared at Lucas through the mirror, clearly taken in by the titillating topic.

"Of course she is." Nan snipped away, hair falling down to the apron and floor.

"Why? If she's done nothing wrong, she has nothing to fear."

"Rachel is afraid of Jared. That man hid his true nature. He's dangerous. She feels threatened by him."

This bit of news changed the course of his investigation. If Rachel had a legitimate reason to be afraid, Lucas might understand her secret. But she still should have come forward.

"What does she think he'll do?" he asked.

Nan looked up from her hands, busy with the scissors and comb, as though he was daft. "Make her look guilty of fraud."

He wanted to understand Rachel's reason for not going to the police; fear of the law didn't cut it. He thanked Nan and left.

On his way to Tieber Transport, Lucas wavered between anger over her secretiveness and a nagging suspicion that something more than the law scared her. The woman he'd met at that pub wouldn't keep vital information on another human being's murder from police out of selfish fear. So what had turned her into a woman who would?

Awkward. Rachel shifted on the chair. She'd left the door open after Joseph had taken her here. He'd offered her a seat at her former desk but she'd declined. Now she sat in the conference room next to his office with nothing to do. She'd have walked away if not for the stalker lurking in the shadows.

But she could not take sitting here like a wallflower any longer. She felt like a stubborn teenager again, dropped off by a foster parent and left to wait. *Don't go anywhere until I get back.*

The demands had driven her to rebellion. Not because of unfairness. Those good people had nothing but her welfare in mind. She'd just lost her way, that was all. A young, impressionable girl who'd become a victim of tragedy, and then a victim of the state.

Rachel tried to forgive herself for succumbing to negativity and dysfunction. She'd let it drag her down. Blamed others for the awfulness that life had splattered all over her existence. She'd seen no way out. Given up. Then she'd realized only she could change her circumstances. Only she could care enough about herself and her future to do something about it. No one else would. No one else would be there to catch her at her lowest. She'd thought she'd found her way when she'd met Jared, when he'd given her a chance and hired her to do a real job. For the first time since her parents died, she'd seen a way forward without them. She'd felt strong. Empowered. And then he'd turned out to be one of the biggest mistakes of her life, possibly *the* biggest.

With Lucas, it had begun to feel the same way, before the discovery of lies. She could have almost believed they had a chance—that she had a chance—for real happiness. Love.

This job. This family. It felt different. Yes, the job had been offered in falseness, but she sensed a genuine offer still stood.

That compelled her to stand and go to the conference room door, peer out into the executive office space and beyond to the lower-level workers, tapping on keyboards, talking on phones and to each other, walking this way and that.

She stepped out of the conference room and took in the expensive art on the walls, interspersed with required corporate informational posters. *Don't get hurt on the job. Personal problems? Call this number.* Mission statements. All Hands meetings. Company events.

Rachel had loved them all when she'd worked for Jared. While the novelty had worn off quickly enough after she'd discovered his infidelity, the security of belonging to something so much greater than her had soaked into her being. She began to have the same sense now. It was what brought her out into the hall.

"Oh, hey, Rachel."

Rachel turned to see Marcy approach, holding her cell phone and a notepad cradled on her forearm.

Keeping her opinion of the woman to herself, Rachel smiled. "Hello."

"Are you back to work?"

Unable to confirm or deny that, Rachel said, "Lucas said he saw you at HealthFirst."

Marcy's too-sugary demeanor faltered a bit. "Yes, he did."

"He also said you left with Jared." Rachel didn't feel she had much to lose. And she rather enjoyed Marcy's mellowing. For a moment she saw through to the real woman, one who could be broken just like everyone else.

"Is he up to his old ways again?" Rachel asked during Marcy's stunned silence.

That snapped Marcy out of her stupor, and the regal corporate cat reemerged. "Are you seeing Jared again?"

Of course she'd focus on that instead of why Lucas had waited until she left, spying on her. "No." She didn't add she'd be fifty shades of stupid if she did.

Marcy's cell phone buzzed. She looked down and came to attention.

"Marcy. There you are." Joseph rushed forward with a printout in his hand. "I need you to make me twenty copies of these and bring them to the boardroom." He handed her the pages. "And the receptionist didn't make coffee. Could you take care of the catering? I've got that potential client in today, you remember? The Alaskan touring company."

Marcy looked down at her phone and then back

at Joseph. "I'm sorry, Mr. Johnson just called me, I have to…"

Joseph harrumphed a sigh. "Then go find that receptionist. What's her name?"

Rachel snatched the pages from Marcy. "I'll take care of your client, Mr. Tieber." Seeing his softening regard, she walked away.

She started the copies in the machine and made coffee at the same time. While those processed, she called the bakery just down the street from the office and asked them to rush over fruit and pastries.

Joseph's meeting had already started by the time she herded the receptionist to help her set up coffee while she passed out the copies. A projector screen displayed another presentation, the copies a supplement to that.

The pastries arrived by the time she finished passing out printouts. On her way out the door, she caught Joseph's smile and nod of appreciation.

Not ready to forgive just yet, Rachel left the room and went to her desk, sitting down and livening up her computer to see what needed catching up.

An hour into going through emails, she caught sight of Lucas. He strode toward her with a storm of tension. Wherever he'd gone, he must have talked to someone close to her. She'd suspected as much when he wouldn't let her go with him. She prepared herself for the worst. She had gotten good at that, preparing herself for the worst, expecting the worst. Disappointment didn't take her down. She'd been disappointed so many times, it was a familiar feeling; so familiar that she had desensitized herself to it long ago. But somehow, Lucas's anger affected her differently. She cared too much what he thought.

She stood.

"Come with me." He took her arm a little too firmly and guided her to the conference room she'd vacated. Inside, he shut the door with a bang.

"Fraud?" he shot at her.

Hiding a flinch, she stepped back and put her hand on the back of a chair. Wherever he'd gone, he'd learned a lot.

"I couldn't prove anything."

"And *that's* your reason for not going to the police with case-altering information?" he roared.

Taking in his furious face and pained by it, she moved away, going to the window with a view of cloud-shrouded mountains. Apprehension kept her tongue still, kept words from tumbling out. The same had overcome her years ago, her life threatened if she said anything to anyone.

"Where did you go? Who told you? Nan?" It had to be. Nan was the only other person she'd told about Jared and her suspicion.

"I went to see her."

While Rachel felt betrayed by her closest friend, Nan hadn't meant to cause her trouble. Lucas was a smooth talker when he wanted information.

Turning from the window, she asked, "Are you going to run down all of my friends and interrogate them? I'll save you some time. Nan is the only person I talked to about Jared. How did you find her?"

"Kadin."

"Ah, yes. The ever-resourceful Mr. Tandy of the great and mighty Dark Alley Investigations. You're not even a real homicide detective. How are you qualified to work for an agency like that?"

"I'm determined. And I know how to hunt criminals."

Narcotics were a lot different than murder investigations, but he hadn't shown any signs of that hindering him in any way. In fact, he struck her as an expert in the field.

"Why did you keep something like that to yourself for so long?" he asked.

Unable to meet his imploring eyes, she faced the window again, rubbing her arms. "I tried to get back into HealthFirst after I quit, after I got my things that first week, but couldn't." The security had been too tight, and she was no Lucas Curran. "I wanted to see if I could find something to prove what I heard was true." That had earned her an attack that still haunted her, it had terrified her so much.

"Four years, Rachel."

She heard him come up behind her. She didn't fault him for his anger. She didn't respect herself, either, for not being braver.

"Four years have gone by that my sister's killer has gone free. You could have changed that by going to the police."

Rachel closed her eyes to the hurtful truth. "I didn't want to go to jail." As an adult, she'd do serious time, and with her juvenile record, the judge may not be lenient.

"Why would you go to jail?"

Four years ago, she'd faced the same decision. Risk her life by telling all? Or keep quiet?

"Rachel. Why?"

The anguish in his voice did her in. She turned and started for the door. "You don't understand." She left the conference room, grabbed her purse from under her desk and then jogged to the elevator.

She pressed the button, fidgeting as she waited for the doors to open. Lucas strode toward her, low-browed and unrelenting.

The doors opened and she got inside, pressing the lobby button and then the one that would close the doors. This time Lucas caught them, sticking his foot between the doors and pushing them back open with his hand.

Inside the elevator, he moved toward her.

Rachel backed up against the wall.

He put his hand above and beside her head. "Make me understand how you could let a killer go free."

She hadn't *let a killer go free.* That dug deep. "I didn't know enough." That was what she'd kept telling herself back then, when one shock after another hit her. Luella's murder. The discovery that she was Jared's wife. Realizing all of his lies and his utter disregard for her as a person, his lack of respect and integrity. She'd had real feelings for him. To be shown his gutter-rat nature so abruptly and horribly... She'd spun in a fog of uncertainty. Add to that the fraud and threats, and no wonder she'd run into isolation.

"My word is all I had to offer," she said to Lucas. "It wasn't enough. No one would have believed me. I may not be a hotshot detective like you, but I know that much."

"It's enough now. You're not alone anymore. You don't have to be afraid. You have me."

Warmth fell through her until she realized she

couldn't trust him. He blamed her for withholding information—possibly rightfully so. But now he was back to manipulating her to get that information. The closer she looked into his eyes, the more she saw his simmering anger.

"Tell me everything," Lucas said.

He'd not settle until she did.

The elevator doors opened and she walked out, numb, scanning the lobby. He walked beside her. His long, graceful strides made her too aware of his attractiveness. His intelligent mind, although cornering her now, only stimulated the sensation. Like the temptation of dark chocolate. Sugar. Mmm.

Outside, she saw a black sedan waiting. They'd be driven wherever Lucas wanted to go. She'd either go with him or face her stalker.

Lucas shoved her the same time glass shattered behind her. Rachel landed on the concrete front entry of Tieber Transport. Tempered glass from the window beside the door scattered.

To her left, the driver of the sedan dived into the front of the car. Bullets sprayed.

The windshield broke. The back passenger seat window next.

Lucas had his pistol out, and was crouched between her and the car. He grabbed her forearm and hauled her to the sedan for shelter from a continual pelting of bullets.

Leaning against the rear tire, Rachel covered her head. She peeked to see Lucas rising up enough to clear the hood and fire at the shooter.

Then he opened the back door and got in, tugging

her after him. The driver pressed the gas and raced away with Rachel's feet still partially out the door.

Lucas fired his gun through the broken window as they raced away.

When the gunfire ended, Rachel saw the driver rise up in his seat and felt the sedan steady. Lucas looked down. She lay flat on her back, his knee between her thighs, his other on the floor.

"Are you hurt?" he asked.

Oh, God, so sexy. His voice, his face, the urgency in his eyes. How could she get hot over him now?

"No."

Relieved, he moved off her. She sat up, pushing her skirt down as Lucas sat beside her. When her feet were inside, the driver maneuvered a turn to pull the car door shut.

"Okay, that was exciting." She tried for humor but it fell a little flat.

"Why is someone trying to kill you, Rachel?" Lucas asked.

"He thinks I know something," she said. "Just like you do."

"You know enough. Tell me everything. Start with the night you had sex with Jared in the conference room. Don't leave any detail out."

Rachel looked at the driver. Wind whipped through the jagged front window even though they were no longer going very fast.

"He's cleared. Highest security level." Lucas nodded up at the driver, looking at him in the rearview mirror. "Isn't that right, Bernie?"

"Yes, sir. I've worked for your father for twenty years. He's a good man."

He may say that if he had to.

"Bernie is a loyal member of Joseph's closest staff," Lucas said.

As though directed, Bernie rolled up the privacy glass, and only the wind coming through the broken back window disturbed them now.

"Like I said…loyal."

Rachel didn't mistake his pointed look.

"After the conference room. What happened?"

Rachel turned to watch the landscape go by. She didn't feel safe revealing this to anyone, her deep, dark secret.

But the time to make things right had come. And one thing Lucas had said, she clung to. She had *him* now.

"I told you. I saw Luella in Jared's office." She met Lucas's eager face, his intense eyes. "I didn't know she was Jared's wife. I didn't know her."

"And then what? Keep going."

"I confronted Jared a few days later. He told me not to tell anyone about us. That made me mad, so I told him what I heard about the fraud. Then he showed me some files that he said were on my computer. They were evidence of a fraudulent insurance policy."

"He blackmailed you?"

"His last parting words were, *Think twice before interfering.*"

"Interfering in what?"

"In his personal affairs, in Luella's murder. He thought I knew about his fake policies."

"You did know."

Rachel turned her back, guilt pressing her down. "No. I didn't. He said he had my computer and everything on it. I worked for him. I handled a lot of his transactions. It's possible I sent some things I shouldn't have." She hadn't paid much attention to what she sent. The business dealings of insurance policies were boring. If he'd actually had her send fraudulent documents, she didn't know for certain. She couldn't imagine he would risk involving her, but what if he had?

"Did Jared plant the files on your computer?"

"I can't prove it."

"I can."

"Jared isn't the one who shot at us." He had to be made aware of that.

"He may as well be the one. He could pay someone to do that, and to threaten you, but that doesn't make him innocent. I can protect you. You don't have to be afraid anymore."

Rachel leaned her head back without moving her eyes from Lucas. He made her feel so safe…and warm…and…hot and tingly. Was she a stupid woman to allow this sweet softening?

He noticed, his manly, fiery gaze taking her face in, connecting with and heating the energy between them.

"You should have told someone." He said it as though doing so would put a wall up to keep him from going to her, taking her into his arms and kissing her.

Every time the glow of love ignited, reality stopped it. He would never let himself be with her that way, especially not now. Closing her eyes, she turned toward the window. "You'll get no argument from me on that."

Chapter 9

Lucas tried not to be angry with Rachel. She had done what she'd done out of fear and blackmail. Now someone tried to kill her, and him, too. The threats four years ago were no longer just threats, and Lucas had to be the reason why. He'd come with serious backing to solve his sister's case. The killer knew what he was up against.

The security camera on the northwest corner of the HealthFirst building came into the crosshairs of his rifle. He sat in the back of a windowless van, a small square cut out of the side for this very purpose. Rachel sat against the metal wall beside him. She'd been quiet since her confession. He felt her distrust. He doubted she'd trusted anyone since discovering Jared's treachery.

He pulled the trigger, and a quiet shot took out the

security camera. Setting the rifle down, he opened the back door. Rachel stepped out behind him and he led her along the edge of the parking lot, following a path only the corner camera could see—if it worked. At a side entrance, he took out a badge he'd stolen the day he'd been here.

"Where did you get that?" Rachel whispered.

"A cook from the cafeteria dropped it as he was getting into his car. I planned on returning it."

"Unless an opportunity arose?" Rachel asked with a note of cynicism.

"Of course." The door unlocked and he pushed it open.

She entered first. At nearly ten, the lights had been dimmed, and no one walked the hall.

Lucas stopped at the entrance to the stairwell. He led Rachel up to the sixth floor and carefully peered into the hall. Brighter lights illuminated the reception area of the executive offices. Jared's office was dark.

Stepping out of the stairwell, Lucas made sure the door closed silently. Then he and Rachel walked toward the offices. Hearing someone in Eldon's office, Lucas stopped. A janitor emerged, turning off the light.

Rachel gripped Lucas's shirt and tugged him back into a cubicle.

The janitor pushed a wheeled cart by, and Lucas leaned forward to stay out of sight, pressing into Rachel, who'd backed up as far as she could against the desk. The janitor passed, and Lucas looked down at Rachel's upturned face.

Her eyes flashed in the dim light, alive with awareness. Now wasn't an appropriate time to be thinking about kissing her.

The ding of the elevator signified the janitor would take it to another floor. Lucas moved back from Rachel, shaking off the heat to focus on the task at hand.

Taking her hand, he led her to Jared's office. The door was locked. He took a pick and tension wrench from the small tool pouch clipped to his belt. Inserting the wrench into the keyhole, he applied pressure in the clockwise direction. Feeling the cylinder stop firmly, he turned the wrench the other direction. The cylinder turned and stopped, but felt less firm. Next, he inserted the pick and felt the pins, lifting each to set them in position. When he set the last pin, he turned the wrench, and the door unlocked.

"You're frighteningly good at that," Rachel said as they entered.

"I locked myself out of my apartment during college so much that I had to learn." He shut Jared's office door and closed the blinds on the window facing the reception area.

"Was it cloak-and-dagger fascination that led you to want to join the navy?"

He handed her desk keys that Jared foolishly left in his center office drawer. "No. I liked blowing things up as a kid."

She took the keys and knelt before the two file drawers in the desk. Lucas sat on the office chair next to her and went to work on the computer.

"Detective work came later," he said.

"Narcotics."

"And then SWAT. The explosives got the best of

me." He grinned and saw her smile back before bending over the files.

"Will you stay at Dark Alley after you solve your sister's murder?"

He liked how confident she sounded. *When* he solved it, not if. "I haven't thought that far ahead. I think maybe I'll take a break for a while. Figure out what I really want to do with the rest of my life."

"You don't want to be a cop? A detective?"

"I wanted to be a navy SEAL." That still made him bitter.

"You can't blame that woman the rest of your life. You said it yourself. You both made a decision. She didn't make the decision for you to quit."

"No, but the truth would have helped me make a wiser one. She tricked me into marrying her."

"Does that make you…?" She didn't want to choose the wrong word. "Skeptical with other women?"

"Skeptical?" He took out a USB device from his tool pouch. "Wiser."

"Distrustful," she said.

"Careful," he countered.

"Okay, careful. But you must realize that not all women are liars."

He inserted the drive and started searching for files, not liking the way her comment made him compare her to his ex. Rachel exuded a sense of integrity, whereas his ex had just been fun to be with. He hadn't looked beyond his ex's looks and the good sex they had. Rachel had more substance. But she'd also lied.

Or withheld the truth.

He'd lied to her, though, so how could he hold that

against her? He began copying file folders. As he waited for the save to complete, he noticed Rachel had gone still. She held a notebook and stared at the contents.

"What is it?"

"This name... I've seen it before."

Lucas leaned over to read the name. *Angie Johnson* had been written down, along with a date and time. Lucas faced the computer again and opened Jared's calendar. Going back several months, he found the date and saw the time had been blocked for a meeting with Angie Johnson. She must have come to see him. The letter by itself didn't incriminate, but details of her account might. And whatever the topic of their meeting had been.

"Who is she?" he asked.

"I don't know. I just remember the name, that's all. I think it was on some documents Jared asked me to send for him."

So Jared hadn't been lying when he'd threatened her. He'd deliberately routed the fraudulent files through her, making it appear she had knowledge of the transactions. What Lucas wanted to know was how Jared expected Rachel to get back together with him after threatening her. Maybe he thought he could trust her. She hadn't gone to the police in four years, after all.

He searched the email account, but any record older than three months had been deleted. He started saving the sent folder when a light came on outside the office.

Lucas removed the USB drive and shut down the computer.

Rachel stuffed the folder back into the drawer and stood with him. He took her hand and brought her to the wall beside the front window. Peering through a crack in the blinds, he saw a security guard walking in the reception area. And he headed right for them.

Lucas looked around the office and saw a small red dot blinking. Motion detectors. Silent. Damn. He hadn't had time to prepare for that level of security, not that it would have mattered. He'd have come here anyway.

He searched for a hiding place. Jared's office was open and didn't offer much. He couldn't shoot his way out of here, not against an innocent security guard.

The man reached the office door. Lucas and Rachel ducked out of the way of the window as he peered inside, or tried to. Then he used keys to unlock the door, only to discover it already unlocked. The guard became instantly alert, going for his radio and gun at the same time. While he took the safety off his pistol, he spoke into the radio.

"Code 22 in Jared's office," he said, his voice muffled but audible in the quiet building.

Code 22 must have been the security staff's communication for a break-in.

The officer pushed the door open.

Rachel gripped the back of Lucas's shirt, preventing him from making his move right then. The guard saw him and began to turn the gun. Lucas swung his arm, connecting his forearm with the other man's wrist hard enough to knock the gun free. Then he grabbed the man and hauled him into the office, sending him falling toward the desk.

Rachel ran out of the office ahead of him, but the ding of the elevator stopped her. Lucas took her hand again and ran faster to the stairwell. They reached it as the elevator doors slid open.

"You! Stop!" one of the guards shouted.

There were four of them. One of them saw their coworker getting up from the floor, having hit his head on something when he fell. "I'm okay, go! Go! Go! Go!"

Lucas pushed Rachel ahead of him on the stairs and raced down after her. Footfalls and squeaking shoes and shouts chased them down to the fifth floor. He let her fly down another floor before grabbing her arm and taking her through the door. He ran through a maze of cubicles. A late worker stood up from his lonely, poorly lit desk area.

"There they are!" a guard shouted from behind.

The office worker cringed back into his cubicle as they raced past, mouth slack in shock and eyes wide.

Lucas veered to the left and then right through the cubicles, coming back out to the main hall toward the stairs. Careful to avoid the late worker, he crossed to more cubicles, crouching so his height wouldn't expose their location. At the wall encompassing the elevator shaft, he slowed and crept along. Not hearing the guards, he figured they were in stealth mode, too.

Bobbing his head out into the hall, he spotted the guards with their guns drawn, making a slow approach, one of them signaling for two of them to go the direction Lucas and Rachel had just gone. He leaned back against the wall and glanced at Rachel.

"We have to surrender."

"What? No!"

"It'll be all right. I can get us out of this."

"We broke into this building. We'll be arrested."

"But not charged. Come on." He took her hand.

She resisted. "Lucas, no. I can't. Not with my record."

Her intense fear stopped him. Only then did he realize how much her past shaped her future, why she went to college, why she sought professional men.

"Trust me," he told her.

Just then, a guard appeared from around the corner of a cubicle. "Don't move! Don't move! Hands in the air!"

Lucas turned, raising his hands.

Rachel did the same.

Rachel fumed over how easily Lucas had given up. She'd gone with him willingly to Jared's company, so she couldn't blame him for her part in the break-in, but how could he be so blithe about this? She waited in a windowless room, sick with the repeated echo of the police officer reading her rights. The handcuffs. The ride in the police car. She'd tried so hard to change the course of her life, to avoid ever being in this situation again. Now here she was, right where she'd striven not to be.

The door opened and an officer entered, holding a file folder.

"Ms. Delany." The man stepped to the chair across from her and sat. "I'm Detective Suarez. I'm here to ask you a few questions about what happened tonight."

He'd waste his time if he thought she'd talk.

"You've got quite a history." He put the folder down and opened it, making a show of checking the contents. But surely he must have already read it. "Haven't changed your ways, it would appear. All those times in jail didn't change you?"

Rachel slapped her hand down on the table. "I have changed my ways. And I was arrested twice as a teenager."

"And you were arrested now, as an adult." He looked up from the file. "Why don't we talk about that."

Rachel kept quiet.

"What were you doing in the HealthFirst building?"

"I don't have to answer any of these questions."

"We could clear this all up in a matter of minutes," he said. "All you have to do is cooperate." He looked down again. "It says in here that you cooperated. Why not continue that trend? This will go a lot easier for you if you do."

"I can't tell you why I was in that building," she said.

"Why is that?"

"Because if I do, I'll be killed." Someone was already trying to kill her. She could talk to this detective, tell him all she knew about Jared. But that left her with breaking and entering charges. Nothing she said would make that go away, and anything she said would be held against her.

"Who will kill you?"

"The only way I say more is with an attorney present." She leaned back against the chair and met the detective's savvy gaze. "We can sit here all day and I won't say a word until I have an attorney."

"No, if you want to request an attorney, I can arrange for you to call one."

"I can't afford one, so you'll have to appoint one to me."

"Very well." He sighed as he leaned back. "Are you sure you don't want to do this the easy way and just tell me all about what happened?"

"Easy for whom?" she asked.

A knock on the door interrupted. A tall, lean black man in a suit and tie leaned in.

"Let her go."

"What?" Detective Suarez dropped the page he held and looked incredulous.

"We received a call from Chief Williams. Let her go."

Detective Suarez turned to Rachel. "The chief? Why'd he call on her behalf?"

Clearly, Rachel didn't have the reputation or the connections to pull that off. She watched him assess her.

"Let her go, Suarez. Stop asking questions I can't answer. The chief called and demanded we let her and Curran go. So do it." The man left the room.

Detective Suarez stared at her for long seconds. "Who do you know who could call the chief and have him set you free as though no crime had ever been committed?"

"No one," she said.

He continued to stare at her. Then he finally stood. "Well, you heard the man. You're free to go."

Rachel stood and went to the door in a surreal fog. Once out in the hall, she walked past darkened offices on her way to the front of the station, where only two officers worked, one at the desk, surfing the internet, the other typing at his computer across the room.

Lucas stood by the double doors, looking as fresh as though he'd just emerged from a shower.

Backing up, he pushed a door open and beckoned her to precede him.

Rachel walked past him, not appreciating his nonchalance. Outside, a car waited—one of Joseph's, with dark-tinted windows and sleek, black paint.

"How did you do it?" she asked.

"The chief supports a charity on missing children. Kadin explained what we were doing here, and the chief asked Jared and Eldon if they really wanted to press charges. They both said no."

"Just like that?" She stopped at the back door of the sedan.

Lucas faced her, putting his hand on the car behind her, his muscular arm close to her head. "I'm sure he also asked if he needed a search warrant to finish what we started."

"We shouldn't have had to call him. I thought you were a hotshot detective. You could have gotten us out of there." She couldn't help lashing out; his nearness stimulated her in ways she didn't welcome. The detective had made her feel the way she had so often felt after her parents died. Helpless. Worthless. Guilty. Lucas had thrust her into that situation. She believed she'd go to jail. She'd believed she'd lose everything. Even a college degree wouldn't help her with a felony on her record.

"Thanks for your high opinion of me, Rachel, but I wasn't going to shoot innocent people to get us out of there. Those guards thought we were criminals.

They didn't deserve to die for that. I knew I could call Kadin."

"You could have taken on four guards all on your own?"

"Yes."

She took in the rugged planes of his face, made sophisticated by his buzz cut and clean shave.

"I could have gotten us out of there."

But at the cost of lives. Rachel had to agree his strategy had been the best, given the circumstances.

"You could have told me you were going to call Kadin." That would have spared her a lot of anxiety.

"When? While the guards were telling us to put up our hands?"

Rachel averted her eyes.

With his free hand, Lucas touched her jawbone, gentle and warm. She looked up at him at his coaxing.

"I asked you to trust me," he said.

Rachel moved her head away from his touch and turned to open the door. Lucas went around to the other side.

"Did they take the USB device from you?" she asked after he closed his door.

"No. Still have it."

Good. She'd put all her energy into that, not him as a man. Maybe she could redeem herself for staying quiet all these years. Maybe she could at last have the courage to stand up to a killer.

The driver took them to Lucas's house, and Rachel went with him into his office. She sat beside him on a chair she'd dragged close, and together they inspected each folder.

Most of the contents were business related and seemingly legitimate. Some personal items came across the screen. Emails to women. Pictures, some of Jared at a party, two women on each side of him.

"I can't believe I was ever interested in him," she said.

"You didn't know him like this," Lucas said.

She thought of how deftly Jared had fooled her. He'd portrayed himself as an honest, hardworking family man. Successful. Charitable. Wholesome. He didn't have kids yet but he wanted them. He'd taken her to dinners and movies like any other normal date. He'd been a dream, until she'd been shocked into reality.

"I tried to break into HealthFirst after I found out about Luella," she said. He needed to hear the rest of this as much as she needed to finally say it.

He stopped looking through files.

"I stole someone's badge, just like you did." She propped her chin on her palm, elbow on the edge of the desk. "I made it to my desk but my login was already changed. I went through Jared's desk until someone walked in and asked where Jared was. I didn't recognize him, and he didn't recognize me. I said he was in a meeting if he'd like to wait. The man waited and I left.

"Jared paid me a visit after that. He behaved strangely, asking me if I'd been to his office. I said no, of course. After that I followed the case in the news and even struck up a friendship with a reporter. They never discovered anything new. A year went by, and I began to feel compelled to risk going to the police. I drove to the station and noticed a car following me. I left, and the car followed. I drove until the car turned and then I went home. A few days later I came home to a package on my doorstep. Inside was my dead cat." She looked over from the computer screen to Lucas. "I never stopped looking over my shoulder after that. I still contemplated going to the police, looking for opportunities to slip in and tell all, but I didn't know what would happen after I did. After I told the police what little I knew, what would they be able to do with the information? They'd have to get evidence. What if they didn't get any? What if Jared didn't kill Luella? What if he wasn't the one who threatened me?"

"I'll say it again, Rachel. You have me, now."

She melted into his blue-gray eyes, letting herself enjoy the sweetness for a time before putting a clamp on it. He'd support her through this investigation, but what about after that?

"I just wanted you to know that I did try. I tried, Lucas."

"I believe you."

"Do you?" He resented her for not going to the police no matter what.

"You were afraid," he said. "That I understand. But you need to stop being afraid, Rachel. You don't have to isolate yourself or hide from the law. You're innocent. You may not have been when you were a teenager, but you are now."

She suspected he left unspoken, *unless you prove me wrong.*

"Do you think you're unworthy of your friends?" he asked.

"No." Why did he ask?

"You haven't seen Nan in a long time."

She turned away. Okay, so she did have issues with that.

"You don't have to climb out of poverty to earn worthiness. Your friends are your friends no matter what. Nan would probably like to hear from you, but you've been in hiding."

"I've been busy." Not hiding. There was a big difference between fighting for a future and hiding from life.

"Busy getting a college degree you're convinced will make you worthy."

"All right. A college degree will help me get a good job. That will make me a worthy contributor to society. What's wrong with that?"

"Nothing, except you let it consume you. Just like, I'm sure, Luella's murder did."

Luella, though a complete stranger and the wife of a man she'd thought had true potential, had touched her. That Lucas brought it to light disconcerted her. Did he do it out of manipulation or sincerity? He knew her secrets now, so why manipulate? Maybe he didn't trust her. Or…maybe he felt he could, and that had him at odds.

"I've told you all I know," she said. "No more games, please."

His gaze fell to her mouth as she said the last, as though tempted to fall for those words, so easily spoken but so much more difficult to practice.

"I'm not playing right now. I'm sharing observations."

That she'd secluded herself because of Jared's fraud, out of a sense of unworthiness. Partly true.

"I believe worthiness is earned," she said.

"In some cases, yes."

"Have I earned it with you?" That should put him on the spot.

Just as she suspected, he turned his head.

She had not earned her worthiness with him. Her path had woven different curves than his. He had the privilege of a loving home growing up; though scarred by the loss of his father, he still had two parents who loved him and brought him into adulthood with strength and integrity.

At last he faced her again. "I only mean that I can see it took a lot out of you not to come forward with Jared's fraud before now. And that you're still plagued with guilt."

"I wouldn't be human if I wasn't."

"Some can easily walk away from that burden if it makes their lives easier. I don't see that in you."

Did he mean that? He did. "Lucas…"

"I wanted to be angry with you, to resent you, to blame you," he said. "But I can't. Because I see you now."

Rachel felt dangerously close to falling deeper into an intensifying eddy of desire. Did he mean that? She asked the question to herself again. Did he? She teetered on the edge of giving in to whimsy. The whimsy of being one of those women she often saw, those women who always caught her eye, the ones whose energy beamed love. Those women were loved by their men. They shopped for groceries with a slight upturn to their lips. They said hello to her with confidence and an overall joy of life. Their laughter infected others. Their hair, skin and eyes glowed with health and abundance.

Never had Rachel felt like one of those women. But Lucas, with his piercing eyes so full of masculine strength and integrity, captured her heart in this moment.

He leaned down, his chair creaking.

Caught off guard, Rachel drew back a fraction. But his eyes, riveting and willing hers to stay with him, made her stop. Dominating. But in a purely sexual way.

Did he really see her?

Rachel had never met a more intriguing, mysterious man. His depths would take time to explore. The product of distrust? Or a man who required assurance before he gave his heart? She supposed it could be both. In a way, the two of them had key elements in common. Trust being the most significant. And loss. His loss had guided him as much as hers had guided her. Well, maybe not as much, but still a common thread.

He leaned some more, touching her jawbone as he had before, sending shivers through her. He pressed warm, soft lips to hers. After all she'd been through, after having to remain cautious every waking moment, this sprinkle of love made her surrender to its wonder.

She moved her mouth with the magic of his. His hand slid to the back of her head, and then he pressed her more firmly to him. Rachel wrapped her arms around his neck, the arm of her chair digging into her side. The kiss grew hotter.

Lucas stood, hooking his arm around her waist and lifting her easily. He kicked her chair out of the way. She hooked her legs on his hips as he moved them away from the desk. Out into the hall, she kissed him back as he devoured her.

In the living room, he stopped and withdrew. She put her feet down but reveled in the feel of his hard body against her. She could so easily strip naked and do him right now. Just forget principle and let loose her animal passion.

But he put his hand on her face and made her focus on him.

"I need you to help me, Rachel," he said.

She began to cool.

"Trust me now," he continued. "Do you?"

Still hot for him but appalled by what he'd just said, Rachel gave him a shove. "Oh!" She stepped forward and slapped her hands onto his chest. "How could you?" She shoved him again.

"What are you doing?" He grabbed her wrists as she went after him again. "What's wrong with you?"

"With me?" She yanked her hands free. "You did that on purpose!"

"What?"

"Kissed me!"

"No."

"I need you to help me, Rachel," she sneered. *"Trust me now..."* She scowled at him. "Really?"

"Okay, I can see how that seems. I didn't kiss you to get you to trust me. I never planned on kissing you. I do need you to trust me, though. Rachel."

Ooo...

"Trust this." She gave him the bird and stormed off, fully intending to leave. She'd been on her own for four years with a killer stalking her. She was pretty sure she could handle herself now. The only thing that had kept her from getting rid of Lucas before was this annoying attraction she had for him and his fit, manly body.

Fit, manly bodies had led her to successful men who weren't worth the time.

Worthy. She'd put too much importance on her offering of worthiness. She wouldn't make that mistake again. The man who made her feel worthy better be just as worthy.

Lucas caught up to her at the door, taking her hand and pulling her to a stop. She faced him.

"Don't go."

"Why not?"

"I wasn't playing games. I'm sorry I kissed you. I didn't mean to. It just…happened."

Maybe that was a good enough reason to leave.

He tugged her hand. "Come on. We need to find out why Angie Johnson contacted Jared."

She did want to know that.

"And then we need to talk to her. She may know something important, and like you, was afraid to come forward."

She pointed her finger at him. "Don't do that."

"I'm not manipulating. I'm trying to solve a case."

Rachel pulled her hand from him. "Okay, but only because I need this as much as you do."

They went back to the office.

This time Rachel sat at the keyboard, resuming the search. Lucas stood behind her, a distracting force, a sexual one. Rachel wished she could dismiss his effect on her.

"There," Lucas said.

Rachel saw the file name along with him. *AJ*, and the date. She opened it. And together they read.

Rachel inhaled her shock. "Jared denied her claim."

Angie had outpatient surgery, and the policy stated it was covered, but the letter of denial she and Lucas looked at now said otherwise.

"It's a fake policy," Lucas said.

"Why is Jared the primary contact for this?"

"He'd want to cover his tracks. Involving others would be a risk."

"He involved me."

"Unwillingly. You may have sent notifications like this without knowledge of its legality."

The words on the letter blurred for Rachel as she recalled all the correspondence Jared had asked her to transmit. Trusting and eager for her good, honest new life, Rachel had done whatever he'd asked. Little had she known what trouble she'd get into.

"Look at this."

Rachel focused on the screen again. It displayed what appeared to be a background report.

"Is that me?" Seeing the date preceded her first date with Jared, she moved to lean on the desk. It was a sloppy report. Short and lots of typos, but it had all of the pertinent information. *Rachel Delany: Juvenile Delinquent.*

She stepped back, slapped in the face with the extent of Jared's betrayal. She'd been too trusting. Too naive. He had taken advantage of her past, singled her out and pursued her.

Well, it was time to fight back. "What's next?"

Lucas faced the computer again. "We find Angie Johnson. We start with her."

She watched him do a quick internet search. Some people let their addresses be shown in directories onlinc. But with Angie, they didn't need an address. One of the first things that came up on her was her obituary—right after a news story covering her murder... her unsolved murder.

Chapter 10

Lucas woke to bright sunlight and thick brunette hair tickling his face. Blinking his eyes clear, he grew aware of Rachel lying half on him, her thigh draped over his, her arm on his stomach and chest. Her fingers lay on bare skin above the unbuttoned neckline of his shirt. At around dawn, they'd finally moved to the couch, still talking about Jared and about Angie's murder. He'd nearly fallen asleep sitting up. He had fallen asleep when Rachel had leaned against him and they'd reclined out of pure tiredness.

"Rachel." He nudged her. If she stayed there any longer, his body would react regardless of what his brain said.

"Mmm." She stirred, moving her hips as though aching from lying in the same position for hours on the confined space of the couch.

He began to get hard. "Rachel. Wake up." He nudged her again, giving her shoulder a shake.

She lifted her head and moved sleepy eyes to him.

"Unless you'd like to take this into the bedroom, I suggest you get up," he said.

That wiped the sleep out of her eyes.

"Oh." She pressed on his chest as she rose to her hands and knees. Straddling him to get off the couch, she went still in that position, her crotch against his.

She tipped her head down, looking at his body to where they pressed together. When her devouring gaze moved back up to his face, her fire set him alight. He reached up and put his hands on her breasts, their shape pushing out the blue-striped blouse she wore and beckoning him. She arched into the caress and rocked back and forth on his erection.

Lucas tore the blouse open. Buttons bounced off his chest and onto the floor. At some point in the night she'd removed her bra. Beautiful bare breasts enticed him from between the ripped material. He touched them. Rachel inhaled a passionate breath, and another when he stroked his thumbs across her nipples.

She ran her hands inside his shirt and leaned down to kiss him. He slid an arm around her and held her head as he rolled her off the side of the couch. He came down on top of her and kissed her hard. She began tugging at his pants.

They would have sex.

Her secrets had allowed a killer to go free. While he understood her reasons, his sister's murder hadn't been solved because of her. More than that began to cool his desire. The uncontrollable heat of it, and his growing feelings for her, also played into it. He wasn't ready for this serious of a relationship. His sister's murder had to come first. Trust had to come second. Was Rachel trustworthy? What if she withheld more information?

He lifted his head. His erection pressed against her warm center. He could just get their pants out of the way and satisfy the raging passion. So tempting.

But he climbed to his feet with a grunt, looking down at her on the floor, blouse ripped, breasts exposed, long, sexy legs coming together.

She sat up and turned away from him, holding her blouse together.

"We should get going. I'll meet you in the car out front." He walked to his bedroom to shower.

Rachel had her own off the guest room. He'd imagine her in there with him the entire time. He'd have to keep the water cold to calm down his body.

Angie's brother worked at the local elementary school as a kindergarten teacher in a town thirty miles from Bozeman. Rachel stopped at the classroom door. Through the vertical window, twenty kids dried rock salt on paper towels. Some of the kids had moved on to the next step of drawing the outline of a flower or a fish. The last step would be the use of the glue bottles, creating a piece of art on construction paper. She entered the room. Four years older, Clinton slicked back his hair and had the length of it in a tie at the base of his neck. He knelt beside one of the kids, helping to drain food-colored rocks.

He saw them, and after getting the child going, stood and came to them. "Hello. What can I do for you?"

He must recognize that they weren't the parents of any of the kids.

"I'm Lucas Curran, and this is Rachel Delany. You're Angie Johnson's brother?"

The friendly light in his eyes faded. His sister had been gone four years and he was still struggling.

"Are you police? Is there a break in her case? The sheriff didn't tell me."

"I'm a private detective. My sister was murdered close to the same time as yours."

"We think the two are related," Rachel said. "Angie took out an insurance policy through HealthFirst and came to meet with Jared Palmer shortly before her murder."

"Yeah. Sheriff Bailey questioned him and some others there. She had surgery, and the policy didn't cover what she expected. Jared wouldn't talk to her or return her calls, so she wrote the letter to complain. She got no response from that and kept calling him until he finally agreed to meet. He denied ever selling her a policy. She was going to hire an attorney, but police didn't find any policy, which corroborated Jared's claim. She didn't save any copies of the plan because the health insurance company didn't give her any. It was all done over the phone."

"When did she pay for the policy?"

"He arranged a welcome meeting for her, gave her cookies and coffee and took her money. Said he'd mail her copy of the policy. The sheriff has nothing to go on."

Rachel glanced at Lucas. That may have been intentional, Jared not giving policy buyers copies of what they purchased. Charmed them into believing they were getting a great deal and that they'd be treated well, only to rob them.

"We found a letter she wrote to Jared," she said.

Clinton perked up. "Police didn't find that. Jared let them search the customer database, and they didn't find anything."

No evidence of a policy? Had Jared scrubbed the books and eliminated any trace of the money Angie had given him? He'd allowed police to search the customer database, but what about his personal files? She and Lucas hadn't found anything yet.

"I told her not to pay cash for an insurance policy, but she did anyway. My sister wasn't the best with her finances."

"So police didn't think Jared had anything to do with her murder?"

"Oh, no. The lead detective thinks he has plenty to do with it. He just can't prove anything. Couldn't even get probable cause to get a search warrant."

Lucas glanced over at Rachel, and she caught the fleeting accusation in that silent message. It had been awkward ever since she'd climbed on top of him. His angst that she'd withheld information may have been what stopped him from finishing. And she'd have let him. Her passion had carried her that far away in a short period of time.

"Who was the last person to see her alive?"

"Mom." Clinton rubbed the back of his neck. "That's killing her." He dropped his hand. "They had lunch together. Angie left the restaurant and that's the last anyone saw of her until her body turned up."

"Who did the sheriff question at HealthFirst?" Lucas asked.

"A lot of people. Jared, his partner, the administrative staff, people in Contracts and Finance. No one could say anything about fraudulent insurance policies."

A five-year-old boy tugged on Clinton's pant leg. His fingers were covered in food coloring. "I spilled my paint."

Rachel looked to his area on the floor and saw the bowl he'd used to dye his rocks had indeed spilled.

"One second, Kevin," Clinton said to the boy, and then to Lucas, "Are you going to catch him?"

"Yes," Lucas answered, and his certainty convinced Rachel. "I just have one more question."

"Anything. I hope I can help."

"Did the sheriff talk to the Bozeman police?"

The schoolteacher and brother to a murdered sister frowned. "I don't know. He didn't say, so I guess not. Why?"

"My sister was murdered in Bozeman."

Jared's company was in Bozeman. Angie had lived here, in a small town thirty miles from the city.

Sheriff Bailey took his feet off his desk and put the newspaper down as Lucas and Rachel entered. Lucas subdued his excitement at the prospect of what he might learn from this meeting. He introduced himself and Rachel.

"Luella Palmer?" Sheriff Bailey repeated the name Lucas had given as his sister's. "The name isn't familiar."

His investigative instincts weren't as sharp as Lucas hoped. Any good sheriff would check surrounding towns for clues, wouldn't he? This day and age, law enforcement worked together. In his early sixties, the sheriff must've still been stuck back in a small-town mentality.

"She was married to Jared Palmer," Lucas said.

Sheriff Bailey's eyes perked up. "Forgive me. It's been so long, and my wife just passed after five years fighting cancer." He tapped his head. "My head isn't quite what it used to be."

That explained a lot. "I'm sorry," Lucas said.

"You think her murder is related to Angie Johnson's," the sheriff said.

Rachel had wandered to a bookshelf in the office, reading titles.

"Luella may have discovered something that got her killed, yes."

Sheriff Bailey walked around his desk to a file cabinet and opened a drawer.

Behind Lucas, Rachel looked through a mess of magazines and papers on a coffee table in front of an old couch. Was she just curious or looking for something useful?

When the sheriff put the file down on the coffee table, she sat next to him. Lucas walked around and sat beside her. The sheriff opened the file.

Rachel leaned back and averted her eyes when the first photograph of Angie's dead body appeared.

"Sorry." The sheriff turned over the photo.

Lucas picked it up. Angie lay in a low-lying area, shot once in the head. Branches covered her, but wind and weather had moved them over the days she'd lain there. It was strikingly similar to Luella's murder. Shot in the head. Dumped in a natural ditch. Branches put over her.

"No murder weapon. No DNA," Sheriff Bailey said.

"There wasn't in Luella's case, either." He felt Rachel look up at him, the sound of his voice giving away what seeing these photos did.

Sheriff Bailey handed him a few pages. "Jared's statement."

Lucas took the pages and read the first few lines.

"He has a tight alibi for the time frame Angie was killed."

"He's paying someone," Rachel said.

Loving how she lightened his mood by falling into amateur detective mode, Lucas read the report with less gravity. Jared had worked late when Angie had been killed. A janitor and computer data had confirmed it.

"Did you work through Bozeman police?" Lucas asked.

"No. After I checked out his alibi, I didn't see much point." The sheriff leafed through the file. "But in retrospect, I can see that was a bad decision."

"You had no way of knowing Jared's wife was killed."

And his own wife had been dying.

"Is there anything I can do to help?" Sheriff Bailey asked.

Lucas handed the pages back to him. "See if you can find anyone else you might have missed who either saw Angie or spoke to her about the insurance policy. Revisit your case. Start from scratch, except leave Jared to me."

The sheriff took the pages and put them back into the file. He'd have a second chance to make it right.

Next, Lucas handed the man his card. "Call me if you find anything. Day or night."

Sheriff Bailey nodded. "I will."

Back in Bozeman, Lucas and Rachel were brought up from the lobby of HealthFirst after a security guard announced their arrival to Eldon's assistant. At least Eldon hadn't refused to see them.

"You've got balls coming here after what you tried to pull off." Sitting behind a big desk, Eldon Sordi looked at Rachel. "It's good to see you again. I never had a chance to tell you I didn't know you and Jared were seeing each other, and that I thought you were a hard worker."

He hadn't known? She found that difficult to believe, but she couldn't help feeling good about his compliment. In a sleek gray suit and salt-and-pepper hair, he made a handsome example of what she'd once believed she wanted in a man. But he'd turned out to be a womanizer just like Jared. Maybe something a little more earthy suited her best.

She glanced over at Lucas before saying to Eldon, "Hello, Mr. Sordi."

"I was disappointed to learn you were with Mr. Curran here, after he broke into my building."

She'd never had an issue with Eldon. He was older than Jared and a gentleman, except for his excessive taste in women and posh parties, which she hadn't discovered until after she'd learned of Jared's misconduct.

"There's no proof we broke in," Lucas said.

"Just because the camera didn't record you? Are you the one who shot it out? And I don't suppose you know what happened to one of my cook's badges.

Strange, how we only have his word now that the system has experienced a peculiar failure."

Rachel looked at Lucas again. Had his boss taken care of that?

Lucas said nothing and didn't acknowledge her.

"Just what I thought." Eldon turned to Rachel. "I believed you when you said you changed your ways during your interview with me, that you would stay out of courts and jails."

"I meant it."

"You think you can break into my company and get away with it?" Back to Lucas, he said, "You must have powerful friends. I know it isn't Rachel who has them."

The blatant insult went through Rachel. He might consider her a hard worker, but she was a hardworking minion, nothing compared to the movers and shakers in his world.

"There wasn't enough evidence to hold us," Lucas said.

"Yes, I was told you were let into the building and weren't trying to take anything. *Waiting for Jared,* is what they said you were doing. An impressive ruse." Eldon pushed back from his desk and stood. "What were you looking for in his office?"

"We discovered that a woman who obtained a policy through him was murdered not long after my sister," Lucas said.

Eldon stood and walked around his desk. "Who?"

Leaving this part of the meeting to Lucas and his expertise, Rachel wandered over to a bookshelf. There was always something to be gleaned from the contents of a person's bookshelf. Eldon had old-school taste in both literature and decor. Churchill trim and desk and lots of war stories.

"Her name was Angie Johnson," Lucas said. "She wrote Jared a letter saying he sold her a fake policy, and she met with him prior to her death regarding the matter."

"Letter? What letter?"

Rachel saw the two of them standing face-to-face in front of the desk; Lucas calm, cool and seasoned for this type of interrogation.

"Police must have recovered it when they investigated Jared."

With a frown furrowing between his eyebrows, Eldon thought a moment. "Oh, yes. I remember now. It was an accusatory letter with no backing. I was shocked when police came to question Jared. They didn't charge him with anything, so what is the issue?"

"Her claims must be true if she was murdered after accusing him," Rachel said.

Eldon turned to her. "Jared wouldn't waste his time on fraudulent policies. He's got a strong client base. What were you doing in his office? I thought police cleared him years ago."

"He's never been cleared. There's no evidence," Lucas said.

"Has he ever spoken to you about Angie?" Rachel asked from the bookshelf.

"He told me about her claims. We have weekly status meetings, and clients are discussed."

"And you didn't think anything of it?" This question came from Lucas.

"Oh, I thought plenty of it. I spoke to Jared myself. He assured me that she didn't have a policy with us because she hadn't paid for it yet, and he thought she may have been desperate to have her medical bills covered."

"And you believed him?" Rachel asked. Jared hid the payments so that it appeared the customer had never paid.

"I did. I've known Jared a long time. We're business partners. I didn't ask him to join my company out of a lack of trust." Eldon walked over to a wet bar and poured a splash of scotch.

When he held up an empty glass to Lucas, Lucas held up his hand with a shake of his head.

Eldon took a sip.

"Did Sheriff Bailey ask you about Angie Johnson's death?"

"No. I was in Italy during that time. I flew out the day before." He drank more scotch.

Why did some executives think drinking in the middle of the afternoon was sophisticated? Or had talk of Jared's fraud made him uncomfortable? Health-First had been his company. He'd brought Jared in as a trusted friend. That kind of publicity would do some damage to his reputation.

"When did Jared become a partner?" Lucas asked.

He must have wondered the same as she had.

"When he invested half into HealthFirst five years ago," Eldon answered, draining the rest of his drink.

One year before Luella and Angie had been killed. Was it a coincidence?

"Are you sure you've never noticed anything suspicious about his dealings?" Lucas asked. "People he meets? Or maybe he goes out to meet people."

"We do that all the time. It's not unusual. No, I've

noticed nothing unusual about Jared. He knows what I expect, and he's never disappointed me. I can't imagine why he'd risk losing all of this." Eldon opened his palm to indicate his nice office.

"He invested in your company five years ago," Lucas said. "Did he have a difficult time coming up with the cash?"

"No. At least, I don't think so. He never said anything." Putting down his empty glass, Eldon looked from Rachel to Lucas, perplexed and becoming concerned. "Do you really think he could have killed Luella and Angie? Over fake insurance policies? I see the books. I'd know if there was money coming in unaccounted for."

Maybe he would, or maybe Jared had gotten good at hiding it.

"What about Marcy Sanders?" Lucas asked. "Do you know about his relationship with her?"

"Jared?" He appeared genuinely surprised.

"Yes," Lucas said, shrewdness narrowing his eyes slightly. "I saw him with her."

"With her how?"

"Leaving this building. Real close and cozy."

The furrow returned to Eldon's brow. He bent his head briefly and then raised it as his brow smoothed and he recovered from whatever emotion that stirred.

"Jared is that way. He likes women."

Was Marcy one of Eldon's women? The two men were so much alike, Eldon shouldn't be surprised they'd end up sharing one or two women.

"My apologies if that offends you," Eldon said to Rachel.

Taken aback that he'd think of her reaction to hearing that Jared liked women, Rachel said, "I'm not offended. I'm grateful I discovered his lies."

"Is there anything else you can tell us?" Lucas asked.

"No. If I learn anything, I'll be sure to notify the police."

Not them. Lucas's mouth inched up in a wry grin. He leaned over the desk and gave Eldon his card. "If you're inclined, you may call me at the mobile number listed there…anytime."

Rachel preceded Lucas out the door with one last look back at Eldon. He still held the card and watched them go. Would he protect his partner and friend or do the right thing and do as he said? She felt a kinship to him, except instead of protecting someone else, she'd protected herself.

Lucas put his hand on Rachel's lower back. Looking up at him, she saw his accurate reading of what she'd just felt.

"You have me now," he said, low and gruff as they left the office.

Yes, she did have him. For the investigation. To free herself from danger and to catch his sister's killer. As much as her heart clamored for more, that was all it could be for them.

"Rachel?"

She spun her head forward to see Jared standing outside the office, leaning against Eldon's secretary's desk with his arms and ankles crossed. He pushed to his feet, Eldon's secretary's eyes rolling up in curiosity.

"What are you doing here?" He looked to Lucas as he pushed off the desk and approached, stopping before Rachel, eyeing her in a way a man did when he liked what he saw, only in an aggressive way. "Did Eldon ask to see you?"

"No," Rachel said, betting he'd like a chance to exert power over her, to control her. "We came here to talk to him."

Jared's head moved back with the boldness of that. "Why?"

"Let's go, Rachel." Lucas slid his arm farther around her waist.

She moved out of his hold, putting her hands on his chest. "In a minute." She wanted to see how Jared reacted to this. She may not have ever dared go against him after he'd threatened her before Lucas had come to find her, but she dared now. Lucas gave her courage, support.

She faced Jared and saw his tension had increased as he watched how she touched Lucas.

"Why are you here?" he asked her with a note of resentment.

"We asked him about you," she said.

Jared glanced menacingly at Lucas and then back to her. "Why did you break into my office? What were you looking for?"

Was he playing? He had to know.

"Angie Johnson," she said.

Nothing changed on his face. "She didn't pay for her policy."

"That's how it appears," Lucas said.

Jared turned to him, the hint of a response to the innuendo. "So that's why you came here." He bestowed on Rachel another control-needy once-over. "You wasted your time."

Beside her, Lucas waited in stoic silence. He wouldn't give anything away about their investigation. He'd let Jared ramble on if that was what he did.

"Imagine my surprise when I received a call from security saying you were arrested," Jared said. "Was it his idea or yours?"

Mindful she could be talking to the man who'd killed two people—that they knew of—she didn't respond.

"What were you looking for?" he repeated.

"Did you kill Angie Johnson?" Rachel asked outright.

He drew his head back again, as though that was a preposterous thing to say. Jared pushed the lapels of his jacket back as he put his hands on his hips. "I can see someone's been poisoning your mind. What are you doing with him?"

"He's looking for his sister's killer. He's also protecting me. Someone's been trying to kill me…or at least scare me into backing off." She watched for signs in Jared's face, any change to indicate guilt. She saw none, only hints of jealousy, which she found odd from a man like him.

"Backing off? Why are you so interested in his sister's murder?"

"Don't you know?" she taunted.

His eyebrows twitched. "What am I supposed to know, Rachel?"

"Let's go," Lucas said again, reaching for her hand.

She realized he did it on purpose, touched her intimately. His arm around her waist, his gaze, which now regarded her in a way a man would look at a woman he'd slept with. She began to fume over that.

And then cheer him all the same. Jared barely contained his jealousy.

After a few seconds Jared regained his aplomb. "Rachel, have you thought any more about what we talked about?"

His profession of love? She kept what she wanted to say inside her head.

"I don't need to, Jared. You aren't the settling-down kind."

"I would be, with you."

He expected her to believe him? His declaration in such a public setting disconcerted her and exposed a little desperation.

"There's nothing more to discuss," she said. "You aren't the kind of man I see myself with in my future."

Jared's gaze hardened, and he slid it over to Lucas.

Rachel couldn't resist a peek at Lucas's reaction. Nothing could penetrate that face. He simply observed Jared, unmoving and unaffected. And ready to protect her.

Then Lucas moved closer and put his hand on her lower back without wavering his eyes, targeted on Jared.

Rachel felt a tingle chase through her, and it had nothing to do with the intentional display of possessiveness. Lucas meant to push Jared. See if he cracked.

Jared didn't crumble. He did something worse. He let his desperation get the best of him.

"Rachel." He reached for her hand. She withdrew, sickened and trying not to let her nausea show. She did not love this man. Never had. For him to shower her with his perception of that sacred feeling made her squirm inside.

Jared swiped the lapels of his jacket back as he'd done before, hands on hips. It was an entirely non-masculine pose.

"I've apologized for not telling you I was married," he said. "That was a mistake. Rachel, you're different than all the others. If I married you, I wouldn't need anyone else." His sleazy eyes took in her shape again. "You'd complete me."

"It's really time to go now," Lucas said.

Rachel felt the staged words, empty and meaningless. But she wasn't finished with Jared. She played along.

"I'd never be able to trust you again. What makes you think I ever could?"

He let out a frustrated breath. "Rachel—"

"Did you pay someone to come after me?"

"No. Of course not."

He almost sounded sincere. She leaned forward, putting her face up to his. "I may have been vulnerable before, but I'm not now. This is your warning, Jared. Leave me alone. Or else." Straightening, she glanced over at Lucas, her handsome, strong, sexy sentinel. "Now it's time to go."

His kissable lips curved up at the corners. She felt the shrewd light in his eyes all the way to her toes.

He stuck out his elbow, and she hooked her arm with his. Together they walked toward the elevator.

"Rachel."

She didn't turn to acknowledge Jared.

"Don't continue with this, Rachel." He sounded more confident.

Lucas pressed the elevator button and looked toward Jared. No way would Jared try to stop her, not as long as she was with a man like this. But what would happen if she no longer had Lucas?

Rachel recognized limits. A woman with a slender build, she didn't have the strength to go up against a man stronger than her, especially one with guns or hired guns and one who didn't think twice about threatening the weaker sex. Lucas liberated her.

She liked that. She liked it a lot.

Chapter 11

When Rachel and Lucas arrived back at his apartment, she recognized the old Jeep Wrangler in the driveway.

"You told Nan where to find me?"

"She misses you." Lucas pulled into the driveway beside the Wrangler. "You shouldn't have closed her out of your life."

Nan waved as they passed and pulled into the garage. Rachel got out and waited for her friend. She was still shapely and beautiful, with shoulder-length hair and blond streaks.

"Oh, Rachel." Nan came into the garage and hugged her. "After your boyfriend came to see me, I had to come here."

Rachel rolled her eyes to see Lucas, his head visible over the roof of the car. He shrugged to indicate he had no idea what Nan meant.

Nan leaned back. "When he asked me all those questions, it dawned on me that I haven't been a very good friend to you."

Rachel slid her hands off Nan's long black leather jacket. "Yes, you have."

"No." She shook her head, shiny silver dangling earrings swaying with a slight jingle. "I should have seen what you were doing."

While Rachel still tried to understand what she meant, Nan unzipped her leather jacket. Underneath she wore a beaded, turquoise-and-black V-neck with a black skirt and boots up to her knees. She had always taken fashion seriously. Much more so than Rachel.

"Let's go inside." Lucas had gone to the garage door.

Nan walked there and Rachel followed.

"I lost you after your mom and dad died, and my parents wouldn't let me try to find you," Nan said when they entered the laundry room of Lucas's house. "And then you straightened out and we got close again."

"Of course we did," Rachel said. "You're my best friend. You always will be."

Nan removed her jacket, and Lucas took it from her. Draping that over his arm, he helped Rachel out of her simpler, thigh-length cloth jacket with faux fur-lined hood. She thought his touch a lot gentler with her than with Nan, more intimate, lingering longer.

"You pushed me away," Nan said. Lucas hung up their jackets. "Now I know why." Nan reached out and put her hand on Rachel's shoulder. "You weren't just scared."

"You're right. I did it to protect you."

"Yes, but you also did it because you felt alone. You got used to being alone when you were in foster care. It's what was familiar to you."

"No. It had nothing to do with that. Jared threatened me. Well...*he* didn't, but he paid someone to."

"All noble, Rachel, but it still isn't the core of why you pushed me away. Lucas made me realize that. Not with anything he said. It was more the way he acted when I told him you were afraid of being accused of fraud. I realized he was falling for you."

No wonder she'd called him her boyfriend.

Lucas closed the closet door after hanging his jacket and with a good-humored smirk, walked down the hall toward the great room. Rachel admired the swaggering rise and fall of his butt cheeks before he vanished around the wall to the kitchen.

"Nice," Nan said.

Rachel smiled with her friend and then led her into the great room. At the kitchen island, she saw Lucas take out three cans of flavored iced tea. Sitting on a stool, she admired him some more, the way his muscles moved as he opened the cans and poured them over ice in three glasses.

"How long have you been seeing him?"

Jarred from her preoccupation, Rachel said, "I'm not seeing him."

"I didn't think so at first, either, the way he came to my salon asking questions like he thought you killed somebody." Nan laughed, a breathy, light sound that so fit her. Nan was always optimistic, always saw the bright side of things, no matter how rough they got. "But then I told him that you were afraid, and he changed. He got protective. I doubt he even realized it. Hell, I didn't, either, until after he left and I had some time to digest our conversation—and the fact that he left me his card."

"He does that with everyone." Lucas never left opportunities behind when he fished for clues.

"Hey," Nan teased, "don't ruin my popular moment."

Rachel smiled. "I'm not seeing him."

"All right. You aren't. That's not why I came here. I can't believe I didn't do something about this sooner. You've been hiding away all this time, and I had the reason all wrong. Yeah, you were scared, but you could have reached out to someone. Me. You didn't have to take on Jared on your own."

"No. Then Jared could have used you against me."

Lucas put two glasses down and moved back into the kitchen, leaving them alone to talk. But he could still hear them. Rachel found she didn't mind.

"I'm not afraid of Jared."

"He's trying to kill me, Nan."

"What?" She looked accusingly at Lucas, who hadn't told her that.

"Not at first, but ever since Lucas came to town, he's sent a man after me. And Lucas."

"Are you sure?"

Lucas met Rachel's eyes, and together they communicated they were.

"Okay, I can see why you went away, but you did that as a teen, too, Rachel. No one was after you, but you ran away from anyone who tried to get close. That's why I came here. You have to stop. If you ever want to find happiness and live the life I know you dream of having, you have to let go of your past and not be afraid of letting someone get close to you. You used to have so many friends. Then you went into foster care and that all changed." Nan put her hand over Rachel's. "I'm really worried about you."

"I'm fine."

"I took it personally, the way you shut me out. I felt like you blamed me for not doing anything to help you when Family Services took you away."

That came as a surprise to her. "I never blamed you." Nan had been a teen, just like her. What could she have done?

"I've always regretted never asking my parents to take you in."

"Would they have?"

Nan's parents had a rocky marriage. They fought a lot and had struggled financially. They couldn't have handled another kid, especially one as traumatized as Rachel.

As they sat exchanging silent thoughts, Rachel laughed at the same time she did.

"No way," Nan said between laughs.

"I'd have become a drunk and a thief," Rachel said, unable to believe she could laugh about that.

After sharing a few more moments of humor, Nan sobered. "I wish I could have been there for you."

"You were. Whenever I thought about you, I felt better. I wondered how you were and what you were doing. I'd picture you dyeing your doll's hair, and all was well again."

"You aren't alone, Rachel. Don't isolate yourself anymore. Promise?"

Rachel glanced at Lucas, feeling a strong pull that he'd be the one to draw her out, to make her trust again. Having the only source of security and love ripped from her life and then thrust into a life of survival had formed a hardness in her she wasn't sure she could soften.

Maybe he'd be able to soften it for her.

And if so, what then? What about what Lucas wanted? What about his ex-wife, who still loved him, or so it seemed.

"Some risks are worth it, Rachel," Nan said. She'd seen her look at Lucas. "Nothing worthwhile is easy, either."

Easy for her friend to say. She wasn't falling for a man who had trust issues and regrets that shaped everything he did with his life.

But then, didn't she? Rachel had trust issues and regrets, too. Did that make them a perfect couple or a disaster?

Nan had given Rachel plenty to think about after she finally left late that night. They'd had dinner and talked; well, mostly Lucas had listened to them catch up on the happenings of their lives. Nan had loved hearing about Rachel's many jobs that always ended with her being fired.

You're meant for something bigger, Nan had said. *You didn't believe in yourself so you took those low-level jobs. Start believing, Rachel. You believed enough to go to college, so finish it.*

I am, Rachel had said with admirable certainty.

Lucas hadn't wanted to let her go into the guest room, not with her dreamy smile and the healing balm spending time with a good friend had delivered. Her strength shined.

He lay on his bed with his arm under his head, staring at the dark ceiling, unable to stop thinking of her. She may have fallen into a pattern of withdrawal, but she wasn't a weak woman. She'd never been that, not when she went in and out of juvenile court, and not when Jared's thug had begun to threaten her. She may have felt weak, and Lucas admitted he'd thought the same, but he knew now that Rachel was anything but weak. She was a true survivor and brave enough to sacrifice time with her best friend to protect her.

An hour faded away before he closed his eyes. And then it seemed only moments later when he woke to breaking glass.

Bounding off the bed, he yanked on a pair of jeans and grabbed his gun before running out of the room. At the loft railing, he saw smoke billowing from a ball of flames that quickly spread across the area rug and climbed the drapes and walls. Someone had thrown a firebomb through the window.

Rachel rushed up from behind him, her hands going to the railing.

"Oh, my God!"

She'd dressed in jeans and a light blue and white long-sleeved shirt, and stared in horror as the flames spread ever wider.

"Let's get out of here!" Lucas took her hand and pulled her down the stairs. Flames jumped to the railing at the bottom, quickly engulfing the lower stairs.

"This way!" He led her down the hall to his bedroom. Another firebomb had been thrown through the window in there.

Rachel ran into the guest room and he followed,

slamming the door shut. She slid the window open. It was a long drop to the ground level.

When she clawed at the screen, he moved her out of the way, punched a hole and then ripped it open. He could hear the roar of flames in the hall as they swallowed the house.

Rachel climbed through the ripped screen and stepped out onto the roof. Lucas stepped out after her. He had mature trees in his front yard. One of them had branches that nearly reached the house. If they jumped, they might make it.

"Lucas!" Rachel peered over the edge of the roof.

He leaned forward and saw flames licking their way up the siding, coming out from the broken front window. Following Rachel along the edge of the roof, he stopped her at the tree.

She looked at him as though he'd lost his mind.

"I can't jump that far!"

Just then, a bullet whizzed past Lucas's head and plugged into the siding. Looking toward the street, he saw a car and a driver with a gun. He couldn't see the driver clearly, but raised his gun and fired back. The driver got a few more shots off before he backed into the car.

Rachel staggered.

Lucas saw blood soaking her shirt, up high and to the left. "Rachel!"

He reached for her but she'd already begun to fall. She landed on her hip on the roof and slid to the edge, grabbing hold of the gutter as she fell over.

Lucas went down onto his stomach and reached again for her. With her hand outstretched for him, she fell.

"Rachel!" He watched in horror as she landed on a bush and rolled onto the ground.

The roof was getting hot. Soon flames would burn through. Bullets hit the shingles next to him. He fired several shots at the driver, making him duck.

Swinging himself over the side of the roof, Lucas hung down and then dropped to the ground, going into a roll and coming back up to fire again at the driver, heading right for him and putting himself between the driver and Rachel.

The driver sped off. Lucas kept firing until he ran out of bullets.

He rushed back to Rachel. Blood soaked most of her shirt now. She was losing a lot of blood.

"Are you hurt anywhere else?" Lucas slid his arms under her and lifted her.

"Lucas." She sounded weak.

He swore as he carried her away from the burning house. Neighbors had begun to come outside. One of them ran toward him, a fortysomething woman.

"Are you okay?" Her breasts and stomach jiggled as she ran, eyes frantic and holding a cell phone. "I called 911!"

As soon as she finished, he heard the sirens.

At the edge of the grass, he put Rachel down and pressed his hand to her gunshot wound. Her eyes had lost some focus. She was going into shock.

"Stay with me!" Dear God, she couldn't die. "Rachel." He put his other hand on her cheek.

"Lucas." As she finished the whisper, her eyes slid closed.

White-cold anxiety shot through him. "No."

Sirens grew louder as a fire truck rushed to them.

Lucas kept his hand over her wound and moved his fingers to her pulse. She had one.

The woman who'd called for help knelt beside Rachel, opposite Lucas. "Is she dead? What happened?"

The fire truck came to a stop on the street. Firemen hurried to get the hose out while two others came to Rachel. An ambulance turned onto the street.

"What happened?" one fireman asked.

"She was shot."

"We'll take her from here."

Lucas reluctantly removed his bloody hand, sick with worry as more blood oozed from the wound. The fireman applied pressure.

Lucas stepped back as the paramedics brought over a gurney. His neighbor, whom he'd never met before, came to stand beside him.

"I saw what happened," she said.

Lucas turned to her and saw that she offered him a sticky note.

"That's the license plate number."

Lucas took it from her, amazed and grateful. "Thank you. Did you get a good look at the driver?"

"No. I couldn't sleep and was sitting at my kitchen table when I saw flames. I went to the front window and saw that car parked in front of my house with a man inside. I thought that was pretty strange, especially since he just sat there watching the house catch on fire. That's when I went to get my phone and a piece of paper."

"Your quick thinking may lead to the capture of the gunman," he said.

"Why was he shooting at her?"

"He shot at both of us." And Lucas would give anything to change places with Rachel.

Seeing the paramedics were ready to load Rachel into the ambulance, he said, "I can't thank you enough."

"I hope she's going to be all right."

Lucas did, too, more than he ever thought he would. Somewhere along the way, Rachel had become incredibly important to him, more important than an instrumental player in the search for his sister's killer.

Sitting in the hospital room on an uncomfortable chair, Lucas watched Rachel lay unconscious with tubes sprouting from her and a bandage on her upper left chest. The doctor said the bullet missed her heart by an inch, and she'd have been dead if she had arrived at the hospital much later.

Lucas kept wondering what he'd have done if she had died. Unable to catch his sister's killer, he'd have lost another woman who meant something to him. Never mind his doubts about her; he cared about her. No, he was *falling for her.* Maybe he'd already fallen.

Her fire when he kissed her, her perseverance despite the bad turn life had handed her, her determination to make a better life for herself, all touched him in some intangible, uncontrollable way. She had a loving, sensitive heart, but also a strong one. Yes, she'd withheld important information about his sister's case, but could he hold that against her? She'd been blackmailed. And after the danger had subsided, she'd been ridden by a moral dilemma. Until her blackmailer had decided threats were no longer enough. Now he'd kill her.

Hearing someone at the door, Lucas turned from

Rachel's beautiful face. No one was there. Who had peered into the room and walked on?

He stood and went to the door, looking one way down the hall and then the other. A man in a suit walked away. It was Jared.

Lucas ran after him.

Jared glanced back and saw him. Rather than run, he stopped and faced him.

"Did you hope to finish her off?" Lucas asked.

"I heard about what happened on the news."

"Disappointed she isn't dead?"

Jared sighed hard and ran his fingers through his hair. Then he looked at Lucas. "I know you won't believe me, but I had nothing to do with this."

How could he say that? They both knew he was involved in fraud, and all that kept him from jail was the right evidence.

The injustice built up in Lucas. How much more could he endure, failing his sister and now Rachel?

"If she'd have been with me, this wouldn't have happened," Jared said.

And what a wrong thing to say to him. Lucas grabbed ahold of his tie and shoved him against the wall. "You go anywhere near her again and I'll kill you."

With round, startled eyes, Jared raised his hands. "Whoa. I didn't come here to hurt her. I came here to make sure she was all right and tell her I had nothing to do with it. I wouldn't kill Rachel. I don't want her dead. I want to marry her."

Lucas scoffed. "You? Why would any woman want to marry you? Why did my sister marry you? Why would any woman like *Rachel* want to marry you?"

Giving Jared another shove against the wall, he let go of his tie.

Jared appeared contrite. "Look, I know I haven't been the most chivalrous man, but Rachel made me see my mistakes, especially that multiple women don't fulfill a man. A good relationship does. I was wrong for the way I treated her. I didn't appreciate her because I didn't know what I had until it was too late. Rachel and I were compatible together. I should have been honest with her."

"Why weren't you?"

Jared looked away briefly, a man contemplating what a jerk he'd been. Willingly. "My partnership with Eldon changed me. He was so charismatic and sophisticated. He had everything I dreamed of having."

"Women."

"That came with it. No, he had money. I followed him, but I shouldn't have followed his ways with women. I want to have the chance to tell Rachel that. When I heard she was shot and might not live, I nearly fell apart. And in an instant, I realized the magnitude of my mistake."

"What do you hope telling her that will gain?" Lucas asked. And what about Luella? Had he never cared for her? If what he said was true, maybe he had at first, until Eldon had changed him.

"Her heart. I want her back. I want to ask her to marry me. I'll quit HealthFirst. I'll start a new life. Things will be different this time."

Until the next woman came along to tempt him? Lucas held back the flare of jealousy. Rachel wouldn't go back to this man.

"That all sounds noble," he said, "but how will you accomplish that when you're in jail?"

A flash of anger hardened Jared's eyes, and he put his hands on his hips. "I'm going to talk to her when she wakes up."

"Not if I can have you arrested first."

After a narrow-eyed sizing up, Jared said, "You're in love with her, too." His singsong voice mocked, the heartless businessman who drove hard for a high bottom line coming out.

Too?

Lucas rebelled against that.

"I've seen you with her," Jared went on in his condescending tone. "You're a real cowboy, aren't you? Just like your boss. Well, capturing a woman like Rachel is going to take more than brawn. You think she'll be satisfied with mediocre?" He breathed a scornful laugh. "I mean, I know your dad makes a lot of money, and you aren't lacking, but your ambition in life is tracking down drug addicts. You have no taste for finer things. Rachel loves finer things." He leaned toward Lucas. "You can't give her that."

While he couldn't argue Rachel had a soft spot for men like Jared—businessmen who made a lot of money—he could argue she did have integrity in that endeavor.

"Is she looking for money to be wined and dined or is she looking for money with a man she can trust?" And love.

Jared's blink and slight drawback of head gave away how close to the truth Lucas had gotten.

"You want to marry her?"

Unlike Jared, Lucas held back his flinch. Marry her? How terrifying.

In his delayed response, Jared said, "You always did like to one-up me."

"What?"

"Any woman I wanted, you took."

What was he talking about? "No, I didn't."

"Oh, you weren't aware of it, but you did. They all wanted you." The sneer that contorted his face was fueled by years of comparison and resentment.

Lucas began to understand his estranged friend's discontent, what had driven them apart, and Jared into Eldon's way of life.

"I never meant to hurt you. I thought you were my friend." Lucas said the simple truth.

To which Jared instantly deflated. He turned his head away. "I know."

Lucas waited. He couldn't believe this change in him. The Jared that had married his sister would never have admitted his insecurities with Lucas.

"Feeling the crunch of the law?" Lucas asked.

A strange, softening, even regretful—deeply so— pause came over Jared. Somber eyes, flat mouth and silent communication with an old friend gave him a glimpse of the real Jared Palmer.

He almost said something, but Jared moved away from the wall. With a terse, "Good luck, Lucas," Jared walked away, down the hall.

Lucas didn't follow. He felt at odds with the silent message he'd received, one that contradicted the Jared of HealthFirst, the heartless businessman who'd do anything to stay rich. No, this man seemed more in line with the friend he'd once known. That didn't change the bad choices Jared had made. Realizing his mistake would only make prison harder.

Chapter 12

Rachel came to slow consciousness and the sound of a woman's voice talking softly with Lucas's deeper, gruffer response.

"You shouldn't have come here," he said.

Groggy and disoriented, Rachel struggled to get her bearings. Where was she? Why did her chest and arm hurt so much? She moved her head and saw the hospital room, the IV in her arm, and everything rushed back. The fire. The gunshot. Falling...

The USB device—they hadn't finished going through all the files. Neither of them had time to retrieve it. They'd rushed out of the house onto the roof. She'd fallen, and Lucas had carried her. That was the last she remembered before passing out, thinking she'd died.

"I heard what happened. I couldn't stay away," the woman said. "Why is someone shooting at you? Is it your sister?"

"Rachel was shot."

Rachel pretended to sleep but through a tiny crack of her eyelids, she saw the woman turn to glance at her, a quick dismissal. Blonde, blue-eyed and curvy, she had stunning good looks. She reached out and put her hand on Lucas's arm, giving him a brief but intimate rub.

"You were lucky you weren't shot, too."

Lucas stepped back from her touch. "Why are you here?"

The woman lowered her arm, taking the rejection with disappointment pursing her mouth. "I've been trying to talk to you for weeks, and you keep avoiding me."

"I heard all I wanted to hear before I left, Tory."

Tory Curran. The woman who'd shared his last name. Lucas's ex-wife. Rachel had not prepared herself for her gorgeousness. She had never possessed that kind of model beauty. Not unattractive, and not average, either, Rachel considered herself beautiful in a real kind of way, not a showcase-quality, hip-on-a-shiny-sports-car, evening-gown-with-big-diamonds way. This woman struck her as that type. Her well-made, wrinkle-free, knee-length pencil dress and crocodile purse and matching shoes gave away her demanding shopping habits and the money to back it.

"I'm a changed woman, Lucas. I won't hide the fact that I want a second chance with you, but I don't expect one. All I want is to apologize and ask for your forgiveness. I know how much it meant to you to start a family, how excited you were about it. I was stupid and heartless for lying to you."

"What's done is done."

Rachel shut her eyes and listened. Lucas's stiff indifference revealed deep pain over losing something he'd thought he'd had with this woman. What astonished Rachel most was that Lucas had wanted to start a family.

He'd been *excited* to start a family. That differed so greatly from Rachel's impression that she began to reform her view of him. He'd expertly hidden the desire. He'd homed in on his failure in becoming a SEAL and his job as a cop and now an elite detective when in his heart, he'd have given all of it up for a family. Family held that much importance to him.

The revelation came as a pungent shock to Rachel.

"We had something nice, you and I," Tory said. "I blew it. I was so afraid of losing you that I thought I had to lie to keep you."

"You should go now. That's all in the past, and I have no interest in going over it again."

"Did you love me?" Tory asked anyway.

"Go, Tory. Rachel is my only concern right now."

Warmth suffused Rachel at his declaration, but she found his avoidance in acknowledging Tory's profession of love odd, and his tone said he thought Tory rather rude for coming here at a time like this, while someone he cared about lay on a hospital bed after being shot.

"You loved me."

The woman's desperation almost made Rachel feel sorry for her. She and Jared should get together. She opened her eyes. Tory faced Lucas's indifference with sad hope, a beautiful woman who could have been any of those Rachel had seen and admired in the mall. Except without the joy.

"Rachel."

Lucas's urgent voice alerted her to her exposure. He saw that she'd awakened.

He came to her, putting his hand on hers and then leaning over to run his other along the side of her head.

"How do you feel?" he asked.

Rachel basked in his care before heeding their company. Tory looked on, those sad, hopeful eyes not so hopeful anymore.

"I'm fine."

Lucas grinned. "You are not fine. You must be in pain." He picked up the call button to send for the nurse. "You don't have to be brave right now."

Tory moved closer to the bed as though needing to get a closer look at her competition.

"Are you in terrible pain?" Lucas asked. "How are you, really?"

Rachel looked up at the warm concern of his blue-gray eyes and couldn't help responding to it, relaxing her muscles in the safety of his care.

"How long have you two been seeing each other?" Tory asked.

"We're not seeing each other."

"I'm helping him…with his sister's cold case," Rachel said, feeling fatigue weigh her down. She didn't have much energy.

"Aren't you the one who had an affair with Luella's husband?"

"Tory, I'll ask you nicely once more to go," Lucas said. If he had to ask again, he wouldn't ask nicely.

"Of course. Now isn't the time." Before she moved to leave, Tory said to Rachel, "I'm his ex-wife."

"Tory," Rachel said. "I know."

Tory looked sharply at Lucas, taken aback that he'd revealed so much. Rachel must be someone significant to him. If only that was true.

Recovering, Tory turned to Lucas. "I really just came to apologize. In person. I hope that someday you can forgive me and, even if we can't be friends, you don't regard me with anger and resentment. I have changed, Lucas." She glanced at Rachel. "And I do wish you the best. No matter what."

Rachel debated that. How far would a woman take her lies? If Tory told the truth, then honor to her, but a woman capable of such a big lie could easily lie again. Rachel believed Tory loved Lucas. She believed Tory wished for a second chance. But had she really changed that much? Or would she say and do anything to get her man back?

"Thank you, Tory. Coming here had to be difficult. I appreciate your effort. I do."

Rachel heard the *but* in that just as Tory must have. She gave a slight nod and then turned. At the door she paused, and with a dramatic, "Goodbye, Lucas," she left.

As soon as the door shut, Lucas returned his attention to Rachel. "How do you feel, Rachel?"

"Just tired. And in pain." She winced as she moved her shoulder. She felt so stiff, and the sharp stab reminded her that movement would come slowly.

"Rest. I'm just so happy to see you awake. They took you into surgery, and that was the longest three hours of my life."

"It'll take a lot more than this to take me down," she said, trying for humor.

Lucas didn't smile. He'd seriously suffered, not knowing whether she'd be all right.

"Careful, I might start to think you really do care about me." She smiled through her exhaustion.

"I do care."

In a humanitarian way. His heart was clearly locked away, as she'd just seen.

"Did you love her?" Rachel had to ask, now that she understood what made him this way, so off-limits with women, his lack of trust. He may have doubts over her involvement with Jared and how much she knew of Luella's death, but would he feel that way without the betrayal in his past?

"I felt enough to grow into love," Lucas said. "Or, at least, I thought I could."

"And then she broke your heart."

"She stole my future."

"You planned a future with her."

He straightened from the bed, his hand leaving hers cold. "You should get some rest."

"You chose family over the SEALs," Rachel said, her eyes drooping and her voice cracking with weariness.

"Don't go there, Rachel."

"Do you still want a family?" She closed her eyes, feeling herself drifting off into a drug-induced sleep, only then realizing it hadn't been the nurse Lucas had called. He'd given her a dose of pain medication.

"Go to sleep, Rachel. The doctor said he'd release you in a few days."

"That's so sad." Rachel nearly whispered now. "She took your love and any chance of finding something new." With that, she fell into black sleep.

* * *

Although Rachel had reclined her seat for the drive to the mountains northwest of Bozeman, she suffered in pain and exhaustion by the time Lucas drove his SUV onto a gravel road. He had to stop to unlock a metal gate, and stop again on the other side to lock it shut again. As he drove up the winding road flanked by a forest of healthy pine trees and a blanket of snow, she felt safer already. Isolation would do her good. She wouldn't have to worry about that man calling to threaten her, either. Her cell phone had burned in the fire.

Topping a hill, his ranch came into sight and stole her breath. Gabled windows and big logs made up the large structure, surrounded by a thick forest of pine trees and rocky, forbidding landscape. Rugged, like the owner.

He parked. "Don't move."

She didn't think she could even if she tried. So she waited for him to come around to her side. The driveway had been plowed. Someone had maintained the place in his absence. Opening the door, Lucas slid his arms beneath her and lifted her out of the SUV. The movements to do so tweaked her shoulder and sent sharp pain from deep in her upper chest down her arm and through her torso, wearing her down further.

She couldn't repress a moan.

"Sorry." He tried not to hurt her, but just his walking hurt. The front door opened, verifying Rachel's guess that someone had been here. He employed help. Had he done that in anticipation of bringing her here?

"I have the lower room prepared as you requested, Mr. Curran," the woman said.

"Thank you, Beverly."

"Homemade chicken noodle soup will be ready at six."

"Excellent."

"I can eat more than soup. I don't have the flu," Rachel said from the cradle of his arms as he carried her inside. She was rather hungry. Hospital food didn't inspire the taste buds, and she hadn't eaten much with the prospect of going somewhere so remote with Lucas. Finding out his soft spot had endeared her too much.

"There will also be cheesesteak sliders and a salad." The midfifties woman wiped her hands on her apron. "I didn't think I was only feeding an injured woman. I have a strapping man to feed, as well." She winked at Lucas. "It's good to see you again." To Rachel she said, "I worked for his father for years until I retired up here with my husband. We have a place just thirty minutes from here."

"I'm glad to have you while we're here," Lucas said, effortlessly holding Rachel in the entry, his handsome, kind face speaking of the respect he had for the woman.

How many times had she dreamed of what it would be like to have a family of her own? She'd longed to have her parents back right after they were killed. She'd imagined what it would have been like had they still lived. A dream. A fantasy. Something far more magical than reality may have been. Those had morphed into a family of her own. Husband, kids. A boy and a girl, three years apart. Idyllic. And, most of the time, unattainable.

"You get her settled. Just holler if you need me."

Beverly walked back into the house, which Rachel noticed with fuller attention.

The large entry opened to a living room with exposed ceiling and a river-rock fireplace. Antique, rustic furniture accented by light earth tones beckoned cozy nights before a big-screen TV mounted to the log wall. A kitchen ran along the back, a long island dividing the living room from a twelve-seated dining table with a chandelier hanging down in the center. As Lucas carried her across the living room, she saw the wall of windows in the back and a smaller, more private, sunken family room.

Anyone could live here. The signs of money were conservative and leaned more toward a casual lifestyle.

Lucas carried her past a bathroom to the end of the hall. "There are two master bedrooms down here. A loft upstairs and two more masters. I figured everyone should have their own who came to visit."

She managed enough energy to smile at his idle chatter. Was he nervous about carrying her into his home? Maybe he felt the same as her, anxious over spending so much time alone. His housekeeper wouldn't be around 24/7.

"I took the liberty of asking Beverly to fill your closet," he said as he stopped at the king-size bed.

As he lowered her down, she didn't dwell on the thoughtfulness of his action. Her clothes had burned with his house. She didn't have much at her apartment.

She closed her eyes to the wave of nauseating pain.

"Sorry." He gently slid his arms out from under her, and she lay comfortably reclined on the pillows. The covers had been drawn back ahead of her arrival.

She listened to him go into the closet and opened her eyes when he reappeared with a nightgown.

"You'll be more comfortable in this."

Yes, but how would she get into that? Just the thought of moving more made her recoil.

"I can ask Beverly to help you."

"No. Just leave it. I'll manage." Even as she said it, she yelled out in pain as she tried to shrug out of her jacket.

Lucas helped her. "I won't look."

With the jacket gone, she now had an oversize long-sleeved T-shirt that he'd had for her at the hospital, something roomy for ease of removal. He lifted that over her head. Wearing no bra, the cool air touched her nipples.

Though he'd said he wouldn't look, as a man he couldn't stop himself. She understood that. A few awkward seconds passed while he put the nightgown over her head and stepped back as she pulled it down over her, the lower part pooling at her waist.

Rachel struggled to take off the sweatpants he'd also brought for her.

Reluctantly, Lucas stepped forward and knelt before her. His warm hands took the waist and slid them down. Rachel lifted up enough to get them past her butt.

She heard his breathing grow heavier as he pulled them down her slender legs. With her boots still on, she had to wait for him to untie them and take them from her feet. That done, he removed the sweatpants and tossed them aside. Then he stared at the smooth, creamy texture of her skin. He lifted his hand and almost touched her.

Rachel imagined the feel of him sliding down her legs. More. She wouldn't have stopped him. Indeed, his desire was the best pain medicine of all.

With Rachel sleeping on and off over the past three days, Lucas had kept busy reviewing case files, reading, or watching television. He also did patrols around his property and kept an eye out for strange vehicles. No one had come, so he was fairly certain they were safe here. A storm had moved in and looked as if it would stay awhile, too. His housekeeper stopped by once a day to prepare meals and clean, but he'd told her to stay home until the storm passed. Until today, he'd asked her to help Rachel bathe each day, not trusting himself to do it and not enjoy touching her too much. Luckily, Rachel had refused his help in the shower, only requiring him to prepare with a fresh towel and new nightgown he thought best never to see her in. The filmy thing would be see-through in the right light.

Unable to sleep, he left his room across from Rachel's and turned on the television in the family room. He started the gas fireplace, too, fleetingly wishing he had someone to share it with. Rachel.

Shaking off the thought, he found a good action movie. As he turned to go to a recliner and distract himself with car chases and gunfire, he caught sight of Rachel walking toward him. She had her hand on the back of the living room sofa.

"What are you doing up?" He went to her, putting his hand under her arm to support her.

Through the dark living room and drape-free windows, outdoor light illuminated heavy snowfall.

"I'm feeling better now."

Helping her into the family room, he wished he didn't look down and see her breasts in the firelight. He put her on the sofa, grabbing some pillows and propping her there. Next came a throw, more for him than her.

She covered herself with a sleepy smile. "Thanks."

"Are you hungry? You slept through dinner."

"No. Some tea, maybe?"

"Sure." Glad for the diversion—and the distance from her—he went to the kitchen and started some water boiling.

"This is a good movie," she said, sounding livelier than she had since before she was shot.

It struck him that she liked action movies. Maybe not so unusual, but he liked that she had it in common with him. He came back into the room with her steaming cup and put it down onto the coffee table.

She bobbed the tea bag and looked over at him. Those golden-brown eyes enchanted him, peering out from a curtain of shiny but messy dark hair that swung forward over her shoulder.

Her words before she slipped unconscious at the hospital ran through his mind again.

She took your love and any chance of finding something new.

That's so sad...

Had he given up on love? Funny, how he'd never thought about that. He had no interest in involving himself in another relationship, hadn't put a time frame on when he'd try again, and then his sister had been murdered.

"Have you heard from your ex lately?"

Why was she so curious about that? "No."

"You should forgive her."

Rachel was taking pain medication, so he let that one slide. He sat on the recliner and put his feet up, enjoying the companionship.

She sipped her tea, and those lovely, soft eyes shifted toward him. "Why can't you?"

"Watch the movie."

"If you don't let go of that, Lucas, you'll never find happiness."

Lucas picked up the remote and turned the volume up a little.

Rachel didn't stop poking where it hurt. "I didn't know you were excited to start a family."

"Rachel." He pointed toward the TV.

"Seriously. You would have given up your career for that."

His tactic didn't work. "Yes."

"Would you still?"

It seemed a daring question from a woman who distanced herself from her friends. That wasn't enough to stave the pain. He felt himself rebel, unable to control his response. "Would you open yourself up to that?"

She put her cup down and leaned back with a slight wince. "I've had a lot of time to lie around and think about it." She leaned her head back and looked up at the ceiling awhile. Then she lowered it to look into the fire. "Nan was right."

She had taken some time to think.

"I want to plan a party after all of this is over. Invite all the friends I left behind after my parents died."

"Like a reunion?"

"Yes." A big smile spread. "I'd love to decorate a room and dream up some corny games. Play music. Dance." She closed her eyes. "My dad planned the most fun parties when I was a kid. Maybe I'll re-create one of those." She smiled with the warm memory.

"What did your dad do for a living?" he asked, the question suddenly coming to him that she should have had some kind of inheritance.

"He was an auto mechanic. But he owned a shop." Her head fell back again, and into a dreamy past she went.

"And your mother?"

Rachel sighed but not with stress, only relaxed bliss. "She stayed at home. They didn't have any money but they were happy. She also had a lot of friends who'd either come over for reading club meetings, or she'd take me with her to events and craft classes, lunches. You name it. She was always active."

"Like you."

She belatedly noticed his James Dean slouch, jaw propped in hand, lazy leg spread.

"Like me? What do you mean?"

"You know what I mean."

She did. His conversation with Nan and all of this close contact had enlightened him, the same as it had enlightened her about him.

"I lost my way," she conceded.

"That held when you were young," he said. "Not now. You're in a pattern now. One you should break."

She didn't respond, but he saw how what he said

resonated. She hadn't been willing to admit it before, but she could now.

"Plan your party, Rachel."

She looked over at him and smiled. But just as quickly as it appeared, the joy of planning something like that vanished, and she turned away. What had dimmed her light? He suspected he had a lot to do with it. How much of his conversation with Tory had she heard?

Circumstances kept her with him now, but what about later? After they caught Luella's killer, what then? She'd go back to her studio apartment and finish school, continue her quest to improve her life. He'd go back to...what? He'd left his job in California to join an elite cold-case investigation agency. He'd work, pour himself into his career.

Rachel's talk about family had shaken something loose in him, a wall he'd erected that had stood impenetrable for years. When Tory had told him she was pregnant, he'd felt an instant sense of purpose and rightness. He could have easily taken on the role of father. He would have devoted his life to her and their baby, and every other that might come after that. His career with the SEALs had come second. Blaming Tory for losing that had been a reaction to her lie, nothing more.

But times had changed. His sister's murder had changed everything. This kind of purpose he could not walk away from. And he could not forget that Rachel played a complicated role in the crime. Preferably an innocent one, but could he be one hundred percent sure?

* * *

Water trickled down from a fountain in the middle of a lush and flowering courtyard. The fragrance of lilies and man filled her senses. He lay her down on a bed of green leaves, soft and warm under the shaded sun. Shirtless and tan, he was a god above her. Blue-gray eyes demanded hers to engage while he ran his hands down her body, over the curve of her breasts and down. She had on swimsuit bottoms, and he slid those down until she could kick them free. Sweet, forbidden heat kept her prisoner to his touch. Something warned her that a mistake loomed. If she continued, she'd pay the price, a dark price. But she could not turn away from his eyes. They glowed with other-worldly power. She felt tied to him, unable to escape...

Rachel woke to Lucas lifting her from the couch, still floating with the dream, still in that between state, not quite back to the real world. He was the god. Somewhere in the recesses of her mind, she knew the movie had finished and he'd turned off the television. She looped her arm around his neck. Even the slight twinge of pain in her chest didn't bring her back from the dream. He moved fluidly and with gentle arms.

Glancing down, he caught her dreamy look and looked down again, this time staying with her in that place. In her room, he lowered her to the bed. She held on to his shirt, stopping his withdrawal. He put his hand on the mattress and hovered over her a moment, enchanting her until he slowly brought his mouth to hers. The contact gave her a jolt of passion along with zapping her back to the real world. Temptation circled her heart, swirling up a storm of desire too strong to deny. When he rose just a little and she saw his yearning, she thought of him giving up his career for the family he'd been duped into thinking he'd have, and she melted even more.

She touched his cheek, wishing just this once she could have been that woman he'd championed. Only she wouldn't have lied.

He kissed her again, slow and meaningful, as though he'd read her thoughts. Rachel knew she'd not turn back now. This felt too right. This lovemaking had never felt more right to her.

Breaking the exchange, Lucas cupped her breast, the one not bruised from the gunshot, which had penetrated just above the left one. She didn't let it ruin the moment. She marveled at how close to her dream this felt. It was as though she'd never awakened. He kissed her while he caressed. She held his face with one hand, not moving her other arm because it would hurt to do so.

Ending that kiss, he lifted the hem of her nightgown, taking great care as he slid the garment up and over her head. Next, he removed his tight T-shirt, the next best thing to being bare-chested.

Rachel glided her hand over his skin, able to use both hands somewhat.

He kissed her mouth and then moved down her neck to her right breast, then on to her left, where he treated her to soft, healing love.

After a while, he rose up and unfastened his jeans. Rachel watched his arm muscles flex and then his abdomen tighten when he got off the bed. His jeans fell to the floor, and she admired his jutting penis as he returned to her.

Making room for him between her legs, excitement pumped her blood hotter as he moved into position. Staying up on his hands, he rubbed himself on her first. Several teasing strokes later, he finally pushed inside.

White-hot fire took Rachel to another world. Flying away on wings of pleasure, she let out a series of breathy groans as he began to go back and forth. He moved slow, taking his time, pleasuring her with excruciating sweetness. Arching as she climaxed, she barely noticed the deep sting in her gunshot wound, crying out in pleasure instead of pain.

Lucas pushed into her once more, having reached his peak with her.

Settling down after that incredible high, Rachel's chest throbbed in protest of the extra activity.

Lucas lay beside her, pulling the covers over them to ward off the chill. "Are you all right?" he asked.

"Yes." She grimaced as she adjusted her position to get more comfortable. The pain didn't lessen. In fact, it felt as though it would hang around awhile and make for a rough night of sleep.

Lucas got up, bold in his nakedness, and walked to the bathroom. He returned with her pain medication. Rachel pushed herself to lean against the pillows, unable to stifle an audible grunt of pain.

Sitting beside her on the bed, Lucas handed her the glass of water on the nightstand. She took them both, swallowing the pill. When she finished, he put the glass back down on the nightstand and then looked at her again.

"We probably should have waited for that," he said.

She needed more rest. "I'm glad we didn't." If they'd have waited, would it have ever happened?

Maybe it shouldn't have. She turned away with that thought.

Outside, wind blew snow against the window. Rachel wouldn't think about the consequences of this night. She would only think about the wonder of it.

The muffled ring of Lucas's cell phone woke him. Then he realized two things. His cell phone was in the pocket of his jeans on the floor, and he was in bed with Rachel.

On the third ring, he looked over and saw her stirring, dark hair fanned out on the white pillow, beautiful eyes fluttering open.

Damn.

Moving the covers off him, he crouched for his phone, catching the caller just before it went to voice mail. It was Sheriff Bailey.

"Lucas," the sheriff said, "my apologies for not returning your call sooner. I had to follow up on a few leads first."

Lucas had talked with the sheriff while Rachel was in the hospital, telling him the plate number the neighbor had given him after the shooting.

"The plate traced to Jared Palmer," Sheriff Bailey said.

He must have known that for a while. Why hadn't he called sooner?

"I've spent every day since this discovery trying to locate him," the sheriff said.

"He ran?"

"His partner said the last time he saw him was when he left work the night before the fire. A neighbor saw him leave his house around seven that same night. So something made him go out again. I've checked phone records. He received a call from a disposable phone at six-fifty p.m. A false ID was used to activate the disposable phone, and the buyer paid cash. I traced the buy to a supercenter store and have my deputy going through the security tapes. Bozeman police are working a missing person case on him, and I'm sharing what I find with them."

"Have you spoken with Marcy Sanders?"

"She's another person I haven't been able to find. She was last seen at a restaurant with Jared the night he disappeared. They left the restaurant at six thirty, and her roommate said she never came home, nor did Jared drop her off. His neighbor said he left alone, and he didn't see Marcy come home with him."

Within thirty minutes, Jared had left the restaurant, driven home, received an untraceable phone call and then left right after that. Where was Marcy?

Beside him, Rachel climbed off the bed and walked naked to the bathroom, seeming unabashed. If last night troubled her the way it did him, she gave no indication.

Jared missing could mean one of two things. His failed attempt to kill him and Rachel had made him decide to flee, or someone else had more to lose than him. Was it Marcy? She'd dabbled in relationships with both Eldon and Jared. What kind of triangle had she created? And was Eldon involved somehow? He'd seemed genuinely surprised to learn Marcy was seeing Jared. And Jared had seemed genuinely concerned about Rachel, and sincere when he'd insisted he wouldn't hurt her. Was Marcy the criminal in this scenario? What would she have to gain from Jared's fraud? What would she gain from removing Jared from the picture?

Chapter 13

After a week of resting, Rachel began physical therapy. She'd just finished her routine, exercising with gradually increased length and intensity and ending with a bath. She'd started with gentle movements and still wouldn't call what she did a workout, but it was progress. With her hair up in a clip, she slipped into her nightgown.

Not ready for bed yet, she left the room. She still had to walk slow and felt how weak her injury had made her. In the kitchen she put a kettle of water on a hot burner.

With only the light above the sink on, she didn't see Lucas until he stood from the table. He'd been working in front of his laptop. He walked over to her and came to stand behind her.

He hadn't tried to make love to her again since that

first, glorious time. But now he slid his arms around her and put his face beside hers.

"I can see your body through this nightgown," he said.

He could? She glanced down and couldn't see anything, but she supposed the filmy material would be transparent where it fell away from her skin.

He kissed her neck, sending off an array of tingles. She turned in his arms and looped her good arm around his neck. They kissed, with his hand roaming her body over the soft material of her nightgown.

Passion heated up. Rachel sought more of him and he answered her, their mouths a perfect match for satisfying this marvelous need.

"You make me want to believe I can have this," she whispered against his mouth, and then regretted letting that thought out. While she didn't spell out what *this* was, he must have guessed.

Moving back from her, his hands fell away from her hips, and the look on his face made her go cold.

This to her meant family. Love. All the things she remembered about her parents, everything that had been taken from her at a vulnerable age.

"Maybe we should back off a little," he said.

Back off? They'd barely started. Was his commitment level that low?

"Yes, we should." She didn't need to get her heart wrapped around a lost cause. He had too much to resolve personally. She'd been a fool to hope otherwise.

Almost three weeks later Rachel felt like herself again, except for the tension that living with Lucas generated, and the fact that her period was late. The shooting may have caused the delay, her body struggling to recover, but another reason had taken seed in her mind. While having a baby filled her with wonder and love, the timing couldn't be worse. With a man like Lucas, maybe there'd never be a good time. Maybe he needed this to stop him from hanging on to a negative part of his past.

He'd refrained from intimacy since that last kiss. They'd managed to get along like roommates, but there had been the occasional brush of skin and long looks. A few times she'd gotten close to tossing caution aside just to assuage the constant desire to feel again what she had that magical night. But then the reminder of the last kiss doused any flickering flame. Conversations were either related to Jared or Luella or cordial and out of necessity. No one had found Jared or Marcy, so there wasn't much to say about the case.

Lucas's expertise in walling her off disconcerted her. She tried to tell herself it was for the best.

She watched Beverly's husband plow the road beneath sunlight they hadn't seen in days. Lucas couldn't take the isolation anymore. They'd been cooped up inside through three storms. The snow had piled high. Rachel wasn't sure what bothered him more: not being more involved in the investigation or being too close to her. They could have returned to Bozeman over a week ago were it not for the weather. Lucas may have argued that point. Although he'd been aloof, he'd not slacked on her care. He'd seen to her every need, the only thing that had contradicted his need for distance.

Rachel hated that she didn't share that need. If things had gone her way, they'd have had sex every day. She had often caught herself daydreaming about a life with him. Family. And that had only intensified after she realized her period was late. She'd thought more of her life with her parents than she had since she'd been arrested as a teen. The thoughts had not been tainted by sorrow and resentment, either. No rebellion. Nothing but good memories filled her, contentment and yearning for that happy stability again.

"Are you sure you're healed enough for this?"

Jarred from a peaceful state, she turned from the living room window. He must know she was. There had to be another reason for his reservation.

"Yes."

"Maybe you should stay here."

She faced him, curious as to why he'd like to leave her behind. Concern for her safety? Or fear of close proximity? "Why?"

Not a meek-minded man, or a stupid one, he turned as he said, "You're safer here."

"Maybe what you really mean is you'd be safer if I was here and not close to you. Easier to deny what's happening between us."

"What is happening between us?"

Oh, he aggravated her when he did that, acting as though he felt nothing for her. He may not be falling madly in love, but they had a connection. Could he not at least acknowledge that much? "Apparently nothing."

When he didn't respond, she became more irritated. "Now isn't the time to say I think I'm pregnant," she said, just low enough.

But he stopped and asked, "What did you say?"

"Nothing."

A moment longer, subject to his scrutiny, he finally went on his way.

Rachel faced the window again, seeing the big plow disappear down one of the roads on Lucas's property. It would be stored in one of the outbuildings, protected until needed for the next storm.

She faintly heard Lucas's cell phone go off, and then his muffled voice. She couldn't hear what he said, but the rich baritone penetrated her senses. She lost herself in wistful pleasure.

Then his booted feet thudded back into the living room. "Jared's body's been found."

While the length of time he'd been missing should have prepared her for this, hearing the fact spoken gave her a jolt. Jared was dead.

"His car rolled down a steep ravine in a remote area north of Big Sky. His body is fairly well preserved due to the cold. He was strangled."

"He was in the car?"

Lucas nodded. "But the strangulation suggests he was somewhere else when he was killed. The angle of the ligature marks doesn't support him sitting in the car."

That meant someone else had to drive the car to the cliff and put his body in the driver's seat. "Marcy?"

"Still missing."

Had she driven Jared's car to the dump site?

"I have directions to the crime scene. If we leave now, we'll make it in time."

In time for what? Before the investigators completed their evidence-gathering? She didn't ask, just went with him.

Lucas left Rachel in the warm vehicle while he walked down the precarious, snow-covered hill to the ravine below. The car had been partially buried by snow and well hidden by the steep terrain and thick branches of shrubs and trees along the bank of a frozen stream. Only flowing water beneath the layer of ice could be heard. Late afternoon, a good, Montana bite of cold had settled in the air.

Several investigators worked the scene, searching the land surrounding the vehicle, meticulously going through every millimeter of the interior. Jared's body lay slouched over the console, not belted in. His body showed signs of being jostled violently on the descent to the stream shore. The window was down on the front passenger side. The others were up. Had Jared rolled the window down to talk to someone?

Maybe his killer had pointed a gun at him. Marcy? She smoked, so maybe she'd rolled the window down for that and had then drawn the gun.

"Over here," one of the investigators called.

Lucas made his way through the deep snow to a cluster of thick shrubs. Two investigators were careful not to disturb the item, a briefcase. The female investigator snapped photos. The man opened the case with gloved hands and some fine lock picks. A crude hand-drawn map lay on top of folders and papers.

Lucas didn't see any marks in the snow to indicate the case had tumbled here from the car. He also noted how shallow the case sat in the snow. If it had been hurled from the car, it would have sunken deeper. Not only that, had this case flown from the open window in the car, it would have been buried by snow over the weeks Jared had been here.

Someone had planted this, and someone had planted it recently.

"I need a copy of that map," Lucas said. He took a pair of gloves the woman handed him and lifted the map. He recognized the location right away. Luella had purchased a cabin before marrying Jared. A small structure on about twenty acres, it wasn't much in the way of vacation homes, but it had been what Luella liked. Cozy space tucked away in isolation.

The X marked a spot in the back, within the thick forest of trees.

He put the map back down. Whoever had left this had intended for police to find it. Straightening, he met the sheriff and asked him to give him a copy of the report when it became available. The sheriff nodded with a yawn.

After driving back in the direction they'd come, they finally arrived at Luella's cabin. Rachel didn't find it odd that both siblings preferred the wild of Montana's mountains. What was peculiar was that Lucas leaned more toward the expensive and Luella the more conservative. Her choice in men didn't give any indication of that quiet reserve. Lucas's rugged background gave equally vague clues. Rachel attributed that to their humble upbringing. Joseph had experienced incredible success with Tieber Transport, but he'd also stuck to his principles. An honest, good man, he was someone Rachel respected. She supposed his stepchildren had learned from his better qualities.

She watched Lucas look over at the cabin, memories taking him as he led her through the snow to the back. He didn't yet have a copy of the map. He didn't need one. He knew this land. Something about it struck her as familiar, too.

Lucas stopped short.

Rachel bumped into him and stared at something hanging from a tree limb. It swayed in the slight breeze. Rachel had the image of a piece of skinned meat before she moved closer and realized it was much worse.

It was her pillowcase. Something had been stuffed inside. Blotches of blood gave her a sick feeling.

Lucas recognized the pillowcase. She'd had it on her daybed, the lavender stitching distinctive on the white material. Even dirty and soaked through with blood in places, there was no mistake.

Lucas shot an incredulous look back at her, neither accusing nor believing. But his doubt hurt.

He didn't actually think…

How could he?

Incensed, she marched forward to yank the pillowcase off the branch. The ties held sturdy but gave under her pulls. Drawing the top open, she fell backward onto her butt when she saw the bloody clothes inside.

Lucas didn't lift out any of the items. They were Luella's clothes from the night of her murder…or so they appeared. How could the blood have soaked through in places if it was Luella's? Her pillowcase had not been missing that long. But would Lucas believe that? She had extras in her closet.

"These are Luella's clothes." He said the obvious.

She didn't say she knew. That might make her seem guilty. How would she know if these belonged to Luella? He might dismiss natural insight.

Rachel touched the side of the case on one of the blood stains. "Someone put these in my pillowcase on purpose." Didn't he see that? She looked up and saw his turmoil. Finding his sister's clothes inside one of Rachel's pillowcases delivered shock the killer had surely intended.

His lack of response said he did see, at least distrustfully. As a detective, he had to consider the possibility—and it was a good possibility. The clue had clearly been left for them to find.

"Someone is trying to set me up." If Jared had still lived, she'd think it was him.

Lucas took out his phone and made a call to the local police. Then he called the sheriff.

As he did so, he made sure to indicate the pillowcase belonged to Rachel. While he had doubt, he still didn't trust her. She felt so betrayed. How could he so easily throw her under the bus like that? The region of her heart stung and ached. She fought for steely resolve that normally came easy to her, but now it failed her.

Would he just stand by and watch her be arrested for a crime she didn't commit? If other detectives became convinced of the plausibility of her guilt, would he take their side? She had to say yes. She couldn't believe it.

He'd cast her aside that simply? Maybe he thought scaring her would get her to talk. Funny, how previously that tactic would have worked. But now she understood the reason she'd been scared before. And she understood she had nothing to fear.

If ever there was a man who needed an intellectual slap in the face, it was this one. She waited for him to end his call.

"I'm pregnant," she blurted.

His glance froze, and he just stared at her. Gaped.

She let him stew awhile before saying, "I don't know for sure, but all the signs are there."

To that, his face darkened. "You're just saying that."

"No, I'm not." Of course, his past would inch in to steal the moment.

He didn't falter. "Yes, you are. You know where I'm vulnerable, and you're taking advantage of the opportunity."

"Nope. Wrong again." She folded her arms, marveling at how far out of touch he'd become.

He said nothing, his whole body exuding conflict. He had no evidence against her, only a pillowcase that could have been stolen from her easy-to-break-into, cheap apartment. "I didn't kill anyone, nor did I have anything to do with this." She pointed down to the pillowcase. "You're reaching for a way to implicate me out of distrust."

With that, he blinked. "For all I know you haven't been honest with me from the start. There could be more you haven't told me."

As he spoke, she saw his own disbelief in what he said. With a long sigh, he said, "I was hoping you would turn out to be different."

Than what? His lying ex-wife? "I am different. You're just too stubborn to admit it. You're scared of what it meant when we made love. And now you're even more scared."

"I'm not afraid of anything." He started trudging back toward the front of the cabin.

Typical macho thing to say. She trailed behind him. "What if I am pregnant?"

He kept walking, not acknowledging her—probably what he wished he'd done with his ex-wife. Did he have daydreams about how he would have handled that differently?

Screw you, I know you're lying...

Except that didn't fit her impression of Lucas Curran. No, *hero* fit him much better. Hunter of justice.

All of the fight drained from her. If he had to cling to the belief that she had something to do with his sister's murder, she couldn't change his mind. He had to decide what to think on his own.

But really...what if she *was* pregnant? What would he do? Would he hold on to past disappointments...or would he be the hero she knew him to be?

Chapter 14

Two nights later, long after Lucas had gone to bed, Rachel still couldn't sleep. She finished dressing in the hotel bathroom. Lucas had gotten them a two-bedroom suite. His aloofness suffocated and angered her. Just because he'd had a bad experience with another woman didn't give him the right to treat her as though she was of the same ilk. Rachel might have withheld the truth to protect herself, but she didn't lie. She resented him for assuming she did, labeling her, judging. That injustice had led to other thoughts, how off course she'd gotten.

She finally relented to the calling in her heart. Fortunately, the calling had nothing to do with him and everything to do with her. *Take back your life*, it said. The setback her relationship with Jared had caused had diverted her path, but she saw a way to put herself back onto the straight road. Thanks to Lucas, she had a chance now. While she still debated the folly of leaving him, she also couldn't stay. Her roots on the street may not equate to his as a SWAT cop, but she could defend herself. With Jared gone, she didn't have to be afraid anymore. She shouldn't have been afraid before.

Lucas's door was still closed. He'd shut it last night as though shutting her out. Well, he'd get his wish. Quietly, she left the hotel suite and took the elevator to the lobby.

She took a taxi to her apartment.

"Wait for me," she told the driver. This wouldn't take long.

Careful that no one saw her, she entered the building. No one stirred at this hour. The elevator seemed loud in the silence. On her floor, she kept careful vigil down the hallway. Someone's television played as she passed one door. Most of the lights had burned out in the hall. Shadows engulfed her door. She used her key, slowly and stealthily unlocking and pushing the door open.

Peeking inside, she saw the mess. Someone had searched her apartment. She calmed her alarm, not seeing anyone inside. Most likely the apartment had been ransacked before she'd been shot. Stepping inside, she closed the door.

Without turning on a light, she veered around an overturned chair and stepped over the covers that had been yanked off her daybed. At the head of the bed, which had been pulled away from the wall, she found her bedside caddy still hanging from the mattress. Whoever had broken in here had dug through the books and magazines, but the zippered pouch had been left undisturbed. She opened it and retrieved her pistol, flipping the safety off. Grabbing the extra clip, she turned. Her armoire doors hung open, and all her clothes lay on the floor, but her purse still hung from a nail on the inside. She went there, kicking clothes out of the way. The top gaped as though meaty hands had reached inside, looking for something revealing.

She removed the purse and dropped the extra clip and gun inside. Strapping that to her waist, she jumped over clothes and headed for the door. Peering into the dark hallway, she left the apartment and made her way to the elevator. The neighbor's television faded as she passed. She stepped inside the elevator. In the lobby, a man staggered through the front doors.

Seeing her, his face took on a drunken leer. "Hey, I remember you."

"Have a good night," she said and took a wide path to avoid him.

"We could have a good night together."

Ignoring him, she went outside, glancing up and down the street. The same cars were parked on the road. One drove by, the driver oblivious to her.

She got back into her waiting taxi and told the driver Jared's address.

Ten minutes later the driver pulled to a stop in front of the huge house. Only an outdoor light and possibly one interior light shined through the night. Crime-scene tape bordered the perimeter. The team had finished going through the house.

"You sure this is the right address?" the driver asked.

"Yes, this is it." She dug into her jeans pocket for cash. Lucas had given her some when they'd left his ranch, in case they ever got separated. Handing him the fare plus a generous tip, she said, "Don't wait for me."

The driver stared at her a long moment, but saw the thickness of the folded wad of cash and took it.

Getting out, she looked at each neighboring house, spaced far apart. Not seeing anyone watching, or that the taxi's arrival had drawn any attention, she faced Jared's house.

One thing she'd told no one: she still had a key to get in the back door. Keeping to the shadows, she made her way undetected to the back garage door. Using her key, she entered the garage and stepped inside Jared's large, five-bedroom home.

Being here again felt wrong, and not because she'd broken in. The last time she'd been here, she'd thought he lived alone. Luella, his wife, had lived here, too. It felt completely different. Not that she had any feelings left for Jared. She didn't. She just wished she'd have known he was married when she met him.

Going into his den, a room he'd often told her he favored, she went to the photos he prominently displayed on the bookshelf. One whole shelf showcased six. A chill spread through her. She remembered seeing these. They'd struck her as odd; six pictures on one shelf when the rest had nothing but books. Why had Jared put them here? Maybe he had no particular reason.

Moving closer, she studied each one. Jared and Luella were in all of them, captured in varying moments at different events. Rachel estimated the time frame must be two or three years before she'd met him, or before he'd taken her to his house and she'd seen them the first time.

Something else snagged her attention. Eldon was in all of them, too. And in each one, the camera had caught Luella looking at him. Over her shoulder in one, to the side in another. Across the room. Facing each other, Eldon with a stunning brunette on his arm and Jared smiling and talking to her, unaware of the sultry way his wife regarded his partner in that moment. In the last photo, she actually stood right next to Eldon. Her head tilted beguilingly, Eldon grinning as though they shared some intimate secret.

Eldon being in the photos wasn't significant. The way Jared's wife looked at him was.

Rachel saw why police hadn't thought much of these. A few family pictures, harmless by themselves. But piece it together with Eldon...

If Luella had discovered Jared's fraudulent policies, could she also have discovered Eldon's? With Jared murdered, Eldon could have been the one to take action to protect their activities. Jared could have been innocent, or he may have gone along with Eldon's plan up until he'd had a change of heart.

Rachel needed proof. Evidence. If she would ever take her life back, she needed that one thing. Eldon wouldn't know what she'd learned just now, and she could act as though she hadn't. He wouldn't know he was about to become a suspect of fraud and murder.

Taking up all of the framed photos, she put them on the floor, spreading them out in a row so no one would miss them.

Then, after a quick search of the rest of the house

that turned up no other clues, she slipped out, as unseen as she had been when she arrived.

After walking all the way back to town with one stop at a supercenter store to buy a recorder, Rachel waited for HealthFirst to open. She'd hoped to intercept Eldon on his way into the building, but he hadn't shown up. After ten, he probably wasn't going to. She went into the lobby and asked the front desk receptionist if he'd be there today.

"No. He's on vacation."

He'd gone on vacation with his partner missing? "Where did he go?"

The young woman smiled. "They don't tell me that."

"May I speak with his assistant?"

"Sure." The woman picked up a phone and called an extension. "Rachel Delany is here to see you." She listened and then hung up the phone. "She'll come to the lobby."

"Thank you." Rachel left the front desk, and the woman helped a man dressed in a suit who'd waited behind Rachel.

She wandered over to a wall beneath the atrium high above, where wide-screen televisions silently displayed advertisements for quality health coverage. Silver. Gold. Diamond. Three plans for varying levels of income. The screen switched to Ruby and Sapphire plans. Sapphire sold to the lowest-income policy holders. Rachel recalled that Jared had sold a few of those, and she had facilitated sending them to clients. That must be the plan where he'd embedded the fraudulent policies.

"Rachel?"

She turned to see Eldon's assistant approach.

"Can I help you?"

"I hope so. Do you know where Eldon is? I need to talk to him about Jared."

The woman's friendly smile faded as she sobered. "He was devastated when he heard about Jared. Murdered?" She shook her head. "Everybody is so shocked."

"Yes, it is a shock."

"Were you seeing him again?"

"No." She forgave the woman for asking. "But there is something I really need to talk to Eldon about."

"He went to his lake house." She explained where, and when Rachel asked for the address, she wrote it down for her. "He had me mail him some things there. He's on vacation but working when he can. You know those executive types."

"Yes."

"They have no personal life."

Unless they had shady ones, like Jared. But of course, not all executives were like that.

"Why do you need to talk to him?"

"It's personal." She wished she could sneak into his office and hack into his computer, but she'd have to leave that to Lucas's expertise.

She turned to the patiently waiting assistant. "If Lucas comes looking for me, tell him to go to Jared's house." He'd know what to do from there.

She left the building and started walking toward a bus stop. A few minutes later she realized someone was following her. Glancing back, she saw a woman, tall and thin with long, wavy blond hair and sunglasses. A bright, multicolored purse hung from her shoulder. She didn't look like much of a threat.

At the bus stop, Rachel stopped to wait. The woman stopped next to her, casual, nonchalant.

The bus arrived and Rachel boarded, aware of the woman behind her. She chose a window seat.

When the blonde woman took the seat next to her, she turned expectant eyes to her.

The woman glanced at her and then all around the bus. Then she faced Rachel again.

"You're Rachel Delany, right?" the woman asked.

Apprehension reared up as she tried to place the woman. "Who are you?"

"You worked for Jared Palmer a few years ago."

"Who are you?" Rachel asked in a more demanding tone.

"Oh." She stuck her hand out. "Sorry. Chloe Chesterfield."

Rachel shook her hand, picking up on a spunky personality despite her second glance around the bus. What had her so skittish?

"You're working with that detective, right? The one who works for that famous one? Tandy?"

"Well, I'm not really *working* with him. He's looking for his sister's killer."

"And now that Jared is dead, that means someone else probably killed her. I heard it on the news that he was missing, and I just found out he was killed." Chloe did another survey through the bus, and this time included a sweep of the road behind them. Then she leaned closer to Rachel. "I was too afraid to come forward but there's no other way." She lowered her voice. "My mother bought one of those policies Jared sells."

"The Sapphire package?"

"Yes. She went in for a routine checkup and had to pay eighty percent. Eighty percent! Her policy didn't say what percentages it paid, just what it covered. Jared told her she'd pay twenty percent. When she confronted him, he said, no, he told her eighty percent. But of course that's not what he said. I started doing my own investigation." She put her hand on Rachel's briefly. "I'm married, you see, so my name is different than my mother's. I acted like I wanted a cheap policy. He sold me the same one as my mother's." She gave Rachel's hand a pat. "Only I recorded the entire conversation."

As the woman paused, Rachel realized she expected some kind of accolade. "Wow. You're a brave woman."

Chloe beamed, so proud of herself. "Yes, and then later, I told Jared if he didn't refund my mother her expenses, I'd take what I had to police." She did another look-around, again going to the rear of the bus. Rachel did the same, beginning to wonder if this woman had attracted attention she didn't want, either.

"Do you know, that very night my home was broken into? I put the recording in our safe, but it wasn't a high-dollar safe. Someone broke into that, too, and took the recording. But that wasn't all. Whoever did it was still in my house. I was attacked. Beaten. And then the man warned me if I ever threatened Jared Palmer again, I'd be killed."

Something similar had happened to Rachel. "You were afraid to go to the police?"

The woman nodded emphatically. "The threats didn't stop after I got out of the hospital. I found my cat dead on my front porch. I received scary phone calls. I was followed. And that man would talk to me in person. He'd wait until I left work or, once when I went out with friends, he was waiting for me outside my door. I'd had a little to drink that night so I was completely vulnerable. He didn't hurt me again, just warned me that he'd always be watching, that Jared employed him to take care of people like me. I believed him. I also think he enjoyed tormenting me more than he'd enjoy killing me. He was a real creep."

Rachel wholeheartedly agreed. "But now Jared is dead."

"Yes. And you have your detective." Chloe leaned back after another check of their surroundings. Then she dug into her purse. "I kept a copy of my mother's policy, and recently befriended Eldon's secretary. She told me you came to see Eldon. That's how I knew to come after you." She pulled out a USB. "I'm too afraid to hang on to something like this. But you could give it to your detective friend."

"What is this?"

"A copy of everything on Jared's computer."

Rachel took the device, ecstatic she'd have another chance to go through Jared's files. "Thanks." Unfortunately, it wouldn't be enough to implicate the real criminal. Eldon.

"Eldon's secretary never liked Jared."

"Did she have an affair with him?" Rachel didn't really want to know the answer to that, she just couldn't resist the sarcasm.

"She didn't say."

The bus came to Rachel's stop. "This is me."

"I'm staying on until the bus turns around and heads back to town. This one does that."

"Thank you, Chloe. This will be a big help."

"I can't wait to have my life back," Chloe said, getting up to let Rachel out. "Not having to look over my shoulder will be deliverance from Hell to Heaven."

"Yes." Rachel smiled at the woman. She'd feel the same. Taking her life back… That was what this was all about. "For me, too." She said farewell and went to step off the bus. From there she had about a five-mile walk. The thought that maybe she should be doing this with Lucas nagged her. But if he'd never come into her life, she'd have had to face this sooner or later. She would have to take action in order to rid Eldon and Jared from her life once and for all. She'd faced bad men before. Men in the streets. She knew how to fight and she knew how to use a gun. All she needed was a confession. Then she'd get away and head for the nearest cop.

Fifteen minutes into her walk, a car slowed down behind her. Rachel's heart sped up. She hadn't anticipated being intercepted on her way. She'd intended to surprise Eldon and get him to talk. At gunpoint, if necessary.

Looking back, Rachel saw a white BMW pull off to the side of the road. She recognized the driver—Marcy—and went cold inside. The two-lane mountain highway was deserted. How had she found her here? What was she doing this far out of town?

Marcy rolled down the passenger window. "Hi, Rachel."

"Marcy? Everyone's been looking for you. Where

have you been?" She pretended not to think much of the fact that Marcy was on this mountain road.

Marcy grimaced with a repenting smile. "Yeah, I know. I've been staying with Eldon. I was afraid how it would look once it got out that I was also seeing him. I'm on my way to his cabin now. Need a lift?"

Being afraid of exposure seemed like a lame excuse to Rachel. Her affairs weren't really a secret. Rachel looked down the highway where the bus had long since vanished. She wished she'd have seen this coming— that Marcy would be with Eldon. It implicated them both. Marcy had last been seen with Jared and then she'd gone missing. Now here she was, on her way to Eldon's remote cabin.

Rachel had been so convinced Jared had murdered Luella—up until his own murder. Eldon had been taken aback with the knowledge that Marcy had had an affair with Jared. He had seemed innocent. But he could have been acting. He and Marcy could have worked together all along, even during his affair with Luella. But why would both of them want to kill Jared?

Jared's change of heart, of course. He'd gone against Eldon. Eldon was involved in the fraud as much as him. That had to be it. And Marcy had joined in on the crime. She liked money and men in power. Eldon must give her both.

"Are you all right?"

Rachel turned back to Marcy. If she declined her offer, what then? She could walk back to town. And lose this chance to free herself of menace?

"That's where you're headed, right?" Marcy asked. "To see Eldon? Not too many other places out here."

"Yes," Rachel said cheerily. As she moved toward

the door, she opened her purse and took out her pistol as she sat on the passenger seat. "Take me to see Eldon."

Marcy's act of friendliness disappeared, her astonished eyes going from the gun to Rachel's face. "What are you doing?"

"You can stop the act, Marcy. I know you're working with Eldon."

No longer taken by surprise, the real Marcy came out, shrewd and unafraid. "You're making a big mistake."

"I suppose I should thank you for stopping to offer me a lift," Rachel said. "Now I know what I'm walking into."

Marcy smirked at her.

"Drive."

She did.

"Why'd you do it?" Rachel asked.

"Do what?"

"Was it Eldon's charm? Did he need your help?" Clearly, he didn't. Maybe he'd used Marcy. She'd thrown off Lucas. No one had looked at Eldon, only Jared and his involvement with Marcy. He'd known she would be the last person to see Jared alive. She'd look guilty.

"He's using you," Rachel said as the thought dawned on her.

"Hmph. You don't know anything about me and my relationship with Eldon."

"Did you help him kill Luella?"

"He didn't need my help for that. And I was glad to have her out of the way. Eldon and I have been seeing each other ever since."

"Along with all his other women?" Rachel supported the pistol on her forearm, putting on a facade of comfort and courage, both of which she wasn't completely feeling right now.

"I see other men. Big deal. We aren't monogamous." Marcy lifted her hands from the wheel briefly and sounded annoyed.

"And that's okay with you." Rachel didn't buy it for one minute.

"He gives me everything I want."

"He'll give you a prison term."

"I haven't done anything."

"You were with Jared before he was killed. Police will think you murdered him once they realize you're alive and well and you weren't a victim along with him. Don't you think Eldon planned it that way? He wasn't anywhere near Jared when he disappeared." Rachel paused for emphasis. "But you were, weren't you?"

Marcy looked over at her, no longer shrewd.

"Is he the one who convinced you to go into hiding?"

Again, Marcy glanced over at her, somber now.

"You're way out of your league," Rachel said. "Eldon is smart. He's thought all of this through. Now that Lucas is closing in, he's getting scared. If I were you, I'd turn this car around and go tell the cops everything you know."

Marcy laughed cynically. "It's not that simple."

"No?" She must have done her share of fraud right along with Jared and Eldon.

"No." Marcy turned onto a narrow paved road.

Rachel's heart began to slam. She fought the rising anxiety. She had to stay calm so she could think clearly.

"You'll never get away with this," Marcy said. "What do you hope to do?"

"Just park and get out slowly."

Marcy parked in front of Eldon's spacious log cabin. She opened her door, eyeing Rachel, who kept her pistol aimed at her as she climbed out after her. With her purse hooked diagonally from her shoulder, she grabbed Marcy's arm and bent it behind her back, putting the pistol to her head.

Up the porch steps, Rachel said, "Open the door."

Marcy did. Rachel followed her inside, searching for signs of Eldon. The house was quiet. Too quiet. A single light illuminated the Western-style great room with towering stone fireplace and vaulted ceiling.

"Go to the phone." Rachel nudged Marcy toward the phone on a stand between the marble and stainless-steel kitchen and great room. "Pick it up and dial 911."

Marcy picked up the phone and held it to her ear. "It's dead."

Fear that Rachel could not subdue nearly took over her mind. Releasing Marcy's arm, she kept the gun to her head and took the phone from her, pressing the call button and listening. No dial tone.

Eldon had seen them arrive and had taken the precaution. Where was he? Just as she was about to turn to look, she felt a gun against her own head.

"Hello, Rachel."

Going to HealthFirst led to news of Rachel's where-abouts—and more. Lucas had gone to talk to Eldon, only to learn from his secretary that a woman Jared had double-crossed had followed Rachel out the front entrance. And she knew said stranger.

Rachel didn't have a car, so she must have walked to the nearest bus stop. A talk with the driver and Lucas had a scent. The driver said she got off at the last stop alone, and Eldon's secretary had informed him Rachel had been looking for Eldon and that Eldon was at his cabin in the mountains. The bus's route ended in the mountains.

If Lucas comes looking for me, tell him to go to Jared's house...

She must have discovered something. And she'd gone to try to redeem herself. Alone. Whatever she'd found must involve Eldon. Lucas had to find out what before he went after her. Going in blind would do neither of them any good.

Damn her. Why'd she have to leave him? Luckily, Jared's house was on the way to the mountains. Just a stroll through the house and he found what she'd left for him. Pictures, lined up on the floor. They had not been there when the forensics team had processed the house. Rachel had left them on the floor on purpose.

What he saw turned him to stone. Luella. Eldon. *Eldon.*

He couldn't picture his sister with a man like him, even before he'd begun to suspect him, Eldon wasn't the kind of man he'd have paired with his sister. Jared had a cutting edge, a drive, a charisma. Eldon...well, maybe Eldon had hidden his edge, and Luella hadn't seen the lethal side.

He took out his phone for the umpteenth time, then put it back into his pocket. Rachel didn't have a cell phone. If she was in trouble, she wouldn't be able to call him. She wouldn't be able to anyway, in the mountains. With an increasingly sick feeling, he left the house in an urgent hurry to get to her. But he had to remain calm and think like a detective. One piece of this puzzle bothered him. Marcy.

The sun lit up a bright blue sky but did nothing to chase the cold away. Lucas spotted a young woman outside an old Volkswagen, bundled up in a heavy jacket, gloves and beanie hat. That car probably never got warm and it had broken down on the side of the highway. He couldn't leave her there. Despite his urgency to reach Rachel, he stopped and parked behind the car.

The woman looked wary as he got out.

"I ran out of gas," she said.

Walking up to the car, he saw a baby in the backseat. He thought of Rachel. Was she pregnant? He imagined her struggling the same as this woman, and felt his first sting of contrition. He'd treated her terribly when she'd dropped her bit of news, which may not be news at all. She didn't know for certain. He should have believed her.

"There's a gas station up the road. I'll drop you there," he said. She looked from her baby to him.

"I'm a private investigator. I used to be a cop." Taking out his driver's license, he showed her and handed her a business card with his name.

She read the card and compared it to his license. Then she smiled. "Thanks. You can never be too sure these days."

He didn't see a ring on her finger. Single mother.

Obviously she didn't have a lot of money and the father wasn't helping.

He waited for her to gather her things and the baby, then drove her the short distance to the gas station. All the while he kept thinking of Rachel.

Stopping at the gas station, the woman got out and reached for her sleeping baby. The sweet, innocent face melted Lucas. He couldn't leave this woman to fend for herself.

"Wait."

She paused and looked up at him.

"I couldn't help noticing your car."

A crease formed between her eyebrows. "What's wrong with my car?"

"Nothing, if you live in Florida." He chuckled. He got out and went to the back of his SUV, where he'd put his duffel bag. He kept a lot of cash there while he worked to solve his sister's murder. He had several charities, but this would be delivered by him in person. He took out enough to buy a decent car and walked around the vehicle to the woman. He handed her the cash.

"For a warmer car," he said. "And to get you and your baby home."

She took the cash, dumbfounded.

Lucas looked down at the baby, who'd begun to stir, her young blue eyes opening to see him. An electric bolt of affection speared him. The baby girl grunted and gave him a toothless smile with bobbing hands.

"How old?"

The woman smiled, beaming love even in the wake of receiving a windfall such as he'd just given her. "Ten months."

He again thought of Rachel. She may have one of those soon. His baby. And he'd better be on his way to save them both, if saving was what they needed.

"I don't know how to thank you, Mr. Curran."

"No need. Your baby's done enough." Just the sight of such innocence, a pure and stunning glimpse into God's love energy, snapped him back into focus. Focus he hadn't had since before his ex had revealed her lie.

The woman smiled bigger. "They have a way of doing that." She rocked her baby in the carrier. "It's a true wonder." She observed him a moment longer. "May your life be full of joy." With that, she turned and headed for the gas station.

As he watched her go, his cell phone rang. Close to the highway, he had service. He headed for the driver's side of the SUV and answered the call.

"Curran."

"Lucas Curran," a man's voice said. "Of the infamous Dark Alley investigators."

"Who is this?" The voice was familiar.

"You should never let those you care about out of your sight when you're hunting down a criminal."

"Eldon."

"Someone has something to say to you." Eldon didn't hesitate. He'd fully expected Lucas to figure out who had called.

That almost frightened Lucas. Smart killers planned that way. They stayed a step ahead of investigators. They taunted. They played.

But they always made one mistake. They underestimated the tenacity and intelligence of their opponent. They underestimated the law.

Fast breathing came onto the line. "I'm sorry, Lucas."

Rachel.

The punch in his gut threw him. "Rachel."

"I'm all right. I can handle th—"

The phone must have been taken from her.

"I'd like to have a word with you," Eldon said. "Why don't you meet me?"

Lucas didn't say anything. He couldn't. *Rachel.* She'd been captured by Luella's killer. Eldon had played his role well. Smart killer.

"I presume by now you know where to find me?"

Lucas had captured plenty of smart killers before. "Yes. Just tell me the mile marker. I'm down the road."

That caused Eldon some hesitation. He hadn't expected Lucas to be so close, so soon.

"It's not too late to make a deal, Eldon." Lucas capitalized on this opportunity of weakness. "Turn yourself in and I can arrange to have your sentence reduced."

Eldon laughed, but it was forced and too robust. Nervous. "If you want your girlfriend to live, be here in one hour."

"I can be there in ten minutes. Weren't you listening?"

"One hour. Not before." He told him the mile marker.

"Eldon?" Lucas said before he could disconnect.

"Yes, Mr. Curran?" he said with sarcasm.

"You're not smarter." Lucas disconnected.

The weaker he could make Eldon, the better. Eldon's lack of confidence would work to his advantage. But he'd have an hour to build it back up...and hurt Rachel.

No way would Lucas wait that long.

He got into his SUV and started the engine. Eldon would kill them both if he had his way.

He raced up the highway, a fire lit in him like never before…and plaguing thoughts of that baby he'd seen…and Rachel's news.

Chapter 15

"You should have kept quiet." Marcy set down a plate of food and a glass of water on the end of the twin bed where Rachel sat.

Eldon had locked her in a bedroom he'd modified into a prison cell. The window was boarded and the lock on the door one-sided—the wrong side requiring a key. The twin bed was the only furnishing in the room, and Eldon had made her remove her shoes—a deterrent in case she got out of the room and decided to make a run for it outside in the cold. He'd left her socks, though. And her purse. Once he'd had her gun, she hadn't posed a threat. She'd tucked that under the bed and searched the room for a weapon. The clothes rod in the closet offered the only option. One side missed a screw and the others looked loose. As soon as she got rid of Marcy, she'd get to work.

"You know a lot about what Eldon has done," Rachel said, eyeing the plate of mashed potatoes and some kind of meat smothered in light gravy.

"We're in love. Once you and that pest of an investigator are out of the picture, we can go back to our lives." Marcy smiled with overconfidence, not in a way a woman truly in love would.

"You think it will be that simple? That once you get rid of me and Lucas, the law will stop tracking you?" She would not eat that food. She'd get out of there first.

Marcy remained in her delusional world, an innocent pawn who wouldn't be viewed very innocent in court, brow raised, lids low, wistful. "Eldon says the cops will never catch him."

"Lucas will," Rachel said. The truth of that resonated inside her. Lucas. Her hero. Father of her baby…

She had to protect her future. But first she had to work on taking Marcy down.

"Lucas is one man," Marcy said, her brow lowering with the insult.

"Navy SEAL. LAPD Narcotics cop. Top detective for Dark Alley Investigations. Handpicked by Kadin Tandy?"

Marcy leaned back, folding her arms and regarding Rachel as though deciding how she'd punish her.

Footsteps behind her interrupted and ruined Rachel's chance to escape. Eldon looked at Marcy.

"Go watch for our new visitor," he said, cupping her chin and kissing her.

While Rachel's stomach turned in disgust, Marcy glowed from the scrap of attention.

Eldon faced Rachel, his expression changing from false attraction to hard menace. He cupped her chin, much the same as he'd done with Marcy. She refrained from showing her revulsion.

"I always wondered what you saw in Jared," he said with chilling, psychotic sophistication. "He was such a follower. All I ever had to do was suggest something and he'd do it, so desperate to be like me. Successful. Wealthy. He was easy to manipulate."

Rachel heard his deepening voice, and it reminded her of the threatening calls. He'd muffled his voice so she wouldn't recognize him and had paid thugs to frighten her. Then he'd driven one of Jared's cars when he'd shot her.

"Were you trying to manipulate him?" she asked.

"No. Only coerce him to do what I wanted."

Recalling the files Chloe had gotten Eldon's assistant to retrieve for her, Rachel understood what type of coercion he referred to. "Guilty of fraud? Will the police not find any corruption linked to you?"

He only grinned wickedly.

"What about Marcy?" She didn't need to be told. Her purse was in the room with her, and she'd pressed Record while she'd been left alone after being locked in there.

He grunted. "You and your boyfriend delivered some shocking news to me. About Marcy's affair with Jared. I didn't know. Jared didn't have to die until I learned that."

"You're hoping Marcy will be accused of his murder?"

"Not hoping."

His confidence was nearly inspiring. "Once Lucas and I are out of your way, what then?"

Eldon shrugged with staged animation. "I go back to work."

And Marcy would go to prison for his crimes. Warped minds didn't see the holes in their plans.

"Enough now. We don't have much time, and I want to see what all the fuss is about."

Fuss? What was he talking about?

He leaned closer. "Take off your clothes."

Rachel jerked back, away from his hand. She would not do that. Glancing at the closet, she saw the clothing bar and decided to take the chance.

Shoving Eldon as she stood, she ran to the closet while he staggered backward. Reaching the bar, she yanked as hard as she could. It held firm but began to loosen. She had one end broken off when Eldon grabbed her and hauled her back into the room, tossing her onto the bed. She heard the bar fall to the floor of the closet.

"Fight all you want," he said, climbing over her. "I've dreamed of this." Holding her wrists, he came down and kissed her cheek, a gentle touch that terrified Rachel.

Rolling her head away from him, she recalled the interactions she'd had with Eldon and realized he may have been putting out signs of interest. Maybe he hadn't known she'd been seeing Jared. Jared would have kept them a secret, lest his wife find out.

Eldon dug his fingers into her chin and forced her head back under his mouth. But he let go of her wrists.

Rachel punched him and tried to jab his eyes. He slapped her and took hold of her shirt. She fought him as the material ripped, tearing all the way down the front. The straining material dug into the back of her neck and arms. She punched him right on his nose.

He slapped her harder and in her disorientation, had her jeans unbuttoned and halfway down her legs. She grabbed the waist, fighting not to lose them, not only to stay clothed, but to keep the USB device on her. She'd put it in her pocket and he hadn't found it yet.

Taking her hands in a painful grip, he crossed them over her head. Holding them in one hand, he used his other to push her jeans down. She twisted her hands, prying them free. Addressing the immediate urgency of preventing his assault, she tore some of his hair out—enough of a distraction. He abandoned her jeans to block her swinging hands. Then his fist connected with her face, dropping her head back onto the mattress.

He removed her jeans the rest of the way. She kicked him, catching him under his chin and sending him flying backward. She leaped off the bed and ran for the closet, picking up the bar and gripping it like a bat.

Turning, she swung as Eldon charged for her. She connected with his head. He fell and didn't move.

Rachel didn't waste a precious second. She grabbed her purse and slung it crisscrossed over her shoulder before running from the room. Colliding with Marcy as she made it into the hall, she saw the gun in her hand. Rachel took hold of Marcy's arms and shoved her back against the wall, pounding her wrist. Marcy wasn't a strong woman. She lost hold of the weapon and it fell to the floor and out of the way. Even when she tried to hit Rachel, Rachel easily deflected the fine-boned strike.

Taking both of Marcy's arms, Rachel flung her aside, sending her falling to the hall floor, opposite the direction of the gun. Rachel crouched to pick that up and saw Eldon stirring from inside the room.

Marcy climbed to her feet, and Rachel pointed the gun at her.

"Get out of my way," Rachel said.

Moving slow and guarded, Marcy stepped aside, back into the bathroom.

Rachel walked backward down the hall. When Eldon didn't appear, she turned and ran for the kitchen and living room area. Searching for a phone, seeing none, she instead looked for her shoes—or any shoes. Eldon had hidden them. Why wouldn't he? Not seeing those, she looked for car keys.

"There's nowhere for you to go."

She stopped and faced the hall, gun aimed at Eldon as he unsteadily walked toward her, hand to his head and a pistol of his own targeting her. She backed to the door, seeing Marcy cower in the bathroom, only peering out once.

Eldon advanced, the first sign he thought he may have underestimated her crossing his evil eyes.

He'd underestimated her, all right. She'd lived on the street. She'd encountered many questionable characters. But most people didn't know the strength of her will. No one would get in her way. She'd die before letting anyone have that chance.

Firing the pistol, making sure she hit her mark— his hand—Rachel unlocked the front door and ran outside. She put the cold on her feet out of her mind. She'd find some way of getting them warm quickly.

Sprinting to the woods, she saw her first opportunity, a bush. Jumping onto the snow-free branches, she felt the woody parts scratch her, but at least she was off the snow. Kneeling down, she watched from the protection of tree trunks as Eldon emerged from the cabin. He stopped in the light of the front porch, looking one way and the other and then straight ahead, appearing to see her. But Rachel knew he didn't see her. Not in the darkness that had fallen since she'd been locked in the room.

Looking down at her cold feet, she had to fight fear while she realized she'd have to make a run for it, to find some place to wait until it was safe. Frostbite. The loss of her feet. She hoped that wouldn't happen, but if she stayed here, her death would be a certainty.

After Eldon had his fun with her, he'd kill her. No question.

Oh, Lucas...where are you?

Clouds had moved in over the past few hours. Darkness cloaked Lucas as he hiked through the trees toward Eldon's vacation home. He'd called Sheriff Bailey, who'd round up law enforcement. As he made it to the break in the forest, he took note of all the lights on and especially the car—Marcy's car. No sign of Rachel. Was she here?

The front door was ajar. Lucas took out his gun and eased his way there. He heard nothing from inside.

At the door, he put his back to the wall and listened. Someone moved, walking across the room on the other side of the door. He turned and saw a shadow pass before the window. Someone had looked outside.

Lucas pivoted and pushed the door open as he charged inside and aimed his weapon at the person.

Marcy inhaled a startled breath and stared at him and his gun.

Stepping into the kitchen area to put himself behind her, he looked toward the hall. No one emerged.

"Where is Eldon?" Lucas asked.

Marcy said nothing. She faced him with an upturned chin and defiant eyes, hands raised in brash surrender.

He'd never considered her the sharpest splinter, and this moment proved it. She thought Eldon would prevail tonight and that by not telling him where to find him she'd ensure that end. Looking over the cabin, he didn't like some of the items he saw. Rope. Duct tape. A can of gasoline. White powder on a mirrored tray on the coffee table. The kitchen was a mess. It smelled stale in here. Marcy had been living here awhile, since she'd disappeared with Jared.

Lucas went to Marcy and patted her down, aware of her enjoyment of his hands running over her curves. He met her mocking, seductive eyes and felt nothing but resolve for his purpose. Finding Rachel.

"Your father always talked about you," she said. "The hero cop."

He finished searching for a gun and waited for her to finish.

"He had you so pumped up—" her earrings dangled as she shook her head in remembered awe "—so high on a pedestal. I daydreamed about you. Once he said you were coming home for Christmas and I schemed to meet you. I made sure I worked Christmas Eve." She fingered the sides of his jacket, her gaze following the touches. "But you didn't show up. You came in for a brief visit. Your father talked about that, how he wished you'd have stayed longer, and how he understood because of your devotion to your heroic job."

He didn't have time for this. Taking her by the upper arm, he led her with him down the hall. Eldon would have made himself known by now if he was here. If Eldon wasn't here, where was he? And where was Rachel?

"Now, since you've been back, I can see what a waste of perfectly good daydreams you are."

"That's nice." He looked into the bathroom. "Where is Eldon?"

"Eldon is twice the man you are. He isn't afraid of anything."

Pushing a bedroom door open wider, he saw only a bed and a boarded-up window. On the floor, Rachel's jeans. Not caring that his grip was a little hard, he swung Marcy so she stumbled and fell onto the bed.

He aimed his gun at her. "Where is Rachel?"

The smugness left her face as she lay on her elbows, the tight, shiny faux leather dress inching up her white thighs. She meant to entice, and all he felt was revulsion.

Fear he seldom yielded to gripped him. He went to Rachel's jeans, crouching to feel for something, anything, blind hope making him do it. When he did feel something, he went still. And then dug into the pocket to lift out a USB device.

He looked up at Marcy.

"What's that?" she asked.

Probably something that would have gotten her killed if Eldon had known it was there. He stood, tucking the device into his own jeans pocket.

"You'll never get away with this," Marcy said, sitting up, beginning to doubt her secure position at the side of a dangerous criminal.

Storming toward her, he took her arm and hauled her with him back to the main room. Snatching up the roll of duct tape he no longer had doubts about what Eldon had intended to use it for, he forced her to sit on a kitchen chair.

"Eldon isn't a quitter," Marcy said as he wrapped tape around her body and arms, securing her to the chair.

"He'll quit when I make him," Lucas said. Tearing off the end of the tape, he caught sight of something familiar. Rachel's tennis shoes. They were placed on the messy kitchen counter. Eldon had removed them for a reason.

He zeroed in on Marcy. "Where did he take her?"

At first her smugness returned, but then she saw that Lucas wasn't going to be nice anymore. She faltered, a stutter sputtering before she clung to boldness. "He's outsmarted you for four years."

That just made him furious. "His luck is about to run out." He taped her ankles next.

"It isn't luck. You're going to pay for this. You and your girlfriend, both."

Lucas straightened. "I'm not the one taped up."

As she scowled up at him, he didn't waste any more time on the useless chatter. He went to the door, peered outside and took out his compact flashlight. Shining light onto the ground, he followed all of the footsteps in the snow off the porch. Two sets led into the woods. One print confirmed Rachel was without shoes.

Urgency burned in him to find her. Now.

* * *

Shivering, Rachel heard Eldon approach before she saw him through the darkness. Her feet hurt from cold, socks wet and no longer providing protection. Sticking to shrubbery and dead vegetation had spared her somewhat, but now she had no choice. She'd have to make a run for it—before he saw her. If she could make it to the highway…or maybe she should try to get to Marcy's car. If she made a wide arch, she could turn herself back in that direction.

Going back to that cabin didn't feel safe, but what else could she do? She couldn't stay out in this cold much longer.

She stepped off the branches and ran through the trees. Rocks and branches dug into her freezing flesh. One branch cracked loud. Rachel paused, looking back.

Sure enough, Eldon had heard the sound. And he likely tracked her footprints, too. Running again, she tried to stay on patches of dead leaves and pine needles. She tripped as her foot landed on a sharp rock. Righting herself, biting back against what should be a stinging pain from the cut, she continued to run. Her feet were going numb. At a big tree trunk, she took refuge, looking down at the red stain expanding on her left sock.

She wasn't sure she could run anymore. She couldn't feel her feet anymore. Seeing Eldon trudging through the woods, head down, tracking her, she readied the pistol. Taking aim, she waited until he drew a little closer and fired.

He ducked behind a tree.

Rachel leaned her back against the trunk and closed

her eyes for a second, gathering all her strength, trying not to worry about her feet.

She had to get to a car, somewhere warm.

Deciding to try, she sprinted out from the tree, firing her gun as she went and keeping Eldon behind the tree long enough for her to put a little distance between them. She ran, this time not taking care to keep off the snow. She ran through it, using it as a cushion to her cut feet. She couldn't feel them anyway.

Leaping to clear a fallen tree, her knee caught on the bark and she fell face-first onto the ground. Her hands slid in the snow. Rolling, she fired her gun as Eldon reached the log. He crouched.

Her gun emptied of bullets. An electric jolt of dread shot through her. She crawled back as Eldon straightened, slow and sure, grinning.

"I've got you now."

Rachel scrambled to get to her feet.

Eldon tackled her from behind, wrenching her arm back and yanking the gun from her grasp.

She cried out from the searing pain in her shoulder joint.

In the next instant, a looming figure appeared above them, clubbing the side of Eldon's head with a big pistol.

"Lucas."

She rolled to her backside and scooted back as Eldon staggered to his feet.

Lucas could have killed him. He had a close-range shot. But he didn't. He wanted Eldon alive. He wanted him to suffer and pay for killing his sister.

Rachel watched in awe as he strategically moved, anticipating all of Eldon's moves. Jumping for a double kick that sent Eldon's gun flying and plunking into the snow, Lucas went in for the final blow, knocking Eldon so hard with his fist it sent him to the ground, unconscious. He was a man not to be beaten. Nothing would stop him from avenging his sister.

And saving Rachel...

She fell into more awe as he stepped toward her and crouched.

"Are you hurt?" He looked down at her feet and she didn't have to reply.

He shrugged out of his jacket and wrapped her feet. Still warm from his body heat, the jacket began to penetrate the icy cold.

Lucas lifted her, then carried her through the trees, back toward the cabin.

"You found the pictures."

"Yes."

She smiled. "I knew you would." Like he'd done for her, she'd predicted his actions. "Marcy?"

"Probably being arrested by now."

"Are you sure Eldon won't get away?"

"Yes."

He'd knocked him out good. He knew the amount of force to use.

At the clearing, several police cars, unmarked and marked, filled the open space before the cabin, and an ambulance rolled to a stop with its lights flashing.

Sheriff Bailey appeared from the throng. Other officers noticed their approach.

"Sordi is in the woods," Lucas said, explaining where to find him and digging into his pocket for the USB device. Rachel hung on to his shoulders as his support lightened.

"We've got the perimeter surrounded. They'll find him," Sheriff Bailey said.

Lucas handed Rachel the USB. She took it and handed it over to Bailey.

"That should give you all the evidence you need on Eldon and Jared."

He took the drive from her. "Nice work."

"Just taking back my life." She smiled, albeit wearily.

Lucas fell deeper for her as she looked up at him. His strong, brave woman. Beautiful, too.

One of the officers used his radio and spoke to one of the other officers in the woods. "Close in."

Eldon wouldn't get away. He'd pay for his crimes. Lucas felt a rush of gladness. Justice at last.

"I couldn't have done this without you," Sheriff Bailey said. "The Bozeman police were just as eager to catch the killer, but I think they weren't prepared to deal with a criminal like him."

Eldon had been smart in carrying out his crimes, but against Lucas's determination and the backing of a stealth private investigation agency, he'd been outshined and outwitted.

"I'm glad to have a new friend," Lucas said, and the sheriff smiled because he understood what that meant. He and Lucas would be working together again someday…or maybe another detective from Dark Alley Investigations.

After saying goodbye, Lucas carried Rachel to the ambulance. Over his shoulder, Rachel saw Marcy being led out of the cabin in handcuffs. She looked toward Lucas and Rachel sullenly.

Rachel smiled and rested her head on Lucas's shoulder. Her hero, a true hero.

"Lucas?" she said.

"Yes?" He stepped up into the ambulance and lay her down on the gurney.

"I want to take a vacation."

He chuckled. "I'm taking you back to my ranch. Once you recover, we can talk vacations."

"That's all the vacation I need." She felt so drowsy.

"Stay awake. You have hypothermia."

He moved out of the way for paramedics to go to work on her.

When he told her he'd see her at the hospital, she missed him already. And then she remembered how they'd left things. He'd come after her and saved her, but would he ever come after her heart?

Chapter 16

A reporter waited at the hospital when the ambulance pulled up to the emergency entrance. Lucas had arrived just behind the vehicle and now pushed the paramedics aside to lift Rachel and carry her in, looking down at her looking up at him with wary gladness. He didn't have to do this. Maybe his warrior instinct still hadn't dimmed since going after Eldon, hunting him down like prey, saving Rachel. No other woman would die on his watch.

He took her into the emergency room and deposited her on a waiting gurney. She didn't need to be wheeled in like that, but her feet needed immediate attention, now wrapped in a bandage with blood soaking through.

A cameraman took pictures while a skinny, haggard blonde woman asked, "Is it true you single-handedly brought down Luella Palmer's killer?"

He didn't answer.

"Eldon Sordi? Did he also kill Jared Palmer? And what about the others? Didn't they accuse Jared of fraud? Was Jared guilty of fraud?"

Lucas didn't answer any questions and left them on the other side of the door, where he followed Rachel. Security guards stopped the reporter.

"This ain't LA," the guard said to the reporter, who would just maybe make a sizeable income off the story—with Kadin Tandy's growing popularity.

The next day, Rachel was released. She was quiet as the nurse wheeled her to the emergency exit. When Lucas offered her his hand and the nurse offered her crutches, she waved his hand away and took the crutches. She had the energy of a woman who'd done some thinking and had come to the conclusion that her man was lacking. He felt stunned and...yes, the singe of rejection.

His father's sedan waited to whisk them away to Lucas's ranch. Vacation? Sure. He'd go on vacation with Rachel. But he hadn't thought much beyond that. He couldn't bring himself to. Had the doctors tested her for pregnancy? He couldn't bring himself to face that, either. But now he saw he'd have to.

She stood with the crutches and met his eyes, piercing him with soft, sexy confidence and intellect. This woman made her own way, and if those who crossed her path didn't support her vision, she'd go forward alone.

"I'm going home," she said.

And by home she meant her small apartment. "I can arrange—"

She held up her hand. "No."

"At least let me help you with rent."

She shook her head. "I'll find a job."

He believed her. She'd find a job. She'd finish school. She'd find a better job. And she'd be all right. She had probably never been more sure about that. Her experience with him and with Eldon had taught her that.

"I'll have the driver take you," he said. "You'll have a tough time with those on a bus." He gestured to her crutches.

To that she agreed with a soft smile and a nod. "I could do it, but yes, it will be much easier in the car. Thank you."

He studied her face while resistance swirled in him. *Don't let her go.* Every fiber of his body clamored for that, but his mind stopped him. He needed to be sure of what he did from here on out.

When she started to move toward the car, he stopped her from taking the first step with the crutches. "I want to say I'm sorry, for judging you when I first met you."

"You had me judged before we even met."

"Yes. And I'm sorry. I've never met a stronger woman than you. Or a more honest one."

She lowered her head briefly. "I could have handled things differently. But I'm glad it's over."

Was she? Which parts? Was she glad their acquaintance was over? He didn't ask.

"Goodbye, Lucas." With another of her soft, sexy smiles, she crutched to the sedan where the driver helped her inside.

Later that week, Lucas still couldn't stop thinking about Rachel. Right now he stood in his dad's office, staring out the window.

He'd spent the week at his parents' house, catching up with them, showering his mother with attention and making her beam like a proud mom. He enjoyed it, except when she showed him the picture the reporter had taken of him carrying Rachel, red lights of the emergency sign above their heads. Beyond the romance of a man carrying an injured woman into an emergency room, the way he looked down and she up, locked in an intimate exchange, captured hearts.

Apparently, the photo—and the story—had made it to national news. Another unsolved case closed by Dark Alley Investigations. Kadin had been interviewed on a morning show, and had used the advertising to draw more elite detectives to his agency.

One man had been captured walking into the Rock Springs, Wyoming, office. Tall, dark and brooding, he had the look of a man with an unsolved murder that had gotten too close to his heart. He was a giant of a man and the host of a television series on cold cases. Like Kadin, he'd lost someone close—his wife. An ex-detective from a southern Colorado town, something must have drawn him to Kadin. What? Lucas had called Kadin to find out, but the stoic ex-NYPD detective hadn't revealed much, only saying the man had joined the team, and Lucas would be briefed in due time.

"Lucas?"

He turned from the office window to see Tory standing in the doorway.

"Before you tell me to go, please just hear me out, okay?" She stepped into the office and closed the door. "I cleared this with your father."

His stepfather had allowed her the use of his office to corner Lucas? He'd have to have a word with him.

She stopped a few feet from him, respectful and reserved, different than he remembered all those years ago.

"I saw the picture of you and Rachel."

He rubbed the back of his neck. Very little could make him uncomfortable, but that photo sure did.

"I debated whether to come here to talk to you, but then I found out you and Rachel aren't together and I realized I had to."

Lucas lowered his hand. What was this all about? She'd come because he and Rachel weren't together? Would she try to win him back? No. Her entire demeanor said the opposite, that she'd come for a much more noble reason.

"You don't have to keep beating yourself up over what happened," he said.

"I'm not." She smiled genuinely, not a beaming, laugh-at-you type, just an I-finally-woke-up type. "I think it's you who hasn't stopped beating yourself up."

While part of him took that as an insult, he saw her point. He hadn't let go of what she'd done to him. And as he thought that, he also could see how he blamed her. What had she *done to him*? He should focus more on what he'd done to himself.

"Lucas, you're a wonderful man. I saw that about you when we met. But I've grown up since then. All I really want now is your forgiveness, and to know your relations with me aren't going to prevent you from having something good with Rachel."

Now he really listened. She had his attention. "Why would you care whether I'm with Rachel or not?"

"I saw that photo along with everyone else in the country," she said. "You're in love with her, and she's in love with you. And if you aren't already, then you will be." Tory stepped closer and put her hand on his arm. "You have the real thing with that woman, Lucas. What you and I had wasn't real. Don't throw it away because of something stupid I did."

She had him thrown so off balance he didn't know what to address first. The pure joy and excitement of the prospect of going after Rachel to keep her...or the prospect of forgiving Tory.

Maybe he'd already forgiven her, and he had yet to forgive himself.

"For years I blamed you for losing my place on a SEAL team," he said.

"You had every right to be angry. You can't know how sorry I am. If I could reverse time and start over, I'd—"

"No." He stopped her. "I made my own decision. I wanted a family more than I wanted to be a SEAL member. That's what had me upset when I found out you weren't pregnant." Only he hadn't faced it. He'd delved into a career, instead, and avoided serious relationships.

He still didn't know if Rachel was pregnant. He hadn't asked her, and she hadn't volunteered the information. He respected her for that. She deserved him whole, not halfway committed.

What if she was pregnant? He'd have a family. He and Rachel would build one. As he began to leash in his sudden enthusiasm, he stopped that bad habit and let it go.

Leaning forward, he kissed Tory on her cheek. "Thank you."

She laughed lightly. "Does that mean I'm forgiven?"

"Yes. I forgave you a long time ago. You were right. I had to forgive myself."

"I'm so happy for you. You're going to go get the woman of your dreams."

"What about you?" She had wanted him, after all.

"Don't worry about me. I have a date tonight with a good man. Now I can go out with him with a clean heart and a fresh start."

"Did you just make a rhyme?" He chuckled.

She didn't respond in kind. She meant what she'd said. That was how important this was to her—his forgiveness.

"Go and get her."

Lucas opened the office door and almost bumped into his stepfather, who jumped back.

"Yes, Lucas. Go get Rachel."

Lucas sent him a teasing look for eavesdropping.

"And bring her home to your mother and me!"

Chapter 17

Rachel entered her apartment after her third interview for the week. One of them would come through for her, but in the meantime, she'd barely managed to avoid her landlord. She'd registered for her last semester and spent the last of her money on books. Now she plopped down onto her daybed and glanced around her small apartment. It felt so different than before. As if she didn't belong. It had taken her a couple days to clean up the mess.

What was different about this place? It was still a hole-in-the-wall, her very own hole-in-the-wall. What was missing?

Lucas.

She felt so alone without him. How crazy was that? Being alone had never bothered her before. Why now?

Her intercom buzzed. Going to the door, wary the

person on the other end was her landlord, she pressed the button. "Yes?"

"Delivery." It was the lobby attendant, when he decided to be present in the lobby. The deliveryman must have drawn him out of the back office and away from the TV and internet, and now he sounded annoyed at being drawn away.

Leaving her apartment, she went down to the lobby and found the attendant back in his office with a giant soda and a bag of chips and the latest *Thrones* episode on. Chewing a mouthful of chips, he grunted and moved his elbow toward the box.

Someone sent her a package? There had to be some kind of mistake. Unless Nan had sent her something. Lucas had sent her the clothes from his ranch, but that was the only contact she'd had with him.

"Thanks." She took the box.

The man didn't even acknowledge her. She went back up to her apartment. Putting the box down, she took out a knife and sliced the tape. Opening the flaps, she pulled out something tucked in bubble wrap.

A cell phone. As she stared at it, a text message popped up on the screen.

Hello, Rachel.

The sender's name was listed. *Lucas Curran.*

Lucas had sent her a phone he'd not only activated but had also put his name in the contacts.

Tickled more than she liked herself to be, she entered.

What are you doing?

Picking you up in one hour. Dinner. Wear a dress.

She smiled much too wide for her comfort. She'd distanced herself to protect her heart. Now he'd stolen it right back with this gift…and invitation.

What are you doing? she entered again.

I'll explain over dinner. Get ready. I'll be waiting in front of your building. LC.

She found his contact entry and called him. He didn't answer.

Figures.

Rachel lowered the phone and stared across her tiny apartment. *Don't go. Go. Don't go…*

Go.

She hurried to her armoire and rummaged through her clothes, finding a dark blue strapless, moderately low-cut, long and flowing chiffon dress that would pass for formal if he took her somewhere like that. The slit up the front would give tasteful glimpses of her legs as she walked. Lucas had sneaked this in with the other clothes, and when she'd received them she'd questioned his motives. But when he hadn't called, she assumed he hadn't meant to include it.

Ten minutes past an hour, she emerged from the apartment building, feeling like Cinderella.

Lucas rose from the back of a sleek limousine that had begun to attract attention. People from the houses across the street sat out on their front porches. Three tattooed twentysomethings with patched leather jackets and beanies stood at the corner, smoking and eyeing her and the car.

But all of that fell away when she saw the way Lucas took all of her in, his eyes devouring her and following the V that dipped below the straight bodice. She had her jacket draped over her arm, not wanting the old thing to ruin the effect. But, oh, was she cold.

Lucas leaned into the limo and came back with a thick fur coat. Stepping forward, he draped the soft material over her shoulders.

As she slipped her arms inside, he said in his deep, sexy voice, "No animals were killed for this."

She smiled back and across her shoulder at him, his face close and gray-blue eyes twinkling with delight and desire.

She got into the back of the limo. When he sat beside her she said, "What are you doing, Lucas?"

This time she'd get an answer—beyond *taking you to dinner.*

"Tory came to see me yesterday afternoon."

His ex-wife? "Is that supposed to make me feel better?"

"She made me see that I need to let go of certain things from my past."

She could have told him that. In fact, hadn't she? Why did hearing it from Tory change anything?

"She genuinely needed my forgiveness," he said. "I realized it was never her I needed to forgive. It was myself."

"Congratulations." Rachel still wasn't satisfied.

"She also made me realize that having a family is much more important to me than anything I do in my career."

"Okay, that's getting warmer." She smiled ever so slightly at him.

He grinned and put his arm along the back of the seat, moving closer. "Tory may have turned a switch on in me, but it's you who's made me change the most, Rachel. I want honor in my work, and I get that from Dark Alley, but it's you I want to spend the rest of my life making happy. Raising kids. Teaching them the same honor I learned from my dad and Joseph. Loving you."

They hadn't known each other long enough to profess that sentiment yet, but Rachel understood what he said. They had something rare and precious, something that love would grow from. They'd have a happy home because of the rightness of their union. Their kids would grow up to know what real love was.

"I'm not saying this because you might be pregnant, either," Lucas said. "It doesn't matter if you are or not. We'll have kids now or later."

"Well, it just so happens that it's going to be now."

A triumphant grin spread along his kissable mouth. "That's great news." He put his fingers beneath her chin and kissed her—exactly what she wanted.

She put her hand on his cheek and returned his passion. The kiss turned into an instant inferno of insatiable desire.

"Let's skip dinner and spend tonight and all day tomorrow making love," he said.

No. She'd cherish every moment of this night. "I didn't get all dressed up like this just so you could take everything off."

"You can wear it on Friday night. I'll take you to dinner then. Tonight let's order room service."

She shook her head, teasing. "Dinner tonight. Then after, you can make love to me. And we can still spend tomorrow doing the same. And tomorrow night you can order room service."

"Whatever the lady wants."

"I want you."

"Good." He planted kisses on her mouth and along the edges. "Then I'll tell you what I want."

"Oh?"

He told the driver to take them to a fine restaurant.

"First, you're going to graduate from college."

"Easy enough to accommodate." She tingled from his continued kisses, the driver sliding closed the privacy window.

"Then I'm going to buy you a shop. Where you can run any kind of business you want."

"Mmm. I'd love to collect and sell treasures. Antiques. Decor items. Things I've only watched others buy. Okay, that's doable."

He chuckled because he offered her a lot.

"What do you get in return?" she asked.

"You."

He had said he wanted her. "I'll make it my life's mission to always make you happy." Leaning back she met his eyes to make sure he knew she meant it.

"You won't have to try very hard. Just be with me, Rachel. I'll be the happiest man alive."

"And I'll be the happiest woman."

They kissed again, sealing the promise.

* * * * *

JUSTICE HUNTER by Jennifer Morey
Don't miss the next thrilling installment in the
COLD CASE DETECTIVES miniseries,
coming in summer 2016!

And if you loved this novel, don't miss other
suspenseful titles by Jennifer Morey:

A WANTED MAN
THE MARINE'S TEMPTATION
THE ELIGIBLE SUSPECT
ONE SECRET NIGHT

Available now from Harlequin Romantic Suspense!

ROMANTIC suspense

*When pregnant Lizzie Connor is threatened by a serial
killer, she's desperate to keep herself and her unborn
child safe. So Lizzie turns to the one man who can
protect her—sexy cowboy Ethan Colton, who's also the
father of her baby! As sparks fly, danger and true love
rear their heads…*

Read on for a sneak preview of
COLTON'S SURPRISE HEIR by **Addison Fox**
the second book in the 2016
COLTONS OF TEXAS series.

"Did you—" Lizzie broke off, her voice heavy and out of
breath as she came through the door.

"He's gone."

"He?"

"I thought." Ethan stopped and turned back toward the
window. The figure had vanished, but he conjured up the
image in his mind. "He was wearing a thick sweatshirt
with the hood up, so I guess it could be anyone. He was
too far away to get a sense of height."

"The police will ask what color."

"It was nondescript navy blue." Ethan glanced down at
his own sweatshirt, tossed on that morning from a stack
of similar clothes in the bottom of his drawer. "Just like
I'm wearing. Hell, like half the population wears every
weekend."

"It's still something."

Lizzie stood framed inside the doorway, long, curly

waves of hair framing her face, and he stilled. Since he'd seen her the morning before, his emotions had been on a roller coaster through the ups and downs of his new reality.

Yet here she was. Standing in the doorway of their child's room, a warrior goddess prepared to do battle to protect her home. He saw no fear. Instead, all he saw was a ripe, righteous anger, spilling from her in hard, deep breaths.

"Maybe you should sit down?"

"I'm too mad to sit."

"Once again, I'm forced to ask the obvious. Humor me."

He reached for the window, but she stopped him. "Leave it. It's not that cold, and maybe there are finger-prints."

Although he had no doubt the perp had left nothing behind, Ethan did as she requested. She'd already taken a seat in the rocking chair in the corner, and he felt his knees buckle at the image that rose up to replace her in his mind's eye.

Lizzie, rocking in that same chair, their child nestled in her arms, suckling at her breast.

The shock of emotion that burrowed beneath his heart raced through him, and Ethan fought to keep any trace of it from showing. How could he feel so much joy at something so unexpected?

At something he'd never wanted?

Don't miss
COLTON'S SURPRISE HEIR by Addison Fox,
available February 2016 wherever
Harlequin® Romantic Suspense
books and ebooks are sold.

www.Harlequin.com

THE WORLD IS BETTER WITH

Romance

Harlequin has everything from contemporary, passionate and heartwarming to suspenseful and inspirational stories.

Whatever your mood,
we have a romance just for you!

Connect with us to find your next great read,
special offers and more.